BLUE AVENGER
and the THEORY of EVERYTHING

NORMA HOWE

For Randy –
my good and
faithful friend
and fan. Thanks
so much!
Truly,
Norma

CRICKET BOOKS

A Marcato Book

CHICAGO

December '03

Printed in the United States of America

Designed by Anthony Jacobson

First edition, 2002

Library of Congress Cataloging-in-Publication Data

Howe, Norma.
  Blue Avenger and the theory of everything / Norma Howe.— 1st ed.
      p. cm.
  "A Marcato Book."
  Sequel to: Blue Avenger cracks the code.
  Summary: While continuing to ponder the concepts of free will and time,
Blue Avenger becomes involved in the schemes of a quirky
multimillionaire that may determine not only Blue's financial future but
also that of his girlfriend, Omaha Nebraska Brown.
  ISBN 0-8126-2654-0 (Cloth : alk. paper)
  [1. Interpersonal relations—Fiction. 2. Identity—Fiction. 3.
Contests—Fiction.] I. Title.
  PZ7.H8376 Bl 2002
  [Fic]—dc21

                                        2002000597

FOR

MARC ARONSON

CONTENTS

BLUE'S BACK!
(A PROLOGUE)

Avoid prologues. They can be annoying . . .
—Elmore Leonard

You remember Blue, don't you—that skinny red-headed high-school kid in California who changed his name from David Bruce Schumacher to Blue Avenger (after a comic-strip superhero he himself created) and how, after that, his life suddenly took on amazing new dimensions? No more the placid and studious David! No, sir! Now he was Blue Avenger, superhero, an embodiment of his motto, "Secret Champion of the Underdog, Modest Seeker of Truth, Fearless Innovator of the Unknown!"

Blue was even more surprised than Omaha Nebraska Brown herself when, just minutes after assuming his new persona, he found the courage to tell her that he loved her. And later, while they were having coffee at the mall, she astonished *him* by her uncanny ability to form acronyms on the spot, condensing his somewhat unwieldy motto to the more mysterious and foreboding "Scotu! M-sot! Fiotu!"—a secret warning that could prove useful in a number of ways and encompass myriad meanings: *Attention! Beware! Think! On guard! Help!*

Before he knew it, Blue was accomplishing such feats as saving his school principal from killer bees and preventing the demise of his school paper by an inspired bit of straight talk about condoms directed at the naive and unsuspecting staff of the *Gladiator*.

Later on, he was somehow able to reunite Omaha with her long-lost father by deducing where he was likely to be on the anniversary of the death of an Italian martyr named Giordano Bruno, and cleverly arranging for Omaha to be there, too. Pretty amazing, huh? Stranger than fiction, even. The fact that Omaha's reunion didn't turn out exactly as planned was certainly not Blue's fault, and the same goes for his ingenious idea for ending gun violence in the city of Oakland, his hometown. But we're talking realism here— not magic, and spells, and pie-in-the-sky make-believe! And speaking of pies, what about Blue's prize-winning recipe for Weepless Wonder Lemon Meringue Pie? Have you tested that yet? You should! It won't weep a drop—guaranteed!

And there's more! How about when he cracked the code that ultimately resulted in his friend Louie's receiving the credit he deserved for that computer game he created? And have you at least started to *wonder* about the man from Stratford-on-Avon called William Shakspere? (That's right. *Shakspere.*) How in the world was this glover's son able to write all those plays when he could barely scribble his own name? Because, gosh, that's all Blue Avenger ever wanted you to do—just start wondering about it—for now, at least. And if you don't believe he could barely scribble his own name, check out those six signatures of his and decide for yourself.

Oh, and hey! Can you ever forget Vixen the dog, or how Blue fought to stay true to Omaha while he and Drusie were on that gondola in Venice?

Ah, yes, those were the days, but—whoops! Hold it! Just hold it right there! We can continue rehashing Blue's past and maybe even hint about his future in a minute, but first let's take a peek at what was going on with Omaha Nebraska Brown *at the precise moment in time* that Blue was being dropped off at his house by Mr. DeSoto, who had picked up the kids at the airport in San Francisco just before midnight on the evening of 24 March, when they had just arrived back home after their four-day sojourn in Italy.

$ $ $ $ $ $ $

Actually, at that precise moment in time, Omaha—always a night owl—was not doing much of anything. She was just lying in bed in the dark getting ready to shut off her radio and go to sleep. But as she was raising her head off the pillow and starting to remove the cheap, flimsy headset that her father had given to her a couple of weeks before he had walked out on her and her mother five years ago back in Tulsa, Oklahoma—just as she was removing the headset, she heard the deejay begin to read that commercial for the Unique Construction Company of the Greater Bay Area, whose white pickup trucks featured the word UNIQUE painted on both sides, with the letters formed by acrobatic contortionists dressed in multicolored sequined bodysuits. Omaha had heard that same commercial several times before but had consciously blocked it out. This time, however, she really listened:

The Unique Construction Company of the Greater Bay Area, your dependable building contractor, is proud to announce that they are celebrating their sixteenth year serving your kitchen and bathroom remodeling needs! And to commemorate this special occasion, they are inviting all sixteen-year-olds within hearing distance of this broadcast to enter their Win a New Kitchen or a New Bathroom Contest! That's right! A completely new kitchen or bathroom for your home! Think of it! Imagine how delighted your parents will be when they learn you've won them a brand-new kitchen or sparkling new bathroom! They may even let you borrow the car! Seriously though, if you are unable to accept a new kitchen or bathroom right now, Unique Construction Company will write you a check for $5,000 instead! That's right! A new kitchen or bathroom, or $5,000 in cash! To enter, just tell us in 150 words or less what makes you unique—anything from your state of Texas birthmark to your polka dot hair! It's that simple! So let's hear your story today! The judges will

3

be the five upstanding deejays right here at Radio KFIB, including yours truly—the one, the only—Bobby Briggsmore! So send in your entry today along with your name, address, the school you attend, and your phone number to: I'm Unique, Too! Care of Radio KFIB, Box 1616, Oakland, California. Or e-mail us direct at kitchcontest@KFIB.com! Hurry! Contest ends soon!

Even before the announcement was over, Omaha had quickly switched her light back on and grabbed a pencil, ready to copy down the address. While the prospect of installing a new kitchen or bathroom in the tiny house she and her mother were renting from a witch disguised as a landlady was too far-fetched for words, the possibility of winning five thousand dollars was extremely appealing to Omaha at this particular time in her life. For not only had the witch just raised their rent a shocking amount, but even more alarming, the nurses at the city's hospitals (and that included her mother) were preparing to stage a strike that *could* last for weeks.

In fact, unless the Fates intervened soon, bearing a pile of cold cash, Omaha and her mother would find themselves traveling down that old twisting road displayed so graphically in an uncommonly boring board game that Blue's grandmother had given to his little brother, Josh, called Let's Play Realtor! There Omaha would be, throwing the dice and counting out the squares, passing by Ffth Avenue Mansion, Secluded Shangri-La, and Two-Acre Beachfront, pausing to look longingly at Split-Level Ranch, Charmer with Pool, and Old-World Elegance, before driving right past Back-Street Bungalow, One-Bedroom Shack, and Abandoned Fixer-Upper, only to land directly on Subsidized Housing, miles and miles away from San Pablo High School and that one-in-a-million guy known as Blue Avenger.

Omaha didn't even have to ask herself in what way she was qualified to enter the I'm Unique, Too! contest, for no sooner had she heard the announcement on the radio than the hitherto repressed answer just came whizzing out of her childhood memories like a sudden beacon of light shining on a sinking ship. But in spite of her first reaction (*Oh, God, no! Not that!*), Omaha was now prepared to at least consider the challenge. That five-thousand-dollar prize could mean the difference between staying where they were or moving away from her neighborhood, from her school, and—worst of all—from Blue.

As far as Omaha knew, no one outside of her family was privy to the particulars of her unique physique. (Unless, of course, we count the doctor at Tulsa General who removed "the abnormality," four staff nurses, three round-the-clock desk clerks, two secretaries in the accounting department, the HMO doctor who approved the surgery, the hospital's chief lab technician plus his trainee assistant, and the fourteen relatives who came to visit the other child in Omaha's two-bed room, every one of whom managed to sneak a peek at the chart hanging on the end of Omaha's bed while she was napping—and who, after reading it, whispered to one another, "Wow! Did you see *this?*")

Even so, could Omaha really disclose such a private and personal fact about her body to five creepy deejays from Radio KFIB, compounded by the knowledge that Lenny Briggsmore, the even creepier son of the creepiest deejay of them all, sat directly behind her in Miss Wooliscroft's English class?

Omaha began to think about the possible ramifications of entering this unique contest. If she won, would she be strong enough to bear the inevitable taunting and teasing that would surely result? But even worse, what if she lost? If the word got out then, would she be able to withstand the taunts and catcalls *without* the five thousand to ease her discomfort? But, on the plus side, if she lost the contest, then she and her mother would have no choice but to move away, so it wouldn't matter! Unless, of course, she got a job and was able to contribute enough to the family income to pay the higher rental costs. Omaha's brain was oscillating like a Ping-Pong

5

ball in a championship match. Back and forth, back and forth. Oh, if she could only talk to Blue! But then, would she find the courage to tell *him* about her embarrassing secret?

After reviewing all the possible scenarios, Omaha buried her face in the pillow, clenched her fists, and forced herself to compose in her head the first sentence of her contest entry: *Hi! My name is Omaha Nebraska Brown, and you won't believe what I'm about to tell you.*

Omaha quickly turned over in bed, grimacing in the dark, and whispered to herself, I just can't do it! I just *can't!*

$$\$ \ \$ \ \$ \ \$ \ \$ \ \$ \ \$$$

So much for Omaha, at least for the time being. Now let's get back to Blue. Oh! There he is! See? He's just waved good-bye to Louie and Drusie DeSoto and their father, and he's standing there in the street momentarily stupefied by the sight of their departing automobile bathed in the silvery glow of reflected moonlight, with the dappled shadows of leaves and branches from the overhanging trees making the vehicle appear like a rapidly retreating company of soldiers dressed in army fatigues—an understandably skewed reaction that can be attributed mainly to the fact that Blue is one tired cookie.

The last leg of their flight from Venice was unexpectedly delayed by bad weather, and the journey home from the airport was strangely quiet and melancholy, as each of the three teenagers recalled special Venetian moments they would never forget— Louie, kissing his sweet Angela good-bye; Drusie, blushing at the memory of her meeting with the young Casanova; and Blue, amazed at himself for managing to survive the great gondola fiasco with his honor intact—a feat which, of course, reminded him of Omaha.

Ah, Omaha! What a girl! One might begin to describe her by saying that Omaha is a creature made up of a unique combination of genes, encompassing both the airy philosophical bent of her father and the common-sense practicality of her mother, and that

6

her outward appearance of dark-haired, straight-arrow soberness conceals an ongoing inner dialogue of surprising depth and humor, which remains a constant source of discovery and joy for Blue Avenger, who is as sure as pie that he will love her for all eternity— presuming, of course, that such a thing is possible.

He longs to phone her right now, but the hour is much too late, much past the eleven o'clock cutoff time her mother has stipulated. And that's a shame, because, as we know, Omaha herself is at this very moment lying awake in her bed and wishing desperately that she could hear his voice.

Omaha deeply resents her mother's sometimes unreasonable rules, but in her own way she understands, for she knows that when Margie was a teenager, she had no restrictions put upon her at all, and look where that led! An unmarried mother with one son in jail and a teenage daughter to support with no help at all from the father, that's where.

Nowadays, whenever the subject is resurrected, Omaha says with a sigh, "Yeah, Mom. I know. I know. Getting phone calls from guys after eleven at night can only lead to a life of poverty and degradation. I think I've got the message."

"Very funny," Margie responds, still too ashamed to admit that Travis truly *was* conceived after a late-night phone call and subsequent romantic meeting in the park with a man she barely knew. But such things happen, and life does go on.

$ $ $ $ $ $ $

People with poor imaginations (while they may relish books of fantasy devised by others) have no patience with hypothetical questions, so what say we put yours to the test right now? What if David Schumacher had *not* changed his name to Blue Avenger on his sixteenth birthday? Would he still be in a position to meet Mr. Tractor Nishimura, the boldly irreverent and brilliant young multimillionaire television and motion picture mogul from Rancho Sueño in fabulous Marin County, California?

Oh, possibly. Who knows? Who *cares?*

Okay, then, let's look at it from another angle, which gets rather complicated, so brace yourself: Let's suppose that Tractor, the multimillionaire from Marin, had *not* been edged out of the honor of being named class valedictorian at San Pablo High School almost fifteen years ago by the valedictorian committee's alternate choice for that position—a certain Ms. Holly Hollingshead—a most sincere and sensitive young woman who honestly felt it was her duty to mention to Principal Manning that Tractor was surreptitiously planning to start off his oration by raising his fists in the air and exclaiming loudly, *"Tigers suck!"*—a rude pejorative referring to San Pablo High's crosstown rivals, and which was certainly not in keeping with the solemn nature of the commencement exercises, in the opinion of all those concerned: namely, Principal Manning, the members of the valedictorian committee, and, of course, Holly herself. And let's suppose further that Tractor Nishimura had not been itching ever since to find a way to even the score with Holly before their class reunion this spring. Would he then want to make use of his recently discovered knowledge that Holly is presently employed by the California State Department of Motor Vehicles and charged with the responsibility of ascertaining that personalized license plates conform to a decency standard that forbids vulgar or obscene words or phrases? Of course not! Why would he?

However, the truth is that Tractor *was* edged out of making the graduation speech, and Holly *was* mostly to blame, and Tractor *does* itch to get even. So, keeping all that in mind, is it possible that these various happenings could lead to Tractor's meeting up with Blue Avenger, thus precipitating the incredible events that followed—events involving huge amounts of $$$?

Actually, no. It would take even more than that, for the simple reason that nouveau riche multimillionaire movie moguls tend to move in circles quite apart from high-school kids who live and attend a magnet school in a lower-middle-class neighborhood in

Oakland, California, some of whom have not yet even heard the phrase *nouveau riche*.

So how *will* it happen that the life trajectories of Blue Avenger and Tractor Nishimura will come together the week after Blue returns from four days in Venice during spring break of his junior year at San Pablo High?

Could Mr. Frank Frazier, Blue's high-school counselor, be the connecting link? Well, could be! And when Blue and Trac finally *do* meet up in Mr. Frazier's office, will old Trac discharge his obligation as a multimillionaire should (in accordance with everyone's unreasonable fantasy) and casually extract several hundred-dollar bills from his wallet and toss them over to Blue with a lopsided grin and an offhanded comment about his Gucci® billfold being too stuffed with money to fit into the pocket of his Versace® jeans?

And what about Tractor himself? What can we make of his somewhat perverse penchant for testing and observing the ethical (or, sad to say, the *unethical*) choices made by unsuspecting persons he himself sets up in interesting but sometimes rather costly experiments? (And, in this connection, one cannot help wondering how Blue Avenger will fare when cast in the role of a guinea pig, even though he in no way resembles those small, fat rodents with short ears and no external tails—genus *Cavia*—which were originally brought to England by ships plying between that country, Guinea, and South America, and which are often used in biological experiments.)

As a final query, how will it happen that a totally unsuspecting and surprised personage will suddenly be rolling in dough simply for uttering a form of the rarely used verb *to ply?*

The answers to these and other stumpers will come—all in due time, all in due time.

But first, there is some old business that needs to be attended to—and that is the bothersome question of free will versus determinism. Specifically, did David Schumacher actually *decide* to change his name to Blue Avenger on his sixteenth birthday, or was that action already predetermined from the very beginning of time, whenever the heck that was—or, rather, *if* that was, since some edgy physicists are playing around with the theory that there is no such thing as time, that time *doesn't exist*, a position that puts them in the same basket as that ever growing group of crackpots or wonderfully astute logicians (according to your own outlook on the subject) who believe that the plays and poems attributed to one William Shakespeare were actually written by Edward de Vere, the seventeenth Earl of Oxford. But that's another story.

$ $ $ $ $ $ $

The moon was full on Blue's last night in Venice, and now, in Oakland, California, its still-brilliant light is shining down on a huge blue tarp covering something the approximate size of an elephant, sprawled along the edge of the small front porch of Blue's house and spilling over onto the lawn. Blue smiles at the sight, for he knows what's under the tarp—cartons of cornstarch sent to him by the Wanner Cornstarch Company in appreciation for his Weepless Wonder Lemon Meringue Pie recipe. However, it's obvious that Josh, Blue's ten-year-old brother, was not far off the mark when he sent Blue that e-mail describing the cornstarch hoard as "fifty-four huge boxes bigger than the one the computer came in."

Blue doesn't feel like going into the house just yet, even though it's very late. He sits down on the front step with his left arm resting on his thigh and his chin supported by his right fist, unconsciously mimicking the posture of Auguste Rodin's most famous sculpture. (No, silly—not *The Kiss*—that *other* one.)

If he weren't so absorbed in thought, Blue might have noticed that the late-evening dew had not fallen on a section of the parking area pavement halfway between his house and Marvin Lasher's place next door, leaving dry a large, rectangle-shaped spot where, earlier that evening, a black van had been parked—a black van permeated with the sickly sweet smell of dog shampoo and merciful death.

10

But Marvin Lasher had been aware of the van. Marvin knew that it had been parked there until almost midnight, although he was temporarily absent from his watching post when the mysterious occupant had returned and driven away. Marvin Lasher keeps close track of things like strange vans in his neighborhood and ominous black helicopters hovering overhead, and Marvin Lasher listens to talk radio very, very late into the night, and he marvels at the incredible and bizarre tales he hears coming directly from the mouths of the very persons who experienced them. And, furthermore, like the majority of his fellow Americans, Marvin Lasher does indeed believe in the existence of angels.

After almost ten minutes of rambling philosophical musings, Blue stands up and stretches, finally sick and tired of trying to figure out whether his thoughts and actions are truly *his*, or whether they are really made up of measurable and quantifiable chemicals and electrical impulses blindly obeying every physical law of the universe, regardless of his own personal fears and desires. And that is the reason that he has just this minute decided (*decided?* oh, boy—there's that word again) to put the whole free-will-versus-determinism conundrum on the back burner of his brain and let it stew there until he's good and ready to take the lid off the pot and stir it around some more. As quickly as he does this, however, as fast as a big chunk of his brain is swept clean of free-will clutter, other topics just as puzzling and disconcerting are being sucked into the void, among them:

Why do I sometimes feel that I'm surrounded by crackpots? Am I insane to feel this way?

Why did the simple act of changing my name to Blue Avenger make such a difference in my life? Could something really strange be going on here? Could it be possible that I'm actually morphing into the comic-strip character I created? Oh, please! I'm a sane and reasonable person! How can I believe that? Will I ever be able to dispel this weird and unsettling feeling? Am I actually one of the very crackpots I ridicule and disdain?

Why does it not bother me that I am sixteen years old and have never been drunk or stoned?

Why have I started thinking about time all the time?

And, finally, why does it seem like the best-selling books written for kids my age are composed mostly of simple or compound sentences with no subordinate clauses to challenge our intellect and prepare us to read genuine works of literature, such as, say, the current novels of Nicholson Baker (well, maybe not all of them) and those written by dead guys such as Marcel Proust or Dostoevsky or one of my favorites, William Makepeace Thackeray, whose great masterpiece, Vanity Fair: A Novel without a Hero, *happened to be on my father's bookshelf and which I read last year, with its opening sentence so marvelous that I was compelled to commit it to memory, and which still comes to mind occasionally, like, for instance, now: "While the present century was in its teens, and on one sunshiny morning in June, there drove up to the great iron gate of Miss Pinkerton's academy for young ladies, on Chiswick Mall, a large family coach, with two fat horses in blazing harness, driven by a fat coachman in a three-cornered hat and wig, at the rate of four miles an hour."*

Blue smiles. *At the rate of four miles an hour.* Imagine! Old William Makepeace couldn't resist tacking that on at the end. (Another thing William Makepeace Thackeray couldn't resist tacking on were occasional asides directed to the reader, a habit that is deemed either wonderfully endearing or extremely annoying, according to the intelligence, emotional maturity, and all-around goodness of the same. It should be apparent to the present reader that Thackeray's most fervent fans—those who look forward with eager anticipation to each and every authorial aside—exhibit an overabundance of the aforementioned traits of intelligence, maturity, and goodness.)

Blue reaches in his pocket for his house key. I think I think too much, he thinks, all the while not realizing how truly unique he is—a rare high-school junior who prefers to entertain his own thoughts rather than submit to the mind-numbing hypnotic effect of loud music, a boy who is more familiar with Mozart than with MTV, a nonconformist who has pinned on his bulletin board (as a definitive rebuke of much of the popular music so admired by his peers) an item he clipped out of the newspaper containing a quotation attributed to Voltaire: *Anything too stupid to be spoken is sung.*

In short, either by heredity or environment, or a combination of both, Blue Avenger is one of the fortunate minority of teenagers somehow rendered immune to the siren call of the troublesome phenomenon described by psychologists as peer pressure—a fortunate minority of teenagers who *do* exist, in spite of the many self-absorbed worshipers of teenage angst who insist that no young person can be *that* strong and independent, which is, obviously, an uninformed and erroneous opinion backed up only by their own sorry histories.

Blue turns his key in the lock, walks into the house, and quietly closes the door behind him, gently securing the bolt and then double-checking to make sure it's in place. The room is dimly illuminated by the 15-watt night-light emanating from the bottom of his grandmother's 1950s floor lamp, which is standing alongside his father's old easy chair as steadfastly and permanently as a lighthouse on a promontory overlooking a treacherous sea, but, in this case, the lighthouse is turned upside down and the sea is a prematurely frayed blue carpet in a wavy pattern, manufactured by the misleadingly named TuffTextiles® Floor Coverings Company of Calhoun, California.

As Blue's gaze falls upon his father's bookcase, he feels the old familiar flutter of sadness from somewhere deep within his chest, like a downed and wounded bird attempting flight. The seventh of April, now less than two weeks away, will mark the third anniversary of his father's death, and there still remain twenty-seven of his books for Blue to read before the impulsive vow he made to himself is fulfilled—the pledge to read every book on his father's shelves as a kind of tribute to a parent he both loved and respected. And although Blue is unaware of the power behind this motivating force, his deep desire to honor the memory of his dead father has not only made him a true prince of a son, but has also become a hidden source of strength in his quest to lead an exemplary life.

Blue pauses a moment by the bookcase and impulsively pulls out the next volume from the shelf he was working on, since he had finished reading the travel book about Rome and is ready to start a new one. He stoops down and reads the title by the glow of the night-light from the lamp: *The Treasure of the Sierra Madre*, by B. Traven. He wonders if the book will be as entertaining as the movie (starring the one and only Humphrey Bogart), which he saw with Omaha one Friday night when his mother had invited her for dinner. "We don't need no stinking badges!" Omaha found herself muttering as the final credits rolled, just as thousands of fans before her had done throughout the years.

Blue remembers to stop by his mother's bedroom to let her know that he's home, as he had promised he would when he had called her from the airport during his layover in New York. "Psst. Mom," he whispers, gently touching her arm. "Are you awake? I'm home."

Sally Schumacher opens her eyes and quickly rises up on one elbow. "Oh, Blue! Sorry I didn't wait up for you. What time is it? I'll get up," she says, reaching for her robe. "I want to hear all about—"

"No, no," Blue whispers. "I'm really tired. You stay in bed. I'll tell you all about it in the morning, okay?"

Sally nods and lies back down. She smiles at Blue. "It's nice having you back," she says. "I'll see you in the morning."

ATTENTION READERS!

ARE YOU PLAGUED BY THESE COMMON READING COMPLAINTS?

1. Words Too Hard

2. Sentences Too Long

3. Trouble Staying Awake

4. Material Doesn't Make Sense

5. Other

IF SO, REJOICE! HELP IS ON THE WAY!

Introducing

KWiKYREAD©,

by Simptex®

THE REVOLUTIONARY NEW "SMART" WAY TO READ!

• •

KwikyRead© by Simptex® is a boon for today's busy, top-flight achievers, typically characterized by brief attention spans and limited patience. To demonstrate how KwikyRead© works, the preceding pages have been carefully translated by our language experts into the same, simple writing style found in the most popular books on the market today. If you (or someone you love) found the prologue of this book to be "over your head" and somewhat tedious, KwikyRead© can help! To prove it for yourself, read through the KwikyRead© Simplified Text Version of "Blue's Back!" right now! You will be able to "get the gist" of the longer version in just 4 short pages, with none of the hassle. Guaranteed! Could anything be simpler? We know you will be pleased as punch with the new ease and enjoyment you will find with KwikyRead© by Simptex® as your reading partner! The copyrighted KwikyRead© Simplified Text Version of this entire volume is now available on-line and ready to download at the low, low price of $24.99. (Credit cards only, please.) Find us on the Internet at:

http://www.KwikyRead/Simptex//GalacticWEhiangelface/shuks/hoax.yea

BLUE'S BACK!
(A PROLOGUE)

(KwikyRead© Simplified Text Version by Simptex®)

Hey! Do you remember Blue Avenger and all his adventures? Well, you probably don't, so let's just say he did lots of stuff, and move on.

Blue's girlfriend's name is Omaha Nebraska Brown. She just heard about a contest on the radio. Omaha needs some money real bad. If she wins the contest, she can help her mother pay the rent and they won't have to move away. But she will have to tell a secret about her body. What can it be? (Whatever it is, we won't believe it!)

Blue just got dropped off at his house. He thinks the shadows on his friends' car make it look like guys in camouflage suits. (That's probably because he is pooped.) The moon was out in Venice the night before, too. It was shining on a gondola where weird things were happening.

Thinking about the gondola and the moonlight reminds Blue of Omaha Nebraska Brown. Omaha is a little bit like her father and a little bit like her mother. Blue wants to call her up right now. But her mother gets mad if people call her after eleven at night. Too bad, because Omaha would sure like to talk to Blue right now. He wants to talk to her, too!

Something unusual happened on David Schumacher's sixteenth birthday.

He changed his name to Blue Avenger! But what if he had not decided to change his name? Then maybe he wouldn't have met a man named Tractor Nishimura!

Tractor Nishimura is strange. He doesn't care what anybody thinks of him. He's smart, too. And he makes lots and lots of money from things like television and the movies. He lives in his own little city in California called Rancho Sueño. (So you won't have to look it up, Rancho Sueño means like "Dream Ranch," or, maybe, "Ranch of Dreams." Something like that.)

When Tractor Nishimura graduated from high school, he almost got to be the main speaker at the ceremony. But a girl named Holly Hollingshead found out he was going to start his speech by shouting, "Tigers suck!" So she ratted on him. Then the principal picked her to give the speech instead of Tractor. That made him pretty mad! He wants to get even!

Holly has an interesting job. If someone wants to get a personalized license plate for their car, Holly has to look at it first. If it has swear words in it, she won't let them get it. If it is nasty, she won't let them get it.

Blue Avenger lives in Oakland, California. No really rich people live in his neighborhood. Only regular people. Some kids in Blue's school don't know what *nouveau riche* means.

Do you want to know how Tractor Nishimura and Blue Avenger will meet? Will Blue expect that Tractor is going to give him some hundred-dollar bills because he has an expensive wallet and wears designer pants? Will Blue become a guinea pig? How will somebody get a nice surprise just by saying the word *ply?* Well, you will just have to wait and see!

Blue often wonders if there is such a thing as free will. Free will is hard to understand.

Some people say there is no such thing as time. They may be right. Some people say William Shakespeare didn't write all those plays. They may be right, too.

The moon is also shining down on a blue tarp on Blue's front porch and lawn. There's something the size of an elephant under the blue tarp. Blue knows what it is. It's boxes of cornstarch!

Blue wants to sit out on his front step for a while and think. He looks like a statue. He doesn't know about the black van that was parked near his house a little earlier that night. So he doesn't know the black van smelled funny. (Maybe the black van was full of putrid and decaying dead people with squirming white maggots sucking on their tongues and their eyes dangling from their sockets all moldy and full of crawling worms. That would be cool.)* Blue's neighbor's name is Marvin Lasher. Marvin Lasher believes everything he hears on the radio. He also thinks angels are real. But that's not so strange. A lot of other people do, too.

Pretty soon Blue gets tired of thinking about free will. He starts to think about other things. He thinks that maybe everybody is nuts. Then he thinks that he might be crazy. Could he actually be turning into the comic-book character he made up? Poor Blue! He knows that's crazy, but still he can't help believing it, sort of. He admits to himself that he has never been drunk or stoned, but that doesn't embarrass him. He really likes his brain and wants to preserve it.

William Makepeace Thackeray is one of Blue's favorite authors. Blue likes William Makepeace Thackeray's sentences. They are pretty long sometimes. But they are fun to read, and Blue is smart enough to understand them. Do occasional "asides to the reader" distract you and get you all mixed up? If so, maybe you should try to skip over them until you are a little older and smarter.

---

*Note to Teachers, Librarians, and Reading Specialists: This parenthetical addition cannot be found in the original version. It has been added as a public service in the hope of assisting the path of those readers, predominantly young males, who are in the process of being weaned away from that wildly popular series of books beginning with the word Goose.

Blue gets out his house key. He thinks he thinks too much. He doesn't like loud music with stupid words. He would rather listen to Mozart. Are you always worried about "what the other kids think, or thought, or will think"? Not Blue! Isn't he lucky? He unlocks the door and walks into his front room. The floor lamp was made in the 1950s. It used to be his grandmother's. He notices his father's books. He remembers that he made a promise to himself when his father died. He was going to read all of his books someday!

Blue is really a nice guy. He doesn't know why, but we do. It's really because of his father. He wants to please his father, but he doesn't know it.

Blue wakes up his mother and tells her he's home. He's really tired and doesn't feel like talking about his trip right now. She says, "It's nice having you back. I'll see you in the morning."

Simplified Text by KwikyRead©, a subsidiary of SimptexCorp®, which is owned by the Gutemeyer Conglomerate Group© under the auspices of Galactic Worldwide Endeavors, Inc.©

TIME

But if there is no time, how do we account for the fact that it seems there is? The answer is time capsules. We are contained in a time capsule. The points of Platonia selected by the equations of quantum gravity are precisely the time capsules.
—Simon W. Saunders,
New York Times Book Review

Blue woke up after ten the next morning, and for a few seconds he couldn't remember where he was. He watched, fascinated, as his bedroom door and his window seemed to take leave of their moorings and silently change places several times, jockeying for position before finally settling down in their proper and workaday locations. Hey, jet lag shenanigans! Cool!

Blue closed his eyes and tried to imagine himself back in that little room in Venice that he had shared with his friend Louie just the night before. But wait—was it really just the night before? He turned on his back and raised his hands to his head, running his fingers through his thick red curls. No. No, it wasn't. Actually, it was the night *before* last, since I spent part of last night on the plane and the rest of it right here in my own bed. And tomorrow will make it two days since I was in Venice, because time will have marched on. *Time keeps marching on.*

Blue sighed. He sighed because he knew what was coming. He was going to think about the mystery of time once again. *Time keeps marching on.* Ah, but does it march on in measurable moments,

20

something like the individual images that make up a strip of movie film, where each single frame has captured a tiny increment of what we call time? In that respect, does time work in the same way that energy does as described in the quantum theory of energy that he learned about in physics class? *Energy is not absorbed or radiated continuously, but discontinuously, and only in multiples of definite, indivisible units.* That would make sense, in a way. If so, how long does each unit of time last? What does it feel like? And how is it connected to the next little burst of time, since it's obvious that each little moment has to be connected to the next little moment in some way, or everything would stop. Wouldn't it? And if time *is* divided into short little nanoseconds, then change has to occur only *within* those little moments. So what happens between one moment of time and the next? Because if they *are* separated, there has to be something in between. So are there two kinds of time—real time, and mere space-filling time, during which no change can occur? And what *about* change, anyway? Does change really *need* time, or does it just seem that way to us, because we have no other way of explaining it?

And then Blue—ever sincere, ever the experimenter, ever the hopeless philosopher—tried, yet again, to capture and seize and analyze a fleeting moment of time. And, of course, as always, he failed. Blue sighed again. It just didn't make sense, all that starting and stopping of time. So time *must* be continuous. It must flow along like a river, continuously flowing on and on and on, forever and ever. It must be like a circle, a ring—with no beginning and no end. Just *there*—always present, never-ending—a never-ending nothing.

But hold it! Wait! Maybe that's it! A never-ending nothing! What if there is *no such thing* as time? What if it just *seems* like there is such a thing as time? What if the ticking of clocks merely indicates that *change* is occurring? So who says that change requires time? Maybe that's why time seems to fly when you're having fun and drags when you're bored. Time *can't* be the same for a tiny insect, which maybe lives for only a matter of hours, as it is for a— well, a parrot, or an elephant. And who can conceive of a time when there *was* no time, or of a time when there will *be* no time? The whole concept of time may just be an illusion, after all.

Blue caught his breath, feeling himself once again in that strange, eerie state of mind he sometimes fell into after dwelling upon life's imponderables. But in a few seconds he was back again on more solid ground. The slightest hint of a smile crossed his lips. What if that old witticism turns out to be true—that time is simply nature's way of keeping everything from happening at once? But enough of this time stuff. It's time I got up and gave Omaha a call. Has she missed me as much as I've missed her?

Blue went to the bathroom, and then headed for the kitchen, still in his pajamas.

"Mom?" he called out. "Josh? Anybody home?"

Then he saw the note on the refrigerator: GONE TO STORE—JOSH AT TREVOR'S. In the middle of the table were the two familiar baskets that his mother always managed to retrieve on this particular day of the year from the hidden recesses somewhere in the hard-to-reach kitchen cabinet located above the stove. Although the baskets were not labeled, it was understood that one was for him and the other was for Josh. As usual, the baskets were filled with a mixture of chocolate-covered almonds and jelly beans—his nonchurchgoing mother's traditional token acknowledgment of Easter. Blue grabbed a large handful of the candies from one of the baskets and popped them into his mouth, and then, pausing ever so slightly while his subconscious mind struggled with the ethical choice presented to him, he picked up the *very same basket* from which he had sampled, carried it to the phone, and dialed Omaha's number. (In a similar but highly controlled experiment at the PsychoFood Institute in Pasadena, California—supported by a modest grant from Frack's Confection Company—it was noted that 82 out of 100 youngsters of *normal* weight also carried off the *very same basket* from which they had sampled, while a whopping 92 percent of the overweight subjects promptly claimed the *unsampled* basket as their own, which gives rise to the proposition that Blue's choice was

22

merely the result of his normal weight and should not be construed as a barometer of his moral fiber, so to speak.)

Omaha answered the phone after only one ring.

"Hi," Blue said. "Guess who?"

"Oh, good! You're back! Did you have a good time? When did you get in?"

"I don't know. It was pretty late, though. It was way after midnight, I know that. I wanted to call you, but—"

"Yeah, I know. My mother's dumb rule."

Blue didn't respond to that, since he never did feel right criticizing her mother, even though he agreed that it was, for sure, a dumb rule.

"It was really great getting all that e-mail from you," Omaha said. "But it's funny, you know, how a couple of years ago people believed that all this e-mail and stuff would save a lot of paper? Like it would become a paperless society? Well, right after you left, I talked my mom into getting a printer—they had some really good ones on sale cheap—and anyway, I, personally, have used up more paper in the last couple of days since—well, I don't know since when—but a lot of paper, anyway." She paused for a second, then lowered her voice, adding, "I've printed up all your letters, and I've started keeping them in a special binder under my bed."

Blue swallowed hard and moistened his lips. He couldn't believe that just hearing her say *under my bed* could provoke such a reaction. "Yeah, well, that's funny, because I printed yours, too, in that bookstore in Venice. Actually, they're still in my backpack, since I haven't had a chance to empty that out yet."

Blue suddenly remembered the little amber glass snail he had bought for her at the souvenir stand by the Rialto Bridge, and he was just about to ask if he could come over and see her when she asked, "So, uh, otherwise, what else is happening? Louie and Drusie okay? You know, I'm really sorry I acted so stupid about Drusie. I mean, I've been feeling bad about that—like I don't want you to think—"

"Hey, come on! I don't think anything!" Blue was certain that someday he'd tell her about that last night in Venice, in the gondola

23

with Drusie, but there was no rush. Thank God, at least his conscience was clear, and, actually, the whole thing was starting to seem kind of funny, in a way. But something in Omaha's voice had been bothering him since the beginning of this conversation. He noticed it right away when she first began talking about the paperless society, sort of a nervous cheerfulness, an unusual garrulousness. So before she could start up again, he came right out and asked her. "Omaha? Is everything all right over there?"

The long pause at the other end of the line was a dead giveaway. "Not really."

"What is it? What's wrong?"

"Oh, it's just—all of a sudden everything is such a big, mixed-up mess."

"Like what? What's a mess?"

"Just *everything*—"

Blue waited, expecting she would elaborate, but she remained silent. He wasn't sure just exactly how serious this was. "How about a hint?" he asked finally, trying not to sound too playful, in case it was something *really* serious.

"Well, to make a long story short, it looks like we're going to have to move," she said softly.

Blue almost choked on a chocolate-covered almond. "*Move? Did you say move? Where?*"

"Well, we don't know yet, because—"

"Listen, can I come over?" Blue interrupted.

"Right now? Oh, *could* you? But, listen, my mother's at work, so you know what that means," she said in the singsongy tone she always resorted to when referring to her mother's rules.

Yes, Blue knew what that meant. It meant another one of her mother's decrees was in force—the one that forbids male visitors in the house while she's not at home—a rule that was both humiliating and embarrassing for Omaha, who was, after all, almost seventeen years old and a junior in high school. However, Omaha's way of dealing with this particular proviso was not to sweep it under the rug and hope no one would look there, but, rather, to flaunt it and brag about it, thus diffusing its power. As Miss Wooliscroft has noted, *Omaha is quite a unique young lady—observant, witty, wise beyond her years.*

"Yeah, I guess I know what it means. It means that we'll sit on your porch swing," Blue said, suddenly engulfed again by a hungry and desperate longing for a car to replace his beloved van that was recently totaled by a falling branch of his neighbor's eucalyptus tree—for without a car, there was no permissible opportunity for him and Omaha to be truly alone.

Blue sighed, visions of automobiles still floating around in his head. Finally, he said, "Just give me a few minutes to grab something to eat and I'll be right over."

"Well, hey—I could fix you a sandwich or something over here, if you want."

What was that she said? She could fix him a sandwich? Omaha was the first girl who had ever offered to perform such a domestic-type service for him—surely a milestone in his journey along the newfound road of romance. Blue paused, relishing a sudden feeling of euphoria that seemed to be centered somewhere in his chest, around the area his mother used to massage with Vicks VapoRub when he was little and suffering from a hacking cough. "Great. I'll be on my way in a few minutes then—as soon as I get dressed."

Omaha, all alone in the house, felt herself blushing. She couldn't believe that simply hearing him say *as soon as I get dressed* could provoke such a reaction.

An Introduction to the

WarpSpeed™ Personal Home-Reading Improvement Program

(A Division of SimptexCorp®)

• •

Question: *What is The WarpSpeed™ Personal Home-Reading Improvement Program and how can it help me?*

The WarpSpeed™ Personal Home-Reading Improvement Program (WSPH-RIP™) is a tested and proven plan for individuals to home in on and sharpen their personal reading skills in the comfort of familiar surroundings. Students may proceed at their own pace and in the privacy of their own ReadingSpace™. Pace and Space: Those are the Key Words.

Question: *What is ReadingSpace™?*

ReadingSpace™ is an entirely new concept developed by the ReadRite™ specialists at WarpSpeed™, a division of SimptexCorp®. It is used in conjunction with KwikyKwiz© to enable our customers to check their progress at regular intervals in a highly effective and "fun" way.

Question: *What is KwikyKwiz©?*

Simply stated, KwikyKwiz© is a quicky quiz! It is both the mainstay and backbone of WSPH-RIP™. Amazingly, psychologists have found that readers faced with the prospect of answering Questions pertaining to the material they have just read will pay closer attention to WHAT they are reading so as to not embarrass themselves with a poor evaluation when they are put to the test.

Question: *Well, that is amazing! Can you explain why that is?*

We'd be happy to! Interestingly enough, it's an ego thing, pure and simple.

Question: *Sounds great! When can I try KwikyKwiz© for myself?*

Right now! The very next chapter of the book you are presently holding was deliberately chosen as a DemoVehicle™ for WSPH-RIP™ by our ReadRite™ specialists!

Question: *Well, thank you! That's very nice of you. But I'm curious: Why did you choose the following chapter as your DemoVehicle™?*

To our ReadRite™ specialists, it was a dream come true! Not only is it overly long, going off on tangents every which way and rambling on endlessly with no apparent rhyme or reason, but it is also rife with seemingly pointless dialogue and boring new characters. So what are you waiting for? Let's get started playing KwikyKwiz© now!

Question: *I can't wait! But first, I have one last question: The name WarpSpeed™ sounds familiar to me. Can you explain the reason for that?*

Yes, indeed we can! A much more comprehensive version of WarpSpeed™, known as WarpSpeedPlus™, has been in use in Schools across the Nation for over a decade, receiving "rave reviews" from Principals and Teachers everywhere!

Note: If you are a Teacher, Principal, Interested Parent, or Just Plain Reader and you are not yet familiar with WarpSpeed™ and WarpSpeedPlus™, find out how you and your students can win FABULOUS PRIZES and learn more about these Exciting Home and School Programs by visiting our Web site at:

www.WarpSpeed&/WarpSpeedPlus.Pdq.SIN/hiangelface805060626/ ref=ase/starbright_boksynoahwe/107&%obit753zippy390936 hekcjsu/_://hoax.yea.

• •

DONUTS

Homer Simpson may be America's favorite animated half-wit, but he's definitely in sync with the national obsession for doughnuts. Breakfast? Snack? Dessert? The doughnut has rolled past most pigeonholed food items to become a high-calorie round-the-clock icon of Americana.

—Rick Aristotle Munarriz,
The Motley Fool

For the next few moments, while Blue is busily occupied brushing his teeth and getting dressed for his ride to Omaha's place, let us experiment briefly with the mysterious fluidity of time. It can be simply done, with only words and thoughts, and a willingness to try.

In the blink of an eye, we can go back in time to thirty-five years ago, to the first school day of that year following spring break—or *Easter vacation*, as it was called back then—when 583 fifth graders in the United States of America were asked to write and present a report to their classmates about a scientist by the name of Carolus Linnaeus (pronounced Lin-*knee*-us). Of the 396 fifth-grader reports that were turned in on time, all but 32 of them cited as Carolus Linnaeus's main claim to fame his idea of binomial nomenclature for plants and animals. In other words, he was the instigator of *genus* and *species*. Before Linnaeus, one might say, there was no such thing as *Homo sapiens*—an ambiguously thought-provoking idea, indeed!

Blue has finished brushing his teeth now, but he's still deciding what shirt to wear, so we have time to read just the first sentence of one of those fifth graders' reports, chosen at random. It was written by a certain Jonathan Barger, age ten, of Allentown, Pennsylvania, who got the information for his report from encyclopedias he found in the library, since this was in the days before the invention of the Internet. Jonathan's all-abiding interest in things scientific could later be traced directly back to this sentence: *Carolus Linnaeus was born in 1707 and became interested in botany early in his life.*

Although young Jonathan mispronounced Linnaeus's name during his oral presentation—calling him Lin-*nay*-us—he still received an A from Miss Seiber, his teacher. Miss Seiber did not enjoy teaching one bit. What she really wanted to do was follow her dream, singing and playing an old family-heirloom stringed instrument given to her by her grandfather from Kentucky (which he mistakenly called a dulcimer, but which was really a kind of zither) for loose change in the underground metro stations of Europe.

As for Jonathan Barger (now *Dr.* Barger, head of the pioneering Jonathan Barger Proteomics Research Center in Colorado Springs, Colorado—a nonprofit organization), one of his chief concerns these days, apart from his own pet research projects, is writing grant applications, hoping to keep the money flowing in so that he and his associates may be able to continue their study in the next step *beyond* the human genome, which is the complicated composition and purpose of the tangle of the more than 500,000 proteins that are responsible for the variations found in each and every human being.

One of the center's current projects is the ongoing search for either (or both) of two specific combinations of proteins and the genes that produce them. Put in its simplest terms, Team One is hard at work looking for the highly elusive but long-suspected "religion" or "faith" gene—the lack of which could be responsible for persons known variously as freethinkers, secular humanists, agnostics, or atheists—while Team Two continues to search for the "reason" gene, the lack of *that* one resulting in persons believing in such things as perpetual motion machines, astrology, the existence of extraterrestrials on earth, and—we must be very careful of our wording here—let's just say persons drawn to certain "religious cults," and let it go at that.

As things now stand, the only point the frazzled researchers can agree on is that all bets are off until a definite breakthrough occurs, and when that will happen is anybody's guess. (Just recently, several of the white-coaters, referred to as the Young Turks by some of the older technicians, have caused quite a stir around the lab by suggesting the intriguing possibility that a certain number of human beings may possess both the "faith" *and* the "reason" gene! This, as the Young Turks contend, could account for the often puzzling and confused dichotomy displayed by religious scientists and doubt-plagued theologians.)

Meanwhile, in a little room at the end of the hall, Dr. Jonathan Barger himself is deeply immersed in his own private research effort. Never "one of the crowd," yet a devoted friend to a chosen few, Dr. Barger has been fascinated since his school days by the overwhelming importance attached by the great majority of young people (both at home and abroad) to the opinions of their peers. For the past several weeks he has been outlining a proposed study plan and will soon begin research on the possible causes and often excruciatingly painful ramifications of the seldom-studied force he calls Peer Pressure Power, or PPP, in the vernacular.

And Miss Seiber? Well, the weekend after little Jonathan Barger's report, she met a young man at a morris dancing club, and six weeks later she was engaged to be married. When her students asked her what morris dancing was, she explained that it was an old English folk dance in which the dancers often dress in costumes associated with the Robin Hood legends. She persuaded her beau to come visit her classroom in his Friar Tuck costume, and the children received him with enthusiastic whoops and hollers.

Miss Seiber quit teaching soon after her wedding, and the happy couple journeyed abroad, where they spent two miserable years making fools of themselves for loose change in the underground metro stations of Europe before coming home and settling down in Berkeley, California. And for a time, they found they could actually make more money in one day on Shattuck Avenue in Berkeley—with her playing the zither and him clowning around in his Friar Tuck costume—than they could in a week down in the subways of Europe. Their only son, Jared, was born the year after they returned to the States. Before they knew it, he was in college, where he had a special major in something called "Free World Economics in Emerging Third World Countries," but, eventually, he found a job as a traveling salesman for Oral-B® toothbrushes. To the disappointment of his parents, Jared, now thirty-one years old, was never the least bit interested in morris dancing or dressing up in costumes. He was, however, from an early age, addicted to donuts. Jared joined forces with some salesmen friends who happened to be similarly afflicted, and together they started the world's first Donut Shop Collectors Club. In its heyday, the DSCC boasted the five charter members plus two Johnnies-come-lately and three hangers-on, one of whom was computer-literate and started up the colorful and entertaining Donut Shop Collectors Club Web site, which, at last count, had racked up 5,382 hits.

$ $ $ $ $ $ $

Blue decided to take the fastest route to Omaha's house, even though he would have to travel for over a mile on one of the busiest avenues in the city. Just as he was riding past Donut Pros, his favorite neighborhood donut shop, it happened—a cyclist's worst nightmare. Without any warning, the door on the driver's side of a parked yellow Mercedes 500 SLC swung open and a man stepped out into the street, directly in Blue's path. The surprised driver barely managed to flatten his 215-pound six-foot frame against the side of the car as Blue braked and swerved wildly, and a collision was narrowly avoided, but by the time the man realized what had happened and was able to yell out, "Sorry, kid!" Blue was already trying to negotiate the busy intersection ahead, and all he could do was raise an arm in a gesture of forgiveness.

It will take Blue exactly seventeen minutes and eleven seconds to make it all the way to Omaha's house. As he continues on his way, once again we are free to digress, trusting that we will rejoin our hero the moment he arrives at his destination.

$ $ $ $ $ $

Donut Pros, the scene of Blue's close call, is owned and operated by a hardworking Cambodian husband-and-wife team, who, even after eight years in the business, have not quite mastered the knack of sizing up their potential hired help, usually following their hearts instead of their heads, and therefore often ending up with unreliable counter help and semivagrant donut makers.

Even so, Donut Pros has managed to remain open for seven days a week, including holidays, for the entire eight years of its existence. As the handmade sign in the window proclaims, OPEN FROM 4 A.M. UNTIL THE DONUTS RUN OUT—the peculiar wording of which has provoked myriad comments throughout the years, from haughtily patronizing to genuinely tickled, according to the mood and temperament of the observer.

When the yellow Mercedes 500 SLC pulled up and parked in front of the shop on this particular Easter morning, neither Lynnie, the counter girl, nor Bryan, the donut maker, was aware of it, since they happened to be standing so close to one another they could feel each other's heartbeat, and they were so much in love that they wouldn't even have noticed if a flying saucer belching clouds of purple smoke had just set down in front of the store.

The two men who had just emerged from the car, the hefty driver (who would henceforth be certain to check for oncoming traffic before opening the door) and his smaller companion, were dressed almost alike in wrinkled khaki pants and long-sleeved knit shirts with double pockets, and appeared to be just regular guys out looking for donuts on an Easter morning. In reality, however, they were none other than Timothy Sims and Tractor Nishimura, two of the richest young men in America today.

Timothy Sims, the driver and owner of the car, had been the junior partner in their wildly successful company since its deceivingly commonplace beginnings twelve years ago at another donut shop—a favorite student hangout in Berkeley called the Donut Demon. It was there, at the corner table by the window, that Tim and his college roommate, Tractor Nishimura, formed T&T Productions, a business partnership that has grown to be a legend in the highly competitive and volatile entertainment industry, even though both men prefer to keep extremely low profiles outside of their immediate social and professional connections and have never responded to requests for public appearances of any kind.

Their partnership was textbook perfect from the start, an ideal merging of divergent talents and personalities. While Tim took charge of the increasingly complicated business end of the company with unflappable ease and unquestioned integrity, Tractor more than adequately fulfilled the restless creative promise he had demonstrated from his early childhood.

Trac (as he is sometimes called) is the only son of Hiroshi Nishimura, a Japanese American who was born in 1943 inside the barbed-wire fenced area at the wartime Japanese internment camp in Mansanar, California. Tractor's first full-length film—a documentary called *Life at Mansanar*, made while he was still attending college—won him the prestigious Rooney Award, and was instrumental in getting his fledging career off the ground.

As Trac remarked in his very moving acceptance speech, "The

irony of this situation does not elude me. The fact that my success stems directly from the grave injustices endured by my parents and grandparents—as well as thousands of other American citizens of Japanese ancestry—is almost too much to bear." (At the reception after the award ceremony, an aging movie director by the name of Antonio DiVittorio pointed out to Tractor that certain Italian Americans were afforded similar housing arrangements during that same time period in our nation's history.)

It didn't take long for such an astute observer and quick study as Tractor Nishimura to discover the real secret behind financial success in the motion picture industry, and he had no qualms about fulfilling what he clearly saw as his destiny: forget about making documentaries exposing social and political injustices; instead, devote your time and energies to producing the kinds of films that fill theaters, such as action movies that are disgustingly crude and violent, sappy sagas about dead baseball players or guardian angels, or light sex farces combining as much nudity as the traffic will bear with enough raunchy situations and language to satisfy even the most hormonally challenged thirteen-year-old boy. The fact that several of T&T's most recent blockbusters were written by Tractor himself demonstrates all too clearly that he still dwells in what Tim jokingly refers to as the Wonderland of Adolescence.

Thin and wiry and of average height, Tractor is still boyishly handsome at age thirty-three, with jet-black hair and a complexion as smooth and clear as the maple topping on a perfect buttermilk bar. His relaxed and natural appeal to women has always puzzled the more rugged males of his acquaintance, who just shake their heads and console each other with wild and unfounded speculations. A habitual but harmless flirt, Trac inherited the Nishimura family mark—a disarming dimple on his left cheek which quietly lies in ambush, ready to smite the heart of even the most dispassionate of females whenever Tractor deigns to smile.

$ $ $ $ $ $

Before arriving at Donut Pros this particular morning, Tim and Trac had just completed negotiations with an old high-school buddy of Trac's named Barry Goode for the purpose of purchasing a dozen vehicles destined for certain destruction in an upcoming action film with the working title of *Mangled Metal, Battered Bodies.* Just as Tractor had found his calling in the motion picture business, Barry Goode had found his own little niche in the highly competitive used car market. His secret was to own the only lot on Auto Row open and "dying to deal" not only on Sundays, but also during every holiday in the year. This day, being Easter Sunday, found him sporting pink bunny ears and a fluffy white tail pinned to the seat of his pants.

After concluding their business, Tim and Trac continued with their morning agenda, the next item being coffee and donuts at the nearest shop they could find, where Trac was looking forward to staging one of his favorite stunts—the one he refers to as the Found-Wallet Caper. (If anyone knows how to enjoy being rich, Tractor Nishimura is the guy. No stashing it away for a rainy day for him! No squandering his millions on gold-digging women or high-stakes gambling at Vegas or Monte Carlo. And, definitely, no snorting expensive cocaine! No sir! The multimillionaire from Marin has better ideas than that.)

With a donut shop or two situated on practically every block in America, finding one in the vicinity of B. Goode's Used Cars, even on Easter, was a real no-brainer, especially for a couple of brilliant guys like Tim and Trac. All they had to do was drive down the avenue, keep a sharp lookout for the word DONUT (or, more rarely, DOUGHNUT, or, rarest of all, DO-NUT), and be ready to duck into a convenient parking space on a moment's notice.

So there they were, parked right smack in front of Donut Pros, when Tim, glancing into his right rearview mirror and wondering whether he had parked close enough to the curb, neglected to check for oncoming traffic on the driver's side and almost caused an accident.

After calling out his apology to the kid on the bike, Tim, still breathing heavily, strode to the entrance of the donut shop and patiently waited while Tractor pulled a small camera out of his front pants pocket and snapped a quick photograph of the Donut Pros sign hanging above the door. Then, after shoving the camera back into his pocket, Tractor signaled Tim with a quick wave of his hand, turned on his heel, and headed directly for the telephone in front of the shop, at the same time extracting an expensive new brown leather wallet from the rear pocket of his khaki pants—a wallet decorated with a small inlaid mother-of-pearl male caribou, and containing an identification card listing a man's name and a post office box number, a worn snapshot of a tired-looking woman with a toddler tugging on her skirt, and eighty-five dollars in cash.

"Oh, no!" Tim sighed aloud. "Not that stupid Found-Wallet Caper again."

After briefly glancing around to ascertain he was not being observed, Tractor quickly placed the wallet on the little shelf under the phone and then hurried back to where Tim was waiting, now holding the door open and motioning for Tractor to enter the shop.

Of all the people who have happened upon Tractor's special decoy wallets, not a single one of them has recognized the highly disguised woman posing for the photo—even though she is none other than Tractor's own discovery, his super megastar, Miss Insiston Filofax®. Miss Filofax® is not only a top box-office draw in her own right, but she also holds the dubious distinction of being the very first representative of her profession to become an actual living advertisement—an idea whose time had come, but which was actually conceived and hatched in the fertile brain of Tractor Nishimura.

After Insiston Filofax®, Exxon® Gasoline—né Ronald Bone—who has been called the most exciting teen heartthrob since that guy on the *Titanic*, was also christened at Rancho Sueño. But after Mr. Gasoline, the trend quickly spread to Hollywood, resulting in such stars as Viagra®, a rising young child actor condemned to go through life with just one name, and an embarrassing one at that; Honda Accord®, "an easy sell," according to her agent; and Campbell's® Cream of Mushroom Soup, whose contract stipulates that Miss Soup's full name must appear in all advertisements, both print and audio. It is interesting to note that movieland gossip hounds were all agog at the news that Campbell's® Cream of Mushroom Soup and the outrageous young comedian Ball Park® Franks have been seen necking incessantly in their private hideaway booth at Denny's of Studio City, and may soon replace Brillo® Pads and Charmin® Tissue as "the couple to watch," a development so upsetting to both Brillo® and Charmin® that it may cause them to sever completely their already shaky relationship. And even jaded Hollywood insiders were bemused to learn that Chesterfield® Cigarettes had been cast in a starring role in the upcoming remake of *Smokey Bites the Dust!* Naturally, established actors are up in arms at this latest example of shameless advertising in the entertainment industry, and while they outwardly deplore it, many are making quiet inquiries as to how they, too—even at this late stage in their careers—can also "milk this little gold mine," to quote an out-of-work member of the Screen Actors Guild.

$ $ $ $ $ $ $

Blue, still pedaling along valiantly, was not making good time. The traffic lights had all been against him, and he'd only covered three more blocks on the way to Omaha's house by the time Tim and Trac found themselves seated at a wobbly brown Formica® table next to the window, each with a mug of coffee and a small assortment of donuts arranged in two identical red plastic baskets.

"Think we should hang around until the donuts run out?" Trac asked with a little grin.

"Huh?"

Trac didn't feel like explaining. "Never mind," he said. Then, filing away the name Formica® Table for possible future use, he briefly inspected the powdered-sugar cake specimen in his hand before gingerly taking a bite. As an experienced donut connoisseur, Tractor was all too familiar with the insidious ways of powdered sugar. Being sure to sustain a steady but slow exhaling action, he was able to bite into the rounded morsel without mishap, while at the next table over, a not-so-astute young lady was temporarily overcome by a mild choking fit, brought on by a fine dusting of powdered sugar in the vicinity of her windpipe—an action that caused not only an exchange of sympathetic but slightly impatient glances from those already in the know, but also an interruption of her incessant haranguing to her friend about the trouble she was having with her straying boyfriend.

"Hmm. Not bad," Tractor said, simultaneously chewing and nodding his head. "How's yours?"

"Passable, I suppose," Timothy replied. "But nothing to write home about."

Tractor took another swig of coffee, all the while keeping an eye on the telephone kiosk outside the window.

"Is this place a new one for your collection?" Tim asked politely, raising his eyebrows and smiling in a humorously condescending manner.

"Officially, yes. I mean, I was here a couple of times before I actually started collecting in a systematic manner, with photos and all." Tractor patted his front pants pocket, double-checking to see if he had replaced the little camera.

"So, how many shops do you have in your collection by now?"

Tractor quickly removed a tiny computer from his shirt pocket and struck a few keys. "Well, if we're talking *official* collection here—you know, when I actually started photographing the shops and keeping an official count—well, then my official grand total, as of today, is—let's see here—oh, wow! It looks like it's ninety-two!"

"*Pretty* amazing!"

"Yes. I think so," Tractor said, disregarding the tone of friendly ridicule he thought he detected. "And I can pinpoint just when I started, too. It was when Brillo® gave me his little spy camera. It's the one he used in *The Brothers & Meany Jones*. Remember? That's when I first got the idea to photograph the shops and keep count." Tractor shook his head and whistled under his breath. "Man-oh-man. *The Brothers & Meany Jones*. That was some little moneymaker, wasn't it?"

Tim nodded in agreement. "I'll say. Hey, did I tell you it'll soon be out on DVD? Advertising's working on the campaign now."

"That's great. You know, that reminds me. I was just thinking the other day—why don't we see about the possibility of buying advertising space in books? Like, for instance, we could target some of those new books that are coming out for teenagers, and buy a whole page. I just saw on the Internet that the kids are actually reading more these days, and—" Tractor shrugged and raised his coffee cup to his lips. "It's just an idea, that's all."

Tim didn't speak for a moment. He just sat there, with his chin resting in his hand, slowly shaking his head. "How do you come up with this stuff, anyway?"

Tractor looked puzzled, and a little hurt. "You don't like it?"

"I love it! It's a great idea! I'll talk to advertising myself, first thing in the morning."

$ $ $ $ $ $ $

Blue has now rounded the corner just past Rudy's Market and has less than a half mile to go before he arrives at Omaha's, so we'd better hurry.

After a slight pause, Tractor picked up the last donut in his basket, a slightly misshapen chocolate-with-sprinkles. "Hey, Tim, not to change the subject, but did you hear what Goodie said about Holly Hollingshead when we were over at the car lot?"

"Holly who?"

39

"Hollingshead. Well, actually, she got married. She's Holly Langsford now, but I've told you about her before. You know, she's that babe who blabbed to the school principal about how I planned to start off my graduation speech by saying, 'Tigers suck!' Remember? I told you about it. The principal was offended, and so Holly was picked at the last minute to give the speech instead of me. Jeez! I never should have confided in her! The kids would have really eaten it up. I don't know if you recall or not, but fifteen years ago, the word *suck* was still pretty edgy."

"Yeah," Tim answered dully. He had always considered the word crude and boorish and never used it himself. "Well, what's new with Holly?"

"Goodie told me she's working over at the DMV in Sacramento now. She's the censor-lady for personalized license plates, of all things! What a perfect job for her! God, what a prude she was. Actually, that was the topic of her speech."

"What was? The fact that she was a prude?"

"No, you idiot. It was about how all civility or good taste or some damn thing is disappearing from our language. Can you believe it? Afterward, half the frigging class came over and told me they thought her speech really sucked."

Tim looked up and caught a glimpse of Trac's giveaway grin. He laughed and reached across the table to give his friend's arm a little shove. "Hey, get over it, fella," he chided. "That was fifteen years ago. Time you forgot about it."

"Easy for you to say, but you know, I'm going to get even with her someday, even if it—" Trac broke off suddenly. "Ah!" he said. "Here we go! Look! Look there, out the window!" He indicated the phone booth with several short jabs of his thumb. "Did that woman in there get the wallet? Can you see?"

"Yeah! She's sticking it in her purse. I think she changed her mind about making a phone call, too. Yep! See? She didn't even take the receiver off the hook. Can you see her now?"

The two men stared intently at the woman as she seemed to hesitate slightly before hurriedly turning and taking off across the street in long, determined strides.

"Well?" Trac asked, after a moment. "What do you think?"

"Never hear from her again, that's my vote. How 'bout you?"

"Ah! She's a tough one. But I think she'll come through in the end, and so far I've been pegging them right over 75 percent of the time. Did you notice her shoes?"

"No. Why should I?"

"Because they reveal her character, that's why! They were just plain old navy blue canvas sneakers—those old-fashioned kind— even older than jogging shoes."

"God, since when did you become a shoe expert?"

"All I know is she wasn't wearing those new multicolored cloggy things that all the gals are sporting now. She's not a slave to fashion. I'll have that wallet back within the week."

"I don't know. I don't think so—"

"And what's more, I liked the way she walked. She walked like she knew where she was going."

"I'll say she did," Tim answered with a laugh. "The way she was hurrying out of there with that wallet in her purse, she knew where she was going all right." Tim paused a moment, studying his friend's face, as he sometimes did, looking for some new kind of insight into his puzzling psyche. As usual, he failed. "You know, you must have dropped off close to twenty-five of these babies by now. How many more—"

"Well, I have to get a fairly large sampling before coming to any firm conclusions about how accurately I can size up people just by their appearance and body language. There were fifty wallets in that shipment I ordered, and there's only fifteen left, so my little experiment is more than half over. And, anyway, Mr. Sims, this is *my* thing, remember?" Tractor quickly reached across the table and tweaked his friend's ear. "You do whatever you want with your moola, pal, and I'll do the same with mine."

"Get out of here!" Timothy said, laughing his hearty laugh and raising his elbows in a rearguard defensive move. He quickly polished off his third chocolate old-fashioned and wiped his hands on a napkin. "Speaking of moola," he said, "I've been meaning to tell you, I've just gone over our tax forms with Jasper in accounting, and—" Tim paused. This was important to him, and he wanted to present it in the best way he could.

"And? And what?"

"Well, I think it's about time we looked into setting up some sort of charitable trust fund, like all those other rich guys I've been reading about. Did you see that article in last week's *News!*? I mean, our names were conspicuous by their absence! God, who'd have ever thought we'd have this much dough to play around with!"

"Well, maybe someday I'll think about doing that. But for now, I'm having *way* too much fun! A big chunk here, another chunk there. Hey! I like being Santa Claus!"

"Yeah. Santa *Freud*, you mean. You and your psychological experiments. You know, sometimes I think you're actually just using people to satisfy your own warped curiosity."

Trac looked up quickly. "Hey, pal, that hurt."

But Tim wasn't done with him yet. While he was at it, Tim decided to chide his friend and partner once again about another little idiosyncrasy that had always puzzled him. "So what about that crazy World-Wide-Word-Watch of yours? How can you possibly justify giving people five thousand five hundred fifty-five dollars and fifty-five cents just because they happen to utter a certain *word* within your hearing radius? I mean, that's *crazy!* That makes no sense at all, and I mean *no* sense at all! And carrying around a blank cashier's check for that amount in your wallet all the time is stupid. What if you lose it? Whoever finds it can cash it, you know, and he doesn't even have to say your special word." Tim paused a moment, then added, "And why five thousand five hundred fifty-five dollars and fifty-five cents anyway? What's so special about that amount?"

Tractor looked up and grinned. "I just read where some people spend upward of fifteen thousand dollars for one night at certain plush New York hotels. The last time I was in New York, I got a decent room for less than a hundred and fifty. So tell me about crazy."

"Well, I'll bet the hotel maids didn't put special mints on your pillow every night."

Trac grinned. "So what? I sent out for them! And about the five thousand five hundred fifty-five dollars and fifty-five cents—well, let's say some guy hands you a cashier's check just for saying a special word, okay? When you tell your friends about it, what would be more fun—telling them you got a surprise check from some stranger for five thousand dollars, or for *five thousand five hundred fifty-five dollars and fifty-five cents?* Doesn't that have a much more melodious ring to it?"

"You're really nuts, you know that? What's your current word, anyway? *Demented?*"

"Ha! Very funny. For your information, my current word is still *ply.* I've had it for over seven months now. It's a great word. A simply great three-letter word. Ply. To ply. Plying. Have plied. A great word. A beautiful, simple word that nobody ever uses anymore. What a shame. What a waste. So what's wrong with me rewarding some unsuspecting citizen with an unexpected windfall if he or she naturally employs that word, in any of its—"

Tractor stopped speaking in midsentence and raised a finger to his lips. "Listen," he whispered. As a writer who's always on the lookout for new ideas, Tractor has no qualms about eavesdropping on private conversations, while the same activity tends to make Tim feel guilty and uncomfortable.

This time the discussion was between Lynnie the counter girl and Bryan the donut maker. "If only CashLenders® approves our twenty-five-thousand-dollar loan, honey," Bryan was saying, idly running his hand up and down her bare arm. "Then we'll be all set! I can't *wait* to get out of this grease-bin and get that Bites-O-Health® franchise! God, I can't *stand* this anymore—watching all these poor slobs gobbling up all those obnoxious, calorie-laden bombs of fat and sugar, even if I did make them myself."

Lynnie patted his shoulder. "I know, darling," she whispered, misty-eyed. "I know."

Timothy, always a pushover for young love combined with true business passion, leaned forward and squinted at the nametag pinned on the counter girl's white smock. Then he quickly scribbled "Lynnie—$25,000" on his napkin and stuffed it in his pocket.

"Don't tell me—" Tractor said, grinning and shaking his head. "And you talk about *me* playing fast and loose with my millions."

"Shut up and finish your donut," Tim replied, leaning back in his chair and trying his best to look annoyed.

$ $ $ $ $ $ $

After a while Trac stood up and crumpled his napkin. "Hey, listen, pal," he said. "While I'm thinking about it—will you postpone that meeting I have with Hershey's® Kisses' agent tomorrow morning? I've been wanting to visit my old high school and see if Mr. Frazier is still around, and I've been putting it off too long. He was my old counselor, and we actually got to be pretty good friends by the time I graduated. And while I'm there, I'm going to try to talk to this high-school kid called The Blue Avenger. Ever heard of him?"

"Yeah, I did read about him—he's that kid who proposed substituting darts for bullets here in Oakland, right? But I can tell you right now, that idea will never fly! He's not *The* Blue Avenger, though," Tim added. "Just simply Blue Avenger."

"Whatever. Anyway, the kid sounds interesting—changing his name and everything—so I'm going to see if Mr. Frazier can arrange to have me meet the guy, and then maybe I'll talk with Cynthia and her people—see if we can come up with something."

On their way out of the donut store, Tractor, following a sudden impulse, stopped briefly to share a few tips regarding the curious properties of powdered-sugar donuts with the young lady sitting at the adjoining table.

"So, what'd you say to her?" Tim asked as they were climbing back into the car.

"Oh, the usual. Gently exhale as you bite. What else?"

$ $ $ $ $ $ $

"I'm just sick and tired of him lying to me, that's all!" said the woman with the powdered-sugar donut, taking up the conversation where she had left off before being interrupted by the friendly young man with unsolicited but helpful advice regarding the prevention of powdered-sugar-induced hacking.

"He's been lying to you for years," her companion agreed. "So what are you going to do about it?"

"Right now my intention is to just keep plying him with questions until he finally tells me the truth! And if he doesn't, I'm outa there!"

Oh, well. Sure, it would have been thrilling for her to be presented with a cashier's check for $5,555.55 by that pleasant-looking fellow—so knowledgeable about curious properties of powdered-sugar donuts—just because she happened to utter a particular word, but what the hey! In all likelihood she would've just squandered it all on expensive singles' cruises and exotic "adventure" vacations, only to find that the women outnumber the men on those outings by an average of three to one.

$ $ $ $ $ $ $

Something to aim for:
TRACTOR NISHIMURA'S
DONUT SHOP COLLECTION
Donut Demon
All Star Donuts
Golden Cream Donuts
Chris's Doughnut Barn
Winchell's Donuts
Colonial Donuts

45

Fantasy Donuts
A to Z Donuts
Donna's Cross-Country Donuts
Donut Factory
Bargain Box Donuts
Ace Donut Shop
Bella's Treehouse Donuts
Donut Parade
Fancy Donuts
Donut Depot
Donut Heaven
Wayne's Flying Do-nuts
King Pin Doughnuts
Clara's Donut Carousel
Carlos's Donut Caboose
Dunkin' Donuts
Robert Mac's DonutWorld
Alex's Donut Basket
Yum Yum Donuts
O'Henry's Donut Shop
Jamesey's Digital Donuts
Quality Doughnuts
Dr. Bob's Do-nuts
Amy Joy Donuts
Daily Dozen Donuts
Fresh 'n' Tasty Donuts
Vanessa's Donut Den
Sasha's Perfect Doughnuts
Lou's Living Donut Museum
Daily Donuts
M & P's Discount Donuts
The Donut Machine
Nathan's Original Donuts
Izzie's Donuts

Paula's Happytime Donuts
Donuts 24/7
Peter Pan Donuts
Supreme Donuts
Jaumet's Secret Recipe Donuts
Donut Star
King Donuts
Rosa's Blue Ribbon Donuts
Donut World
Manley's Donut Shop
Jeanne's All-Night Donuts
New York Donuts
Baker Bob's Do-nuts
Oh My Doughnuts
Lucky Donuts
Julie's Jazzy Donuts
Donut Land
Tastee Donuts
Donut Works
Ev's Donuts Plus
Krispy Kreme Doughnuts
Daybreak Donuts
Li'l Orbits
Ginger's Donut Hut
Virgin Donuts
The Do-nut Stop
Dave's Doughnut Garden
Baker's Dozen Donuts
Little Robert's Doughnuts
Dream Fluff Donuts
Rolling Pin Do-nuts
Donut Doctor
Jack's Star-Light Donuts
Morning Fresh Do-nuts

47

D K S Donuts
Donut Times
Paloma's Magic Do-nuts
Partytime Donuts
Express Donuts
Variety Donuts
Pat's Buttercream Donuts
Spudnuts Donuts
Danny-Boy's Donuts
Miss Donut
Sunrise Donuts
Dolphin Donuts
Donut Connection
Tim Horton Donuts
Ted's Ragtime Donuts
Pixie Donuts
Varsity Donuts
Donut Pros

KWiKYKWiZ©

Directions: So you made it through the DemoVehicle™ chapter all in one piece! Great! Now it's time for your KwikyKwiz©! Read each question carefully, and then circle the letter that best completes the sentence. Example:

The first letter of the alphabet is—
A. Z
B. Z
C. Z
D. A

Did you circle the letter D? Excellent! See how easy that was! Now, good luck! And remember, KwikyKwiz© always makes reading seem like fun!

(1) One of the main topics of the chapter entitled "Donuts" is—
A. Too much television-watching
B. The importance of regular flossing in a well-managed dental hygiene program
C. Rugby
D. Donuts

(2) In the past, "spring break" used to be referred to as—
A. Christmas vacation
B. Labor Day
C. Yom Kippur
D. Easter vacation

(3) Carolus Linnaeus is—

   A. The leader of the rock group called Carolus
      Linnaeus and the Nomenclatures
   B. A famous rugby star
   C. The inventor of the donut
   D. A dead botanist

(4) Dr. Jonathan Barger is studying the causes and
    ramifications of Peer Pressure Power. "PPP"
    stands for—

   A. Please Pass (the) Pepper
   B. Picture Postcard Perfect
   C. Promises, Promises, Promises
   D. Peer Pressure Power

(5) Tractor Nishimura has a _____ on his left
    cheek.

   A. Fly
   B. Huge zit
   C. Mark of Zorro
   D. Cute dimple

(6) Tractor Nishimura collects—

   A. Refrigerator magnets
   B. Little soaps
   C. Barbie dolls
   D. Donut shops

(7) Tractor wasn't allowed to be the speaker at his high-school graduation because he was planning to shout out—

A. "Bring on the beer!"
B. "Look, Ma—no hands!"
C. "Hey, nonny nonny!"
D. "Tigers suck!"

(8) Since they are very rich now, Tim suggested to Tractor that they think about—

A. Running for president
B. Wearing tuxedos to work on Fridays
C. Buying up all the accordions in the country and throwing them into the Bay
D. Establishing a charitable trust fund

(9) The first person who says _____ in front of Tractor will receive $5,555.55.

A. "Hi, Cutie!"
B. "Boo!"
C. "Rugby, anyone?"
D. "Ply"

(10) If you checked answer D on all of the questions above, you are—

A. A stupid idiot
B. A clueless twit
C. A real dummy
D. Absolutely correct!

OMAHA

*We don't need badges. I don't have to show you any stinking
badges . . .*

—B. Traven, *The Treasure of the Sierra Madre*

Omaha was waiting on her small, raised front porch when Blue
came skidding up the driveway on his bike. He didn't even take the
time to use the kickstand; he just let the bike drop on its side, and
then he bounded up the cement steps and took Omaha into his
arms, picking her up and twirling her around like the exuberant
dancers he once saw in the movie version of *Oklahoma*.

"Whoa! Blue!" she finally exclaimed, after recovering from having
most of the air squeezed out of her lungs. "Watch out! We'll fall
off the edge, right into that cactus plant!"

Although Blue didn't consciously plan beforehand to kiss her
there on the front porch, in plain view of Mrs. Caruso across the
street (who, he noticed, was peeking through the blinds, as usual),
that's exactly what transpired, caused in part by Omaha herself. For
when a girl refuses to release her grip, when she keeps her arms
wound around you tightly and places her hands on the back of
your head and looks so deeply and unflinchingly into your eyes
that you feel that she has somehow managed to penetrate into your
very brain, what else is a poor fellow to do?

"I guess I see your mother's point about going inside," Blue
finally whispered, sweeping Omaha's hair away from her face and

giving her another nuzzling kiss on the ear. "God! It would be so easy!"

He paused a moment, burying his face in her hair and inhaling the faint odor of violets, which would come as a shocking surprise to the marketing people responsible for labeling the particular shampoo she had used that morning as *Wild Rose*.

"But hey!" Blue said, his mouth still close to her ear. "What's to stop us from consummating our love right here and now on your front porch? We don't need no stinking *bed!*" He suddenly looked up and shook his head, as if to clear away the cobwebs. "No. That's not right! Sorry. Misquote. We don't need no stinking *badge*. Yeah. That's better."

Omaha smiled and gently freed herself from his arms. "Bed, badge—whatever," she said lightly. But all the same, she knew that what he was really saying, spoken in that special encoded language of theirs, was that they had better pull themselves together—or, rather, pull themselves apart—before they suddenly found themselves quietly ducking into the house in spite of Omaha's mother's rule.

"So, what's with this moving stuff?" Blue asked, wondering if she noticed the slight tremor in his voice, just one result of the moment of closeness they had just experienced. He cleared his throat and led her by the hand to the old porch swing that her mother had instructed the movers to pile on top of the rest of their meager belongings when they'd left Omaha, Nebraska. "You're not even *thinking* of changing schools, are you?"

Omaha shrugged and shook her head. She could tell by the sound of his voice that he had been aroused by their embrace, even as she had been, and for a few seconds all she could do was stand there and catch her breath while lovely feelings of great tenderness and sympathy washed over her. "Let me get your sandwich first. It's all made. Then we can talk. I'll be right back."

Blue sat down on the swing, leaned back, spread out his legs, and clasped his hands behind his head. He sighed and closed his eyes, and before he knew it, a vivid memory of a long-ago conversation with his father suddenly appeared in his mind's eye, and the six-year span of time that had elapsed between that event and the present moment seemed to disappear. Although Blue had forgotten what had sparked the particularly unnerving lecture that warm July evening, he did recall its peculiar effect, for while part of him was wishing that his dad would just drop the subject entirely (as he was already quite familiar with the details), another part of him was hoping that his father would delve even deeper into this darkly fascinating and mysterious topic. But what Blue remembered most about that talk was what had come after he had endured with admirable patience the guided tour through the tangled briar patch of what is generally referred to as the birds and the bees—although his father managed well enough with sperms and eggs—it was *after* these preliminaries that his father rose to his greatest heights. Placing his hands gently but firmly on either side of David's face (as he was called back then) and looking directly into his son's eyes, he said slowly and very quietly, "You will never forget what I'm about to tell you." David caught his breath and waited, unaware that his father had just employed the very same proven technique that his own father had used on him. *"Remember this, son. You have absolutely no business indulging in sexual intercourse before marriage. Not only does it disrespect the girl, it can lead to—"*

"Blue?"

Blue jumped up from the swing and walked the few short steps to where Omaha was standing on the other side of the screen door, one hand holding a plate containing a huge tuna sub, the other balancing a bowl of chips. She pushed the door open with her shoulder and waited there inside the house while he came up to her, and once again time demonstrated another facet of its versatility as the plate and bowl exchanged hands through the slightly opened door. The memory of that unique moment in time—the tuna sub, the red bowl of potato chips, and the burning touch of their fingertips—

would remain forever intact, capable of being revisited in all its glory by each one of them for as long as they cared to remember.

"What would you like to drink?" Omaha asked, finally.

"Uh, what do you have?" Blue blinked his eyes and gave his head a little shake, surprised that his father's words were still echoing in his mind.

"Oh, there's some soda, mostly diet stuff, I think. And milk, of course—"

"Is the milk cold?"

Absolutely no business indulging in sexual intercourse—Blue was remembering exactly how he felt as his father spoke those words. In one sense, he couldn't imagine that they would ever actually pertain to him. He simply couldn't foresee a time when he would actually be in the business of indulging in sexual intercourse. And still, in some perverse way, he rather enjoyed the memory of the twinge of fear and submission he felt at the sound of his father's voice.

"No, Blue. It's warm milk. It's been in the oven all night, just the way you like it, and—" She paused. "Blue, are you all right?"

"Yeah. I'm fine." He smiled wanly. "I'll have some then, please. If it's not too much trouble."

Blue watched her as she went back into the house. *Okay, dad. I heard you*, he thought, and then quickly tried to retrieve the unspoken words. In the three years since his father's death, he had never gotten used to moments like these. Although he truly disliked giving in to what he felt was childish sentimentality, talking to visions in his head, he really didn't want to give up the only way he had of reconnecting with his father. But this was not the time or place.

Forcing himself to think about other things, he noticed his bike, there on the lawn where he had left it, and recalled the near miss he had had on the way over. On several occasions car doors had opened unexpectedly while he was riding past, but this was the first time the door was attached to a Mercedes 500 SLC. I must be coming up in the world, he thought wryly, and it's about time. Blue put his head in his hands and gave it another little shake. Oh, sheesh! There's that word *time* again. Is there no way of escaping it?

$ $ $ $ $ $ $

When Omaha returned a few moments later with a glass of milk in her hand, swirling it gently so Blue could hear the sound of tinkling ice cubes, he was almost completely back in the here and now. Omaha handed over the glass, and then carefully sat down beside him on the swing. Blue waited patiently for her to start speaking.

"I meant to warm up some soup for you, too."

"Soup?" *Soup? She's talking about soup?*

"Yeah. Chicken gumbo. I made it myself. I don't know why, but I've been having this real craving for chicken gumbo soup lately. At first I was going to leave out the okra, but then I decided that if it was in the recipe, it'd be cheating to leave it out. Actually, it's not bad. Anyway, I was going to heat some up for you, but I ran out and—"

"Omaha, will you please quit stalling around and tell me what's going on."

Omaha turned her head slightly, quickly glancing in his direction. "Well, what happened first was that our landlady raised the rent." She leaned her head on the back of the swing and shut her eyes. "Do you really want to hear all the gruesome details on the sorry state of our finances?"

Blue quickly took another bite of his sandwich. He nodded his head as he chewed, nonverbally excusing his delay in answering. He swallowed, took a long drink of milk, and said, "If you want to tell me, I do. But you didn't answer my question yet. Are you even *thinking* of changing schools?"

"God, I hope not. I mean, San Pablo is the only school in the city with any advanced placement classes at all. Actually, that's the main reason we rented a house in this neighborhood in the first place. Mom inquired about the schools first thing, even before we started looking at rentals. And now with this nurses' strike looming over us—well, there's no way of telling how long a thing like that might drag on. So I just don't know where we'll end up."

Blue nodded. It sounded bad all right. Since he didn't have a handy Blue Avenger solution on the tip of his tongue, and not knowing what else to do, he momentarily directed her attention to his sandwich. "This is *really* good—"

"Thanks. Is the milk warm enough for you?"

"It's perfect."

The porch swing made a distinctive, low-pitched squeak just as it completed its backward motion and began to reverse its direction. Blue loved the sound, and he thought of it often, usually after he was awakened unexpectedly by a passing siren or the sound of laughter and voices coming from Marvin Lasher's house next door at the end of one of his late-night parties.

"Except for moving out of the district, and away from you," Omaha was saying, "the part that bothers me most about all this is that I'll have to quit the swimming team. I don't mean to brag, but I know I'm good. I mean, I *did* beat Bret Olson last week in a special practice session." Omaha tucked a wayward strand of hair behind her ear. "I e-mailed you about that, didn't I?"

Blue's heartbeat accelerated from seventy-three beats a minute to seventy-nine, but there was no apparent change in his demeanor. "Yeah. You did. That was the two-hundred-meter freestyle, wasn't it? Hey, congratulations! How'd you learn to swim so fast, any-way?" Then he followed up quickly with another question, trying to diffuse it with a quirky smile. "And are you *really* the only girl on the team?"

Omaha nodded. "I can thank Mr. Frazier for that. It was his idea. The thing is, even if we do find a cheaper place to live—around here, I mean—I still won't be able to go to all those practices and meets, keep up with my homework, and get a job, too. I just won't have the time."

"Yeah. That's right, I guess." Blue, afraid of being sabotaged by his own body language, was concentrating on holding perfectly still. But still he wondered, would she be able to detect his true feelings just from the sound of his voice?

"Why don't you just come right out and *say* you don't like me being on the boys' team?"

"Hey, whatever gave you *that* idea? I think it's *fabulous* that you're the only girl on the boys' swimming team!"

He knew he was lying, and she knew he was lying, and he knew that she knew he knew, and she knew that he knew she knew, so that made everything okay. And not only was everything okay, it was better than okay, since the blueprint for an even closer relationship had suddenly been drawn, as they moved one step beyond the obvious spoken word, which is in itself a veritable minefield of misunderstanding.

A little while later—after Blue's left arm had found its way around Omaha's waist and her head naturally leaned against his chest—he reached into his shirt pocket for the little glass snail he had bought for her in Venice, and placed it in the palm of her hand.

"Oh, Blue!" she whispered, first fingering the delicate, amber-colored object ever so gently, and then bringing it up to eye level, allowing the light to shine through. *"Love's feeling is more soft and sensible—"* she began, quoting their own special line from Shakespeare. Blue squeezed her hand and finished the sentence, *"—than are the tender horns of cockled snails."* And for the next few hours, as far-fetched as it seems, Oakland, California, was every bit as enchanting as Venice, Italy, could ever hope to be.

$ $ $ $ $ $ $

Blue Avenger was deeply troubled later that afternoon as he reluctantly hopped on his bike and headed back home. Omaha's problem sounded more like an old-fashioned melodrama than a case for a comic-book superhero. *"I can't pay the rent!" "You must pay the rent!" "But I can't pay the rent!"*

Blue rode on, squinting against the slanted, orange-tinged sun-light of late afternoon, sometimes swooping up the sloping curb onto the sidewalk to avoid a slow-moving bus or double-parked car, and then quickly swerving down again to the street. He suddenly caught a swift, passing glimpse of himself reflected in the now darkened window of the Donut Pros donut store, and he was mildly shocked to see a regular teenage boy wearing a bicycle helmet and dressed in jeans and a T-shirt, rather than the real Blue Avenger, attired in his father's blue fishing vest and the flowing kaffiyeh fash-ioned from a large blue bath towel and a piece of rope. But Blue Avenger has never failed yet! If I put my mind to it, if I really, really concentrate, perhaps I can tap into the great unknown and discov-er those powerful and mysterious forces that have existed for every superhero up through the ages! For am I not one of them—a comic-book hero come to life?

Blue was abruptly shaken out of his reverie when a large brown dog suddenly lunged at him, restrained by a short tether secured to a fire hydrant.

Whew! That was close! Blue thought, now jumping down the low curb and once again riding on the street. But what was that I was just thinking—a comic-book hero come to life? Man-oh-man! I've got to stop thinking like that! Totally irrational, that's what it is. Crazy as a loon. Yet, I can't get over this feeling, as if I've been split in half—as if I'm living in one of those peculiar kinds of dreams where I'm acting out my part but, at the same time, I'm still aware that this is, after all, just a dream. Blue swerved to avoid an old shoe in the road. But hey, why not? In a world as crazy and unpredictable as this, maybe I can do both! Maybe I can keep my sanity, and at the same time sustain this dreamlike state. If I can do that, I just *might* discover a secret route, possibly in another dimen-sion, that will lead me directly to a solution for that certain damsel in distress—that lovely maiden who happens to be the one and only love of my life.

"Hey! Move over, you crazy idiot!" A sudden blast of a horn almost caused Blue to lose control of his bike, and he was startled to find himself riding in the middle of the street, directly in the line of traffic. "Sorry," he murmured meekly, lifting his hand apologetically as the steel-gray SUV swerved back into the lane with another impatient blast of its horn and an unpleasant gesture directed at Blue from the man sitting in the driver's seat.

Blue, his hand still raised, wisely resisted responding in kind, as he recalled some recent and alarming instances of unrestrained road rage involving deadly weapons. Instead, he studiously avoided eye contact with the outraged motorist, took a deep breath, and repositioned his helmet. So much for dreamlike states and secret passageways of the mind. A guy can get himself killed that way!

At the next intersection, Blue suddenly decided to get off the avenue and take an alternate route through a more quiet residential area, even though it would cost him a few extra minutes of time. But he had no sooner rounded the corner than he was suddenly engulfed by the sound of a siren and a gust of wind as an ambulance quickly rushed past him. To his surprise, it stopped at a house on the opposite side of the street about halfway up the next block. When Blue arrived at the site, he paused on the lawn of a house across the street and watched as several people frantically called to the paramedics from the garage. "In here! In here!" they shouted, gesturing wildly.

Quite a gathering of neighbors was beginning to mill about on the adjoining lawns, congregating in small groups while keeping their eyes glued to the activities around the garage. The neighborhood children were running around wildly, as if it were a party.

A few minutes later a woman hurried out of the front door of the house in back of Blue, and met her husband as he returned from across the street to join her. "What happened, honey?" she asked, raising a fist to her mouth in a gesture of alarm and concern.

"Oh, it's just Doris again," he answered. "Just Doris, fooling around again."

Blue inched his bike closer to the couple. He leaned across his handlebars and repeated the woman's question. "What happened?" he asked. "Is anyone hurt?"

"No. No one's hurt. The high-school girl who lives there just tried to hang herself in the garage. But she's okay."

"Really!" Blue exclaimed. "What's her name? What school does she go to?"

"Doris. Doris Sunzeri. She goes to San Pablo. Actually, she's kind of a nut. A real theatrical kind of a kid."

Blue couldn't hide his surprise. "But—"

The man looked at Blue, mildly annoyed. "Listen, do you know her?"

Blue shook his head. "No, I don't think so."

"Well, I do. I've known her all my life. Believe me, it was just a stunt. She craves attention." He motioned to the mobile truck from KFIB and the station wagon from the *Oakland Star* just pulling up to the curb. "And it looks like this time she really hit the jackpot."

The man walked over to the magnolia tree by the edge of his driveway and snapped off a dead twig, while his wife continued to watch the goings-on across the street. After a while Blue got back on his bike. "Well," he said, "I'm glad it turned out okay."

As he pedaled along, almost back home now, his thoughts once again returned to Omaha and her problems. Soon he found himself planning out in his mind a marvelous new four-paneled strip, starring, of course, Blue Avenger, his cartoon superhero and sometimes alter ego.

The first panel featured a closeup view of Blue Avenger dressed in his traditional garb, looking quite forlorn, and thinking to himself in a cartoonist's bubble, THERE ARE SOME PROBLEMS THAT ONLY MONEY CAN SOLVE!

The second panel showed Blue as a contestant in a big-money TV show, shaking hands with the master of ceremonies. Blue had just answered the final question correctly, and had won the million-dollar jackpot!

On to the third panel, where an ecstatic Blue Avenger is reading a newspaper headline: *Blue Avenger Named Sole Heir to Shoe Magnate's Fortune!*

The fourth panel, however, gave Blue a problem. How else might a person suddenly become rich? he wondered. The lottery, perhaps? No, that wouldn't work. Like Blue himself, his superhero counterpart is much too smart to even consider playing the lottery, and he must remain steadfast to his ideals. What to sketch instead? Waiting at a stoplight a few blocks from his house, Blue finally settled on an extremely amateurish and unlikely scene showing his hero simply being showered with hundred-dollar bills by an unknown but obviously happy and extremely rich benefactor. By some odd and mysterious coincidence, as Blue would soon discover, this multi-millionaire cartoon figure in his head happened to bear an uncanny resemblance to a young, extremely wealthy movie producer by the name of Tractor Nishimura.

Just out in paperback from OutaControl Books!

A MUST-READ FOR ALL TEENAGERS WHO JUST CAN'T TAKE IT ANYMORE!

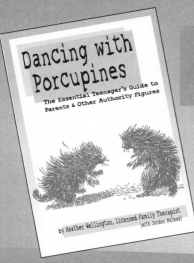

Dancing with Porcupines
The Essential Teenager's Guide to Parents & Other Authority Figures

by Heather Wellington, Licensed Family Therapist
(with Jorden Holmes)

Listen to the Critics Rave!

"Talk about pushing the envelope! This one shoves it completely down the drain! This slim volume (65 pages of dynamite) is absolutely astonishing!"—Dorie Clevenger, *Reviewer's Notebook*

"There are a lot of puny advice books for teens out there that brag about 'testing the limits.' Well, guess what? The test is over, and the limits have gone missing! *Dancing with the Porcupines* is definitely the just-do-it book of the year. The flood gates are open, and kids rule!"—Andy Rider, *The Alternative Librarian Monthly*

"Can you say edgy? Can you say *over* the edge? Can you say best seller! OutaControl Books has a surefire winner on their hands! Watch out for falling debris!"—Boris Bloomer, *The Spitfire Review*

"Sooner or later, it had to happen! Boundaries can only be stretched so far, and then, Whoosh! Smashed to smithereens! After this amazing and shocking book, there's nowhere to go but up. Excellent for those jaded reluctant readers who've been there, done that. Uptight adults need not apply, but we weird blokes at BIW simply adored it!"—Minor League-Pratt, *The Boston Iconoclast Weekly*

Praise from the Kids!

"This book has literally saved my life! Now *I'm* in charge, and lovin' every minute!"—Reggie McCrackin. Junior, Lincoln High School

"I loved the chapter on 'Last Resorts.' Thank God my parents don't give a (hoot) about what I'm reading, or they'd have caught on and spoiled all the fun! I hope there's a sequel in the works! I need more cool ideas!"—Alisha Burns. Sophomore, Sycamore High

Available at bookstores everywhere, or order direct from:
www.outacontrolbooks@hoax.yea

UP WITH READING!

Wearing an old-fashioned swimsuit and an inflatable hippo around her waist, principal Lucienne Wong kept her promise Wednesday to swim in a pool of Jell-O gelatin if her Earl LeGette Elementary students read one million pages.
            —Gwendolyn Crump, *Sacramento Bee*

Let us now take leave of Blue while he continues on his way home from Omaha's house, and, in the interval, take a short trip of our own back in time (or, in case there is no such thing as time, a short trip back in change—whichever you prefer) to that Monday morning in early March when the Special Committee of Twelve was appointed by a subcommittee of the Joint Committee on Reading, which itself was appointed by an ad hoc committee formed as a protest for nonaction on this matter on the part of the Oakland City School Board (in conjunction with a committee commissioned by the City Library Department acting in concert with the State Department of Education's Committee for Reading Readiness) for the purpose of brainstorming ideas for the annual "Up with Reading!" Month. This Special Committee of Twelve was composed of two civic-minded citizens, three educators, two parents, four librarians, one student representative, and a sales rep for a small publishing company in Hayward, California, who was hoping this appointment might possibly afford him a special foot in the door as far as selling books to kids was concerned. (It wasn't until the actual meeting was called to order that the student representative noticed that there were really thirteen people delegated, but after a mild exchange of accusations as to which committee was to blame for this faux pas, the Special Committee of Twelve was allowed to stand, especially after it was pointed out by the sales rep that since Twelve and Thirteen both started with the letter T, the oversight would not necessitate a change in its acronym.) The initial meeting of SCOT was quite productive, evidenced by the fact that the committee members were finally able to agree on a rousing slogan to start the ball rolling: *Getting Our Kids to Read: A New Approach!* The stated purpose of the subsequent meeting was to actually suggest a new approach—something *other* than the usual tactic, which was to conduct a contest to see which school in the district could rack up the "greatest number of pages read" by the end of the designated Up with Reading! Month.

The meeting was being held in a small conference room at the rear of Artie's Restaurant in downtown Oakland, and when one of the committee members carelessly spilled her coffee, a busperson with large beefy arms and limited English was called from the kitchen to clean up the mess. As the restaurant worker was maneuvering her mop between the chairs, she overheard the following sentiments being uttered by the coffee-cup klutz: "Reading is the key, people! It's the magic key to learning! Now if we can somehow get all of these kids reading, I have no doubt that they will be able to attend college, graduate, and attain secure and rewarding futures. In short, with reading, they can make it!"

That sounded so wonderful to the mop-wielder that she actually broke out in a smile. Her children's lives would be so much better than hers, for they could read! They could go to college! They could *make it!*

The meeting was called to order by Mrs. Bernice Ryan, retired fourth-grade teacher and insatiable reader of romance novels, a habit that caused more than a little friction between herself and her long-suffering mate, for whom she had scant time after her daily reading fix. "We must give these kids some *incentive* to read!" she began. "We have to open the barn door and then hold out a carrot. We have to tempt them to take a bite. Just take a bite of the carrot and chew it up. Chew it up real good."

"What if we hold out a candy bar instead of a carrot?" suggested Mrs. Maypole, grandmother of five and an avid reader herself, favoring mystery novels and slashers. "We all know kids are not that crazy about carrots," she added with a self-conscious little laugh.

"I was speaking *figuratively*," answered Mrs. Ryan, somewhat crossly. "I was just trying to get the idea across that they should have some sort of incentive, don't you see?"

Mr. Perth, a science fiction fan himself, objected strenuously. "Baloney, I say! We've tried that nonsense before! We just have to stop mollycoddling these kids! Just lock them in their rooms and tell them, 'Listen, you sit down there and *read*, you little blipsters, or else!'"

After three and a half hours and a break for lunch, a compromise of sorts was reached between these two extremes. The answer would be—a contest! Copies of the rules for the previous years' contests were again printed up and distributed to each elementary school in the district.

OFFICIAL RULES FOR UP WITH READING! MONTH

(1) As a participating school, you must keep an accurate record of the number of pages read by your students during Up with Reading! Month.

(2) At the end of the designated period, please divide the number of pages read by the number of students at your school. Fill out the enclosed form, and drop it in the mail before the deadline. (See attachment for this year's dates.)

(3) The school with the highest percentage of "pages read per student" will be declared the winner. The prize is a brand-new magna-screen TV set for the winning school, kindly donated by Quadruple AAAA Television & Appliance Company. (Please drop by any one of their locations and let them know how much you appreciate their help!)

(4) Principals and teachers are encouraged to "be outrageous and creative!" in motivating their students to rack up the pages.

Back in the broom closet, rinsing out her mop, the busperson was puzzled. Hold it just a darned minute, she thought in her native language. There's a problem here. If *all* the kids learn to read, and *all* the kids go to college and make it, who's going to be left to mop up the floors?

$$\$ \ \$ \ \$ \ \$ \ \$ \ \$ \ \$$$

Concurrently, halfway across the world, on that same Monday in early March, a different kind of book event was taking place. Mr. Johnny Brown, father of Omaha Nebraska Brown and author of a long and scholarly new biography of the sixteenth-century Italian philosopher Giordano Bruno, was celebrating the most exciting evening of his life. The setting was the Pizzeria Trattoria er grottino, in the shadow of the brooding statue of Giordano Bruno on the Campo dei Fiori in Rome—the very same restaurant where he and his daughter had had their less-than-successful reunion just two and a half weeks earlier—and the occasion was Johnny's introduction to his newly appointed editor from BiblioItalia Publishing Company. For Johnny Brown's manuscript had finally been accepted for publication, with an advance against royalties equal to approximately $7,500 in good old American greenbacks. Johnny Brown was a success at last! (Or was he? Anyone care to check with Omaha?)

DR. DEATH

Fantasy: fabrication, improvisation, make-believe, vision, wildest dreams; dream, bad dream, nightmare, bogey or bogy, phantom, ghost, apparition, specter, shadow, vapor; dimness, mirage, visual fallacy, fancy, illusion, optical illusion, trompe l'oeil, delusion, hallucination, chimera, error.

—*Bartlett's Roget's Thesaurus*

When Blue finally coasted up the driveway to his house, he hardly noticed the black van parked in front, naturally assuming that it belonged to a friend of someone in the neighborhood. But he did notice once again the large blue tarp still covering the six-foot-high stack of cartons that had been delivered to his house while he was in Venice—cartons containing a "lifetime" supply of Wanner's Cornstarch, as promised by Mr. Wanner himself in appreciation of Blue's famous Weepless Wonder Lemon Meringue Pie recipe.

Jeez, Blue thought, that letter I wrote to old Mr. Wanner complaining about that dinky little box of cornstarch he sent to me sure got results! Talk about a lifetime supply! With this amount of cornstarch I could make enough pies to feed a large army! I'd better start thinking about what I'm going to do with all that. What *can* you do with that much cornstarch, anyway?

Blue took one last look at the blue tarp and shook his head. Then he wheeled his bike into the garage and entered the house through the kitchen door, and there, sitting at the table, were his mother and a man he had never seen before in his life.

"Oh, Blue!" Sally said, rising quickly from her chair and reaching her arms out toward him. "Welcome home, honey! Listen, I'm *sorry* I didn't get a chance to see you this morning—" She turned her head and addressed the slim, dark-complexioned gentleman seated across from her. "I left for the market before he got up," she explained, adding somewhat sheepishly, "Among other things, we were out of half-and-half again. You know, I have a sneaking suspicion Blue's little brother has been fortifying his cereal with it—leaving only a few drops in the carton for me, even though he knows how much I detest black coffee."

Blue immediately wondered why his mother felt the need to go into such detail for this stranger at the table. Who *was* he, anyway?

"Hi, Mom," he said, as they shared a brief hug.

Sally, blushing slightly, gestured toward the man. "Blue, this is Dr. Chandra."

Blue's face clouded suddenly. "You're not sick—"

Sally shook her head, still blushing. "Oh, no—"

"Actually, we're old school chums," Dr. Chandra said, scraping back his chair and starting to rise. "And besides, I'm not a *real* doctor." He smiled, somewhat apologetically, for it was an old joke. "I'm just a veterinarian."

Blue nodded. "Oh," he said. His eyes—suddenly superhero eagle eyes—immediately noted the two coffee cups on the table, almost empty now, and a few pieces of cheese and several crackers remaining on his mom's best serving plate.

Sally gently chided her friend with a disapproving smile and shake of her head. "Oh, stop that, Rakesh! What do you mean, *just* a veterinarian?" Then she put her hand on Blue's arm and gave it several nervous little squeezes. "And, of course, this is Blue, my eldest son—just returned home last night from Venice!"

The veterinarian reached over to shake Blue's hand. "I'm very happy to meet you, Blue. I read about your weepless pie recipe in that advice column in the *Star*, and I was really disappointed to hear about the possible court action regarding your ban-the-bullets suggestion to the city council. Disappointed, but, I might add, *not* surprised."

At the mention of his seemingly ill-fated efforts to ban bullets in the entire city of Oakland (thus putting an end to the scourge of violent and senseless injuries and deaths caused by handguns), Blue's heart seemed to shrivel within his chest.

"Well, I was both disappointed *and* surprised," he said, shaking the older man's hand. "But according to what I've heard, Councilwoman Peters is pushing to get the issue on the ballot." Blue's face began to redden—as it always does when he's discussing something he genuinely cares about.

"And," Sally added, "unfortunately, that's going to take money—a *lot* of money."

"That's right," Blue agreed, nodding at his mother. "And we all know where the pro-gun money will come from, don't we? But, as for our side—" He shrugged. "We'll be lucky to afford computer-printed flyers tacked on telephone poles."

The handshake was over, but Rakesh was still standing. Blue said, "Oh, sorry. I didn't mean to get carried away like that. Anyway, it's nice meeting you, too, Dr.—uh, sorry, I've forgotten—"

"Chandra. It's Dr. Chandra. But please, just call me Rakesh."

Blue nodded, finding it impossible to look away from Rakesh Chandra's dark and mesmerizing eyes. Finally, since he couldn't think of anything else to say, he raised his hand to his mouth and feigned a slight cough to give himself more time. What's going on around here? Why is she acting so—so schoolgirlish all of a sudden? What does this guy mean to her, anyway?

"Sit down, Blue," Sally was saying, unconsciously signaling with a faint lifting of her brows that she really wanted him to stay. "You must have lots to tell us about your trip."

"Oh, not really. It was just, you know, Venice," he said, somewhat shyly, even though he really had plenty of adventures to relate.

They were all seated around the table now—this Rakesh person settling back down in Blue's usual chair, the one closest to the refrigerator. "Well, personally, I loved the place," he said, running his long, slim fingers along the side of his head, smoothing down his full but slightly gray-streaked black hair.

"So you've been to *Venice*, too!" Sally broke in. "Oh, my! Is there anyplace you haven't been?"

Blue glanced at the ceiling. So much for *my* exciting Venice stories.

Rakesh grinned. "Oh, I can probably come up with a country or two," he said. Then Rakesh looked at Sally and pointed to his watch.

"Oh, gosh," she said. "Is it time to go? Already?"

"Yes, I'm afraid so."

Sally stood up and pushed her chair back under the table, then turned to Blue. "It looks like we're going to have to leave now, so I guess you two won't have time to get acquainted tonight after all. Rakesh has invited me to a little reception for a friend of his who's written a book on animal rights, of all things, and—well, I guess it's time. Right, Rakesh?" She shrugged one shoulder and raised her hands with upturned palms, as if to say this wasn't *her* idea.

Rakesh answered her gesture with a short little laugh that to Blue sounded genuine enough, if a bit strained. "I don't think the topic of animal rights rates very high on your mother's list of priorities," he said. "But maybe after she meets and talks with my friend Steven, she might begin to change her mind. Tomorrow evening he's going to be doing a book signing at Cody's, and I wanted her to get a chance to talk with him before then."

"Yeah, well, I guess I'll see you later," Blue said, thinking how unlike her it was not to even mention dinner.

"Oh, and Blue—" she said, almost as if she had read his mind, "I hope you and Josh won't mind scrounging up some dinner for yourselves."

"Oh, sure, we'll manage. But where is he, anyway?"

"He's around, someplace. I guess he's in his room." Sally lowered her voice and indicated the direction of Josh's bedroom with a toss of her head. "He's still upset with me for getting Mrs. Lawson to baby-sit him last night. He thinks he's outgrown baby-sitters. Rakesh and I went bowling, of all things." She smiled at Rakesh. "Just like we used to do in high school."

"That was almost twenty-five years ago," Rakesh said. "But it seems like only yesterday," he added, with just the right combination of self-mockery and genuine surprise.

They were all standing now, and Blue had to admit to himself that he rather liked this guy. And it was obvious that his mother did.

"Yeah, well, I guess I'll see you later, then," Blue said, realizing too late that he was repeating himself. "Uh, it was nice meeting you, Rakesh."

Dr. Chandra nodded and smiled. "My pleasure, Blue. Good night."

Sally gave Blue another short hug, and he couldn't help noticing a new kind of sparkle in her eyes. "Good night, honey," she said, patting his back.

"Good night, Mom."

Sally turned to leave, but she hesitated for a moment, quickly glancing back at Blue and turning to face him. "I'm really sorry I have to rush off like this—" She nervously slipped her finger under the silver band on her wrist watch, turning it slightly so she could see its face more clearly. "I didn't realize it was getting to be so late. I don't know what happened to the time—"

"That's okay, Mom. I didn't mean to stay over at Omaha's this long, either."

They looked at each other for a moment, with a kind of shared sense of wonder hanging in the air, and then they smiled—not knowing exactly why—only knowing that they felt like it.

Sally took a step backward and peered toward the front door, where her friend was waiting, his hand on the doorknob. "I'm coming, Rakesh," she called. "Just a moment." She turned again to Blue. "I've already told Josh good night once," she said softly. "I think it would only upset him more if I told him again."

73

"Okay, Mom. No problem. I'll—I'll take care of him."

"Thanks, honey. And I can't wait to hear all about your trip. Really."

$ $ $ $ $ $ $

When Blue walked into his room, he found another surprise awaiting him there. It was his little brother, Josh, lying on his back on Blue's bed, reading a book.

"Joshpot! What in blazes are you doing in my room?"

Josh lowered the book. "Well, lookie who's here! Mr. World Traveler! How was Venice?"

"Venice was great. Now what are you doing in my room?"

"Is he gone yet?"

Blue unzipped his backpack and dumped the contents on the floor. "Yes. I think so."

"Stupid Dr. Death!"

"What?"

"That's what he is. Dr. *Death!* He goes around killing animals! He killed Rex, you know—"

"Rex? The Lawsons' dog? No. I didn't know that."

"Didn't you get my last e-mail? I told you about it."

"When did you send it? Maybe it was after I left."

"Well, maybe. But that's how Mom met him. Rex was sick and Mrs. Lawson called Dr. Death to come over and do his dirty work. Mrs. Lawson called Mom, too. I guess she wanted Mom to be there and hold her hand or something while she watched her dog get killed."

Blue sat down on the bed, pushing Josh over to make room for himself. He was suddenly very, very tired. His head felt like an empty—something. He was too tired to describe it, exactly. A basketball? A water balloon? A giant pincushion? Nevertheless, he felt he should set his little brother straight. "We call it euthanasia, Josh. It's not *killing*. It's *putting to sleep*. Rex was old and probably suffering a lot. You'd rather have him suffer?"

74

Josh shrugged and rubbed his eyes, trying not to cry. Josh had never had a dog of his own. His mother had never liked dogs. Rex had been almost like his own dog. He and Rex used to talk, sometimes. Rex had told him—with his eyes—that he really liked *him* better than old Mr. and Mrs. Lawson put together. Rex had told Josh that dogs really don't like old people; they just tolerate them in exchange for food.

Josh rubbed his nose with the side of his hand and then wiped his hand on his pants.

"Josh, that's disgusting," Blue said.

Josh picked up the book he'd been reading and grasped it between his bare feet. Raising it high in the air, he attempted to balance it on the sole of his right foot. "Hey, David! Look at this! One foot! I'll bet you can't do this!"

In spite of his weariness, Blue glared at his little brother with as much severity as he could muster. Why did this kid persist in calling him David! "Come *on*, Josh. I'm in no mood to watch your sorry circus routine. So scram! Now!"

"Whoops!" Josh said, as the book slid off his foot, bounced on the headboard, and landed on the floor.

Blue wondered if he should take a shower. He felt really grimy after his bike ride.

Josh, surprised at not being hollered at again, slowly leaned over and picked up the book from the floor. "You should read this," he said, opening it and thumbing through the pages. "It's really good!"

"What's this? My brother Josh is reading a book! Have TVs disappeared from the face of the earth? Are computer games not yet invented? Am I in a time warp? What's going on?"

"You're so funny I forgot to laugh," Josh said, carelessly letting the book drop to the floor. "And anyway, it's my homework. We have to read at least ten pages every night for this dumb reading contest. Including weekends. If our school wins, Mrs. Lindstrom has to put on a bathing suit and jump in a wading pool full of yucky strawberry Jell-O®. She promised. But then, for spring break, my teacher gave us twenty-five pages to read! They're not supposed to give us homework on spring break, are they?"

Blue looked up. "What? Mrs. Lindstrom is going to jump in a pool of Jell-O®? What's that all about? That's terrible."

Blue had always remembered his old elementary school principal with a certain degree of fondness and respect, and he couldn't imagine her sacrificing her dignity by agreeing to participate in such a stunt. There must be better ways to persuade kids to read.

"Well, she said she would! And anyway, the principal at Hawthorne said he would eat a barbecued rat if *his* school won. And Trevor told me that the principal at his cousin's school will either sit in a cage with a bunch of snakes or wear a big diaper and baby bonnet and kiss a pig, whichever one the kids vote for."

The part of Blue's brain that used to be concerned with the problem of free will—but which now keeps telling him the world is nuts—signaled like crazy for his attention, but Blue was too tired to take notice.

"Listen, I have some stuff to do now, so just beat it, please."

"Who's going to fix my dinner?"

"The dinner fairy, I guess."

Josh started to whine. "But Mom told me you would—"

"Get *out* of here!" Blue said, this time backing up his words with a bit of physical persuasion. "I have a few things I want to get caught up on, and then I plan to take a little lie-down before dinner," he said, using the British term for nap that he had heard on *Fawlty Towers* reruns, broadcast over San Francisco's public television station, *made possible by donations from viewers like you—thank you!*

Blue had his desk drawer open and was already taking out his drawing pencils as Josh glanced back at him before leaving the room. "Oh, no! Spare me!" Josh said, covering his eyes with his hands. "Not another stupid Blue Avenger episode!"

"Coming right up!" Blue answered cheerfully. "And what a doozy this one's going to be!"

Josh scurried out of the room in an exaggerated show of alarm, noisily slamming the door behind him, while Blue hastily sketched out the cartoon panel he had dreamt up on the ride home from Omaha's house. Then, cringing slightly at what he had just drawn, and vowing to come up with something better when he was more rested, Blue stumbled toward his bed and fell asleep three seconds after his head touched the pillow.

$ $ $ $ $ $ $

An hour and a half later, Josh's stomach acids had slowly built up to the limits of their threshold and began to make themselves heard. Josh, giving in to their urgings, quietly crept into Blue's room and ducked down out of sight at the foot of his bed. Then, grabbing hold of the mattress with both hands, he began to shake it violently back and forth, grinning his best out-of-control-maniac grin.

"Huh? What?" A startled Blue immediately sat up and looked around the room.

"Mom says you should fix dinner for us," said a low voice emanating from the foot of the bed.

Blue was confused. "What? Where? Is she back?"

"Nooo. But it is dinnertime at the Schumacher abode."

Blue rubbed his eyes and flopped back down on the bed. "Oh, Josh! Jeez! Why don't you go play out in the street or something?"

"Because I might get run over, that's why! And then I'd have to come back and *haunt* you, that's why! And then you'd probably get really, really scared, and wet your pants, right in front of your girlfriend! And then Omaha would say, 'Oh, Blue Avenger, darling, I hate to bring this up, but I think you just wet your pants!' And then you would say, 'No, I didn't ever! That's just—that's just, uh, well, the cat did it!'" Josh collapsed in one of his silly laughing fits, rolling on the floor and holding his stomach.

Blue was not amused, either by Josh's antics or by his oblique reference to a joke he had recently heard, known as "the cat and the

77

piano story." Blue was fascinated, though, by all the ways in which Josh had managed to work bits and pieces of that story into his general conversation, and also at how he kept searching for new prospects on whom he might practice his budding comedic skills. Blue remembered that when Josh had related the story to Omaha, she had actually laughed out loud—a rare occurrence for her. But then, of course, it was her favorite kind of joke, a silly and outrageous premise concealing a basic and universal human truth—although the silly and outrageous premise was more than sufficient to send Josh into spasms of hysterical laughter.

But Blue, not in the best of moods, was determined to give his brother no satisfaction whatsoever for his vain attempt at cleverness. "I don't see any cat around here," he said, quickly glancing around the room with a blank and emotionless expression. After a few moments he sighed, and stretched, and rose slowly to his feet. Then he looked over at Josh and said, "I guess we'll have a couple of chicken potpies for dinner. How does that sound?"

Josh hesitated, but only for a moment. "Well, that sounds just clucky," he said, grinning broadly and following Blue into the kitchen.

After he put the pies in the microwave, Blue sat down at the kitchen table and said, "Hey, Joshpot. When are you going to grow up, anyway? You could have done this yourself, you know."

"No I couldn't. I don't know how."

Blue tossed the empty box over to his brother. "Here. You can read, can't you?"

Josh grinned. "Boxes don't count. Only pages," he said, deciding not to mention the 323 pages contained in the musty old book that he had recently discovered on the top shelf of his father's bookcase, one that had come as a pleasant surprise to Blue himself three years earlier when he had first started reading all the books on his father's shelves. (Entitled *Ideal Marriage: Its Physiology and Technique*, the sexually explicit but dignified tome—first published in 1928, complete with foldout color plates of both male and female anatomy—had already sent an inordinately curious Josh to the dictionary at least a dozen times, starting with the title itself, and that can't be a *bad* thing, can it? Furthermore, since the Up with Reading! contest rules only specify *pages* read, Josh felt free to skip the more boring sections of the book and concentrate only on the pages with chapter headings appealing to his ten-year-old inquisitiveness about matters sexual—chapters with headings such as—Oh, well, never mind. We really don't need to go there, do we?)

While the pies were in the microwave, Blue went to his room and picked up *The Treasure of the Sierra Madre* and brought it back to the kitchen. He read the editor's preface to the book with a sense of wonder and near disbelief, for here was yet another case of a mystery author! Because the writer known as B. Traven refused to give any personal information to his publishers, the speculation about his true identity was a literary puzzle for years. However, compared to the extremely complicated and highly challenging Shakespeare mystery, the case of B. Traven was mere child's play.

Because he had already seen the movie, Blue started reading with some degree of expectation. He knew he was about to immerse himself in a story about success, money, and greed, topics that just might pop up in his own life in the not too distant future.

$ $ $ $ $ $ $

Blue is not exactly a speed-reader, but he *is* fast. His mind is quick, and he hasn't been cursed with the not uncommon habit of rereading sentences, paragraphs, and even pages just to make sure he got it right the first time. He continued reading right through his chicken potpie and beyond, and when he finally looked up, he was surprised to see that it was after ten o'clock and Josh was still in the den peering intently at something on the Internet.

"What are you doing?" Blue asked, poking his head in the door.

"None of your business."

Blue inched in closer. "What is that?" He looked at the screen over Josh's shoulder. "Stress ball craft? What is that?"

Josh sighed and swirled around on the chair. "Well, see, our class is supposed to think of ways to make money during the final week of Up with Reading! Month at school, and since Mom told me she was going to make you get rid of all that cornstarch, I was just checking here to see if maybe I could make something with it. I mean, there is a *lot* of cornstarch out there."

"Hey, cool! Nice idea!" said Blue, genuinely impressed. "So what'd you come up with?"

Josh straightened his shoulders and his eyes took on that peculiar shine that occurred on those rare occasions when his big brother demonstrated his approval of him or his actions.

"Well, I checked Google-dot-com for 'family crafts' and got some stuff right away. Here, let me show you." Josh picked up a little stack of printouts and shuffled through them.

"The very first site on the list was this, uh, let's see here—" Josh read from a sheet of paper, "*Family Crafts—Free Craft Projects—Holiday Crafts*—see? And then I searched for cornstarch and I found instructions for these stress ball craft things—you know, those squishy things you're supposed to squeeze when you're all stressed out?"

"*Very* cool! That's a *great* idea, Josh!"

Josh was starting to get really wound up now. "See, they're made out of balloons and they use *lots* of cornstarch, which we have, as you know! And then you can write on them and stuff. They seem pretty easy to make, and the kids in my class could do it, and we could write funny stuff about reading and stuff on them and probably sell them for maybe even two dollars each and the only cost we would have is for the balloons! And then, here's the best part. If that's the project my class chooses, I get a special award for thinking up the best idea! I'll be *famous!*" Josh paused a moment while his brain switched to its sarcastic mode. "But not as famous as *you*, of course!"

"Right," Blue said. "But listen. It's after ten, Joshpot. Time to turn in."

Josh turned back to face the computer. "I don't have to go to bed just because you tell me to," he said, with new bravado.

"I don't care whether you do or not. But when Mom and that guy come home, and she sees you're still up this late on a school night—"

That guy! Josh suddenly tipped his head sideways and looked up to the ceiling, rapidly blinking his eyelids as if he were trying to track a spaceship heading directly into the bright sunlight.

Blue's face softened. "What's wrong now, Buddy?"

Josh stood up. "Nothing," he said, quickly walking out of the room before the first teardrop spilled over the edge of his lower lid.

$ $ $ $ $ $ $

Blue woke up at four in the morning, not completely rested, yet wide awake. He tossed and turned for a while, but finally rose up on one elbow and switched on his light. More jet lag. This could get to be a real drag. So I'll read for a while and see if that cures it. Where's that book Josh was reading for the contest at school? Ah! there it is, on the floor, just where he left it. Blue picked up the book and started to read.

Stanley Still and the Curse of the Seven Gargoyles
By Wendy Carver
Illustrations by Lucien Carver

Chapter One

My sister's a big fat slob, my brother is an ugly creep, and my parents look like they live under a rock. I deserve better than this, and that's why I know I'm adopted.

Every fortnight, as regular as clockwork, I have the same fantastically cool dream. My real mother and father appear out of the mists, and together we journey as swift as the wind until we reach the underground tunnels at Dymmwit Park, where their special job is make the impossible happen daily.

Someday, after I overcome the curse of the seven gargoyles, they will find me, and then I, too, can live forever at Dymmwit Park. And if I try extra extra hard to be like them—not to ever think, but just to dream and fantasize all the day long, I could become a special Dymmwit kid, with my own special magic kit, and never have to clean my room at all! Heck! Let the magic do it!

When I go to Dymmwit Park, I can learn how to make the impossible happen just like my parents do—not daily, of course, because I'm just a little Dymmwit, but for sure I certainly don't ever want to be like the Dullards, who refuse to live in Dymmwit Park, and who only do science and math and algebra and think logically and never believe the really true truth—that the impossible is the real, real truth and the seemingly real is really not real at all, only dull and boring and sensible and practical and for sure never any fun. I can hardly wait to live the rest of my life in Dymmwit Park! But first, I know I must journey to many strange lands in search of the seven gargoyles.

Blue put down Josh's book with a sigh. He picked up *The Treasure of the Sierra Madre* and read until he got to the end.

BLEEP

"I was crying all night this book was so sad."

"I definelty recommend this book to who ever loves a good cry."

"I finished the book in class today, and I almost CRIED MY EYES OUT, right there in fornt of everyone!"

"I was crying VERY hard at the end."

"This book is so wonderful that it had me sobbing all night."
—Customer reviews: Amazon.com

Everything was going along just ducky at San Pablo High until Doris Sunzeri pretended to hang herself in the family garage at five o'clock in the afternoon on Easter Sunday, an ill-conceived action that caused a great deal of pandemonium and chaos among the counselors, teachers, and administrators at her school. (Fooling and upsetting her parents was her privilege, of course, but leaving Mrs. Manning and the counseling staff to deal with the fallout was thoughtless and inconsiderate, to say the least.)

The simple fact is that Doris Sunzeri had been feeling really, *really* bored and terribly, terribly *blah* since her fifteenth birthday, mostly because she had received exactly what she had asked for— the entire thirty-volume set of the popular *Never So Miserable* books by Arlene Spaniel, in which the young heroine, Cristella Bassett, copes valiantly with a laundry list of hardships endured by herself and her family—listed alphabetically, those would be: AIDS, alcoholism, anorexia, bloating, cancer, cellulite, drug addiction, genetic stuttering, incest, irreversible brain damage, low self-esteem, ostracism, premature death, paraskavedekatriaphobia, rape, sexual abuse, starvation, suicide, unwanted pregnancies, weak bladder, and white plague—which is another name for TB. The final book of the series, *Watch Me Die!*, remains Doris's all-time favorite, mostly because of its simple yet heart-wrenching plot, which goes like this: after suffering through every single hardship endured by mankind throughout the centuries, Cristella has finally had it, and reluctantly decides there is only one way out. ("'Committing my own suicide is the only door left open,' she sobbed, peering into the mirror.") At any rate, after the deed is done, her afterlife soul is permitted to visit a sort of rest stop on her journey to becoming an angel, all due to the kind intervention of a mysterious stranger—the manager of the Last Starbucks® in the Sky.* It is there, while enjoying a delicious latte and a heavenly madeleine, that Cristella is permitted to view the bitter remorse of her tormentors and the uncontrolled sobs of her allies down below, played out in moving and poetic individual monologues of regret and sorrow. A fitting ending indeed to the series that provoked enough tears among its devoted fans to drown an elephant.

Recently, however, Doris had tired of enjoying her heartbreaks vicariously through the magic of reading and had developed a craving for spreading around some real-life misery. While a faked suicide may have its built-in dangers—the chance of being exposed, for example—it still had its attractions. Besides sparking renewed attention from her parents, it would also enable her to compete

---

Unpaid "feeler" advertisement. (If the advertising director of Starbucks is interested in pursuing the untapped potential of both placement and/or running-head book ads, please contact the author.)

with the continuous supply of grief and pain her provisional friends bring to school each day. Trish Lowe, for example, is still getting mileage from her mother's debilitating bout with carpal tunnel syndrome, which obliges poor Trish to cut down drastically on her TV-watching and pitch in more with the household chores, and Kelly Peters continues to entertain the other girls with her on-going saga about that unfortunate accident at the soup factory, involving her sister's ex-boyfriend's stepfather and the missing digits.

In short, Doris was long overdue for her turn in the spotlight, and, as it happened, two recent events at school provided her with both an excuse and the ammunition for turning to more risky measures. Not only did both Kelly and Trish neglect to make room for her at their usual table at lunchtime, but they also ridiculed her new scarf, a Sara Salinas exclusive for which she had paid a great deal of money. Poor Doris was so clueless she hadn't been aware that SaSa, as her press agent had dubbed her, was totally, but totally, gone. But now a new Doris, bursting with attitude, was ready for the attack!

$$\$ \ \$ \ \$ \ \$ \ \$ \ \$ \ \$$$

Along with the *Never So Miserable* thirty-volume series, Doris also received on her birthday a popular self-help book for teens called *Dancing with Porcupines: The Essential Teenager's Guide to Parents & Other Authority Figures,* which was unwittingly given to her by her mother, who had somehow mistaken it for a *Chicken Soup for the Soul* book.

Three days before Easter, when Doris was feeling particularly put-upon, she fixed herself a turkey sandwich on a sesame seed bun and took it to her room—even though she had already had dinner with her parents—Chinese stir-fry with rice, a dish she hated, but which didn't bother *them*—and began to read *Dancing with Porcupines.* It was hard going at first, since there was nothing in those slim pages that brought even a hint of moisture to her eyes, and unless Doris was moved to tears, reading held no charm. However, with a combination of skimming and sheer will power, she soon found

85

herself at the final chapter, which was entitled "Last Resorts," and which began with this admonition:

> **Okay. So you've had it!** You've tried absolutely everything we've suggested to get your share of the personal attention, special privileges, and the material objects you deserve from your parents, siblings, friends, and teachers, and nothing has worked. Don't despair! We've got one final trick up our sleeve that's guaranteed to bring success, *provided you follow our directions to the letter.*

Doris was captivated on the spot. She fixed herself a large bowl of ice cream, topped it off with lots of chocolate syrup, and was soon busily planning her own "big event."

HOW TO STAGE YOUR OWN SHAM SUICIDE

> **1. Choosing a date and time.** Be sure to plan your sham suicide for a time when someone will be there to discover you! THIS IS VERY IMPORTANT! Holidays and weekends are preferable because they are generally slow news days and you are apt to receive wider TV and news coverage, which is a good thing.

TV and news coverage! Wow! Easter Sunday might be a good time. Doris quickly went into the den to check the family calendar that was kept on the desk by the phone. "What are you looking for?" asked her mother, who happened to be talking to Doris's older sister, who was away at college—and who always *was* their favorite. "Nothing," Doris said.

> **2. Method.** We do NOT (repeat, NOT!) endorse overdosing!! It is unreliable and messy, and will most certainly result in a stomach-pumping, which is not a pretty sight, not to mention extremely unpleasant. Guns are much too dangerous, and sometimes difficult to come by. Throwing yourself out

of a window or under a speeding train is, of course, out of the question. Our preferred method, therefore, entails only a length of rope, a belt, or a scarf, and a suitable crossbeam over which to drape it.

My SaSa scarf! Perfect! Doris finished the last of her ice cream and pushed her empty bowl aside. So far so good. Except for one thing! The scarf happened to be at the bottom of the trash bin, where Doris had tossed it after her so-called friends had insulted it during lunch on the last day of school before spring break. A few minutes later found Doris, flashlight in hand, searching through the trash can just outside the kitchen window. "What on earth are you doing out there?" her mother called out. "Nothing," Doris said.

3. Preparing for your Event. Garages make perfect locales for your Event. Procure a sturdy box or platform on which to stand. Drape your chosen length of material over a suitable crossbeam and secure it LOOSELY around your neck, being certain that your box or platform is steady and secure. (Important: Do NOT attempt to kick the box or platform away, even in fun!) For added realism, you may want to prepare ahead of time such accessories as diaries, letters, or notebooks detailing your misery. Hint: Teardrop stains are always effective.

Doris planned to prepare a notebook and a suicide note, as suggested, within the next day or two, but for now she went out to the garage to check for crossbeams and rummage around for a sturdy box. Her mother, hearing the commotion, went out to investigate. "What in the world are you doing out here this time of night?" she asked. "Nothing," said Doris.

4. Hints for obtaining greater realism. At the moment that you are discovered, it is important that you feign (pretend to be) choking by making strange choking and gurgling sounds, and holding your breath until your face turns red. Practice these procedures until they come more or less naturally.

After a few minutes, Doris's mother rattled the doorknob and walked into the room without even knocking. "Are you all right? You sound like you're choking to death! What's wrong?" she asked. "Nothing," said Doris.

$ $ $ $ $ $ $

The day of her Event soon arrived. Doris, while never helping with the laundry, knew her mother always performed that chore on Sunday afternoons, Easter or not, and would be trooping in and out of the garage at regular intervals. So there she waited, patiently standing on a sturdy box with her SaSa scarf at the ready, listening to the spinning cycle of the washer and the constant whir of the dryer while envisioning her soon-to-be status as the main focus of attention among her family, neighbors, and friends.

As expected, her mother appeared shortly, laundry basket in hand. Mrs. Sunzeri immediately let out a piercing scream at what she thought she saw, thereby alerting the neighborhood children who were gathered on the lawn next door, and who were in imminent danger of coming to blows over a disagreement regarding the proper procedure and purpose of a so-called Easter Egg Roll—one faction insisting that they could not conduct a proper Egg Roll because of the absence of a hill, while the others opined that the eggs could simply be rolled around like bowling balls, with no incline needed.

In the ensuing confusion, the police were called and an ambulance arrived shortly thereafter. One enterprising neighbor quickly dialed up the special "Citizen News-Alert Hotline" at the *Oakland Star,* lured by the promise of a possible cash reward should the unfolding event be deemed sufficiently newsworthy, which, to his delight, it was.

$ $ $ $ $ $ $

"Who the heck is Doris Sunzeri?" asked a distraught Mr. Frazier, when Mrs. Manning, the high-school principal, called him at home early that evening to break the news, which in turn had been relayed to her by Margaret Jennings, the reporter for the *Star* who had been called to the scene, even though it was, technically, a holiday.

"Well, you have the S's, Frank! Think a minute, for God's sake!"

Mr. Frazier took off his glasses and rubbed his eyes. "Not the *seniors*, Fran," he reminded her. "You gave the seniors to Vicky, remember? So what is she? A freshman? A sophomore? What?"

Mrs. Manning had started doodling on the scratch pad next to the phone. She had minored in art in college, so, as one might expect, her doodles were much more professional-looking than average. "A sophomore. She's a sophomore. A solid B student, according to her parents, who, I might add, were very, *very* upset."

"Wait a minute. I think I remember her now. She's the one whose name was spelled wrong in my files—Sunseri, with an *s* instead of a *z*. So she kind of got lost in the shuffle. That is, until we got it sorted out. A rather plain, heavyset girl, as I remember."

"Well, listen, Frank. After she was discovered by her mother—just in the nick of time, apparently—this reporter from the *Star* asked her if by any chance she had written a suicide note. And, sure enough, the girl produced one that she had earlier tucked inside one of her notebooks. You know, this could be really incriminating for us at San Pablo."

"For us? How so?"

"Well, according to the reporter, Doris not only felt neglected at home, but she also had some sort of traumatic experience at school with a scarf just before Easter vacation." Mrs. Manning pursed her lips and shook her head. "I mean *spring break.* Why do I keep getting that wrong?" she asked rhetorically. "Old habits die hard, I guess. Anyway, from what the reporter told me, some of the kids—some of the other girls—were making fun of it—"

"Making fun of what? I don't understand."

"Her scarf, Frank. A Sara Salinas scarf, if I heard correctly.

Anyway, Doris admitted to the reporter that she felt just too embarrassed to return to school tomorrow. She confessed that the girls she wanted to eat lunch with considered her 'out of it,' and 'boring,' and the scarf thing only added fuel to the fire. And she just couldn't get used to sitting with the nobodies—the blobs, as she called them."

"The blobs? That's a new one."

"Yes. Well, the whole point, I think, is that at age fifteen, Doris Sunzeri considers herself a failure."

"A failure? What does that mean? She's only a kid."

"Listen, Frank, *you're* supposed to be the counselor. Surely you must be familiar with the way some of these children feel when they perceive that they're not being accepted in the particular crowd of their choosing. They think their life is over. Surely you must be familiar with that!"

"Hmm."

"Well, the reporter who called me said that the police implied that Doris was not really intending to—to, you know, finish the job—but that she was not going to report that implication, especially since Doris's notebook did remind her of the one *she* kept during *her* high-school days, and that she could certainly sympathize with what Doris had written. Well, the reporter just kept going on and on about this *notebook*. She even mentioned that the pages looked a bit tear-stained, and the orange cover was pockmarked with little moon-shaped indentations, obviously from Doris's fingernails."

Mr. Frazier pictured the orange, pockmarked notebook in his mind's eye. Poor kid, he thought.

Mrs. Manning was alarmed to see that while she was telling Mr. Frazier about Doris's notebook, she had been sketching a large and detailed noose, fashioned from a scarf, on her scratch pad. She allowed herself just the tiniest smidgen of time to admire her handiwork before quickly scribbling over it. Then she heaved a big sigh and shook her head, remarking, more to herself than to Mr. Frazier, "But just imagine, that poor child trying to *hang* herself with it—"

"Really? With her notebook? Jeez, how'd she ever—"

"No, Frank! Not with her *notebook.* How could she do that? Use your head, for God's sake! Her scarf! Her *scarf!* She tried to hang herself with her SaSa scarf!"

"Well, yeah. Now that makes a lot more sense—"

"But here's the thing," Mrs. Manning continued. "The reporter—I think her name was Margaret something—told me that she obtained permission both from Doris and her mother to print this story, and it's going on the front page in tomorrow's *Star.* From what I could gather, SPHS is going to bear the brunt of the responsibility, along with the book Doris was reading before this uh, unfortunate incident occurred. Just a minute here, I wrote down the title. Oh, yes. It's called *Watch Me Die!* Mrs. Sunzeri is going to complain about allowing such books in school, while the newspaper is taking the position that it's the duty of the school counseling staff to be on guard for this sort of behavior, and to nip it in the bud before it reaches such a critical stage."

"Oh, they can't really believe that!" Mr. Manning exclaimed, following up his statement of incredulity with his all-time-favorite four-letter expletive.

"Frank!" Mrs. Manning scolded. "See there? I've caught you again! Now you've simply got to train yourself to stop using that kind of language—and worse—especially in front of the students. I've warned you about this before, and I don't intend to do so again."

Mrs. Manning paused, waiting for a response from Mr. Frazier. But before he could reply, she added, "We *have* gotten complaints, you know, so this has to stop!"

Mr. Frazier sighed. "Yes. Okay, Fran. I'm sorry. It's just that at times like this I start to wonder why I didn't choose some other line of work, that's all. You know, I *could* have gone into the acoustical ceiling business with my brother-in-law, counseling credential notwithstanding—"

"Well, be that as it may, if you would only do as I've suggested and substitute the word *bleep* when those other objectionable words come to the fore, you could conquer this thing."

"Okay, okay. I'll try. How's this? *Bleep, diddily-bleep bleep bleep!*"

$ $ $ $ $ $ $

While Mr. Frazier was busy bleeping, a significant and crucial personality change had mysteriously befallen Omaha Nebraska Brown. She had no idea how or why it happened; she only knew that somehow she found within herself the courage to shed the last vestiges of Peer Pressure Power that were lingering in her psyche. What could have caused this sudden shift in her PPP? Did a dormant gene suddenly come to life? Could her recent craving for chicken gumbo soup have played a part? The okra, maybe? Have scientists thoroughly examined the vitamin and mineral content of that often maligned vegetable? Or was this merely the result of her body's natural maturing process, hastened by the urgency of her financial situation? Whatever it was, Dr. Jonathan Barger of Colorado Springs, Colorado, would certainly have loved to witness and harness it in the controlled confines of his laboratory.

No longer hampered by the haunting fear of the reaction of her peers to the knowledge of the uniqueness of her physique, the newly emancipated Omaha quickly decided her best bet would be to assume a breezy what-do-I-care tone in her contest entry. She copied down from memory the sentence that she had thought up in bed the night before, but after thinking about it for a while, she decided to jettison it and begin anew—eventually coming up with the following entry, composed of exactly 150 words:

I believe I am uniquely qualified to enter your I am Unique, Too contest.

Judges, ask yourselves this question: "How many women do I know who happen to have three breasts?"

Then ask yourselves this question: "How many women with three breasts would I <u>like</u> to know?"

Don't answer that question!

Well, I'm here to tell you that Mother Nature <u>does</u> make an occasional mistake. In my case, the mistake was located between my "others" and my navel. Actually, it was no big deal. But hey, neither are my others!

Sorry to say, I don't have it anymore. It was removed by surgery when I was quite young. Now all I have to show for it is a little scar, and the knowledge that I do possess a unique physique! I hope you'll agree!

Well, I've used up all my words. Now I could sure use the $5,000.

Thank you!

Omaha read over her entry several times, trying to put herself in the judges' place. What would they think? Is it unique enough? Like Mom told me, the doctor who removed it said that while it wasn't something he saw every day, it was not all *that* uncommon! But is it too offbeat? For those weirdos on KFIB, probably not! But what if I *should* win—will they ask for verification? Will they want to feature me in future ads for the Unique Construction Company? Will I have to give interviews? Answer embarrassing questions? Will my picture (enlarged from the waist up!) suddenly appear next to those contortionists on the sides of their pickup trucks?

Do I *really* want to send this?

DIACRITICAL MARKS

schwa (shwä, shvä) **n.** {*Ger* < *Heb* sheva, *a diacritic marking silence instead of a vowel sound*} *the neutral mid-central vowel sound of most unstressed syllables in English: the sound represented by* a *in* ago, e *in* agent, i *in* sanity, *etc.*
—*Webster's New World Dictionary,*
Third College Edition

On Monday morning before school, Blue removed the rubber band from around the *Oakland Star* and began to read the following front-page story:

Local Girl Attempts Suicide in Family Garage

San Pablo Sophomore Struggles to Strangle Self with Scoffed-at SaSa Scarf

By Margaret Jennings, Staff Reporter

Note to our Readers: It is against the policy of the Star *to publish the names of suicide victims except when explicit permission is given. And even though no actual suicide was committed, both Doris and her family have given that permission, with the hope that their experience may open up much-needed*

94

discussion on this serious topic. Please write or call the Star *to voice your opinions and suggestions.*

A grisly scene came too close for comfort for the parents of 15-year-old Doris Sunzeri yesterday afternoon when they discovered their only daughter moments before hanging herself from the rafters in the family garage.

The young near-victim guided this reporter to a suicide note which she had earlier tucked inside her notebook, a notebook filled with tear-stained pages describing the heartbreaking story of a modern-day high-school outcast.

Lying open on the teenager's nightstand (alongside an overdue rented video of the cult movie *Harold and Maude*) was a well-worn copy of *Watch Me Die!*, a grim, award-winning teenage novel chronicling the constant barrage of tragedies, disappointments, and utter hopelessness of yet another high-school outcast who yearned to be a member of the popular "in crowd," thereby gaining the envy and hatred of other losers such as herself, according to Trudy Deene, children's book reviewer for the *Star*.

In a particularly poignant aspect of the near-tragedy, Miss Sunzeri tearfully confided to this reporter that she had recently purchased a Sara Salinas scarf in an effort to curry favor with a popular group of girls with whom she wished to sit at lunchtime in the school cafeteria. Apparently, however, coinciding with SaSa's plummeting CD sales among notoriously fickle teenagers, the scarf was hopelessly out of fashion, and only caused derision and ridicule. (It was this very same scarf that was found tightly bound around the neck of the young victim-to-be, just in the nick of time.)

Reached for comment by the *Star,* Mrs. Fran Manning, SPHS principal, expressed her deep relief at the outcome of this incident and pledged to devote more time and effort to bolstering the self-confidence and mental health of all the students at San Pablo High. "I am deeply cognizant of the universal turmoil and torment endured almost constantly by today's adolescents, and we at San Pablo High pledge to do whatever we can to explain this to the children. If they are not suffering, they are decidedly abnormal," she concluded sadly, "and we want them to know we're here to help."

However, another view of the volatile teenage years may be slowly gaining favor, according to Dr. Igor Vandergraft, a controversial professor of child psychology at Bangor College in upstate New York. "Society's invention of the 'teenager' is a fairly recent phenomenon," remarked Dr. Vandergraft during an appearance last week at the yearly meeting of the CPFC in Berkeley. "It's high time we put to rest the persistent myth that all teenagers must of necessity suffer through the so-called hormonal whirlwind of adolescence. In point of fact, many well-adjusted youngsters survive their teenage years with enduring good humor and surprising ease. So let us stop dwelling on the inevitability of teenage angst, which, in many cases, becomes a self-fulfilling prophesy. The way things stand now, we're giving our kids the green light for indulging in unacceptable behavior under the guise of 'raging hormones,' when, in fact, human beings have been developing peacefully from childhood to adulthood for millenniums without such pandering as afforded our young people today," he concluded, to the warm but guarded applause of his audience.

Had she been successful in her attempted suicide, Doris Sunzeri's tragic death would have marked the fourth suicide committed by a Bay Area teenager since the beginning of the year, although hers would be the first death by hanging. In the most recent case, a 16-year-old boy threw himself into the path of a slow-moving freight train hauling new Harley-Davidson motorcycles to local distributors. It was later revealed that the boy was retaliating against his parents' refusal to purchase a Harley for his birthday. According to Clive Herndon, executive editor of the *Star,* "This revelation seemed to strike a chord in the hearts and minds of many guilt-ridden parents and their equally put-upon kids, and sparked the largest number of 'Letters to the Editor' since the *Star*'s cancellation of the controversial Doonesbury comic strip during the Nixon-Watergate affair in 1973."

The remaining two juvenile suicides committed this year were caused by self-inflicted gunshot wounds, acts which garnered much criticism and placed Save Our Guns League spokesman Percival "Ace" Blodgett under extreme pressure. In regard to this current tragedy, Mr. Blodgett remarked gleefully, "Well, it appears our work is cut out for us now! Not only must we register all scarves, but we must also declare a three-day waiting period for their purchase!"

Employees at Grace's Boutique, where the scarf in question was purchased, would not comment, except to say that they have a great collection of authentic, copyrighted celebrity scarves, and that consumers should beware of the sudden influx of cheap ripoffs from unlicensed suppliers.

Blue couldn't believe a newspaper reporter would end a story about an attempted suicide with a blatant advertisement for a boutique, but there it was, in black and white.

He walked into the kitchen, newspaper still in hand, and checked the time. The clock on the wall indicated that it was sixteen minutes and twenty-five seconds after seven.

Since Blue was still trying to get used to the novel idea that there may be no such thing as time, he decided to go through what he had begun to call *the drill*. He shut his eyes and tried to picture himself—and the whole universe—enveloped by a vast and enormous colorless expanse of absolute stillness, silence, and timelessness. In other words, an expanse of nothingness. As anyone who has ever tried it will agree, nothingness is extremely difficult to envision. But Blue found that if he concentrated hard enough, letting go of all of his preconceived notions, he was (at times) able to get an extremely fleeting feeling for it. And while he was there—in this limitless expanse of no-time (for which he soon coined the word *notime*), he could see change in action—clock hands moving, young

97

people getting older, leaves falling from trees and decaying into compost right before his eyes. While the minute hand on a large clock tower in his mind went around just once, a little baby grew into an adult, and, somehow, every single leaf drifted slowly down from the huge maple tree. And the strange thing was that time had nothing to do with it, because there was notime. It was just things happening in the absolute stillness and silence of nothingness.

After performing *the drill*, Blue turned to the classified section of the paper and scanned the used cars ads—just as he had been doing every morning while gulping down a Junkpuff or a piece of toast. He really, really hated not having a car. Ever since that branch from the Lawsons' eucalyptus tree had fallen on Wayne's Samwich Wagon and totaled it, he had been yearning for a replacement—but not a converted lunchwagon this time. No, this time he wanted a real car—a private and secluded place on wheels where, finally, he might once again find himself alone with Omaha.

$ $ $ $ $ $ $

Mr. Ridenaur strode up to the board grasping a piece of chalk in his hand as if he intended to stab someone with it. Monday mornings were always the most difficult, and the one following spring break was doubly so.

"When are you people ever going to learn the difference between the accent grave and the accent acute! Can it be that *difficile?*" he asked—for this was, after all, a class in beginning French. Sighing audibly, he proceeded to write a short list of French words on the board, some with accent marks and some without. "All right, now," he said. "Heads up. Let's take a look at these together."

But Blue was having trouble staying focused on his French lesson. Aside from his continuing concern about Omaha's financial situation and her possible move, he couldn't help thinking about Doris Sunzeri. He guessed he could understand how people could sometimes flirt with the idea of killing themselves, just fantasizing about how certain people would sure be sorry *then*, seeing you in your coffin and everything. But how could anyone be so miserable and so utterly without hope that they could actually attempt it? Well, in Doris's case at least, help had arrived before it was too late. But what could be going on in the brain of someone that depressed? Could it be identified in a PET scan? Could it be detected by an analysis of her brain chemicals? Or might it be discovered buried deep within an elusive gene, just waiting to pop out?

A delightful little shiver suddenly rushed across Blue's shoulders and down his spine. Of course! Gene research! And the biochemical makeup of the brain! That's where I'm headed! Why not? It's the wave of the future—a whole new field opening up, just in time for me! Maybe to actually begin to uncover *real scientific answers* to questions like free will—find out once and for all if our thoughts and actions are *truly* our own, subject to our desires and actions, or—

"Blue?"

Blue bolted up in his seat, quickly coming out of himself and back into the classroom. "Yes, sir?"

"Well? What do we need here?"

Blue blinked. "Uh—"

"Come on, pal. *Faites attention!* Acute or grave?"

"Oh! Uh, acute?"

"That's correct. Good. Now, this one—class?"

"Grave!" The entire class joined in the answer. Hallelujah! They had finally aced it!

Mr. Ridenaur glanced at his watch. No time to start a new chapter, so may as well try to teach them some more common accent and diacritical marks. It's a cinch they won't be exposed to them in any of their other classes.

He proceeded to write the character ç followed by ô, ü, æ, ñ, and ū. And then, finally, he wrote an upside down *e*, like this: ə.

"As some of you probably know, these here symbols—or characters, if you prefer—are called diacritical marks. Now please pay

99

attention, because someday you may win an unbelievably large amount of money on a television quiz show—or some such thing—if you're able to recognize and name these particular examples."

He tapped the first symbol on the board with the point of his chalk. "This is called a cedilla." He moved on, tapping each mark in turn. "This one is a circumflex, then an umlaut, a ligature, a tilde, a macron, and, finally, a schwa. Please copy those characters and their names in your notebooks. Besides your regular assignment for tomorrow, I expect you to look up the functions performed by these marks and be prepared to explain them in class. Any questions?"

No questions.

Mr. Ridenaur replaced the chalk and lightly brushed off his pants.

"Mr. Ridenaur?"

Oh, no. It was Lenny Briggsmore, with his hand raised and that innocent look on his face. Mr. Ridenaur braced himself. Lenny Bruce Briggsmore, the son of Bobby Briggsmore, head deejay at Radio KFIB, was named in honor of Lenny Bruce, the now dead, contumacious comedian who changed forever the definition of humor in America, if not the world. Although it took a bucketful of high-powered bargaining before Bobby was able to persuade his wife to name their firstborn in honor of the legendary *enfant terrible*, even Bobby himself never imagined just how weird and unpredictable his own kid would turn out to be.

"Yes, Lenny?" said Mr. Ridenaur, checking his watch.

Lenny posed his question with a deceptive little smile playing around his lips. "Well, I was just wondering, uh, how long do you think it would have taken for Doris Sunzeri to actually die? I mean, if her mother hadn't have gotten there when she did?"

"Ugg! Lenny!" Several of the girls gasped and covered their mouths, and Blue actually winced in pain.

Some of the other kids looked at each other with expressions of disbelief, murmuring, "That's disgusting!" or "Leave it to Lenny!"

Regretfully, three of the boys thought the question was sort of funny, in a gruesome, computer-game kind of way.

Mr. Ridenaur was not caught completely off guard. Lenny's future had recently been discussed in a lively and informal, off-the-record session in the teachers' lounge. The participants had split into two factions; one predicted he would end up living out his days in a cardboard box under a bridge, while the other saw him as the obnoxious CEO of a highly inflammatory, lawsuit-prone, tabloid-publishing conglomerate. Mr. Ridenaur had not expressed an opinion then, but if he had to wager now, he'd put his money on the tabloids, no question about it.

$$\$ \$ \$ \$ \$ \$ \$$$

Mrs. Manning prefers that memos to her staff at San Pablo High be printed on her trademark blue paper. That way there will be no mistaking them for ordinary fliers or miscellaneous throwaways. Mr. Frazier groaned audibly that same Monday morning after spring break when he finally got around to reading her latest communiqué. *Oh, no! Not that Starship San Pablo bleep again!*

INTEROFFICE MEMO
To: All Personnel Aboard Starship San Pablo
From: Captain Manning
Re: Hallway Monitoring

This is to remind you that we have now entered the Final Zone before summer vacation. Acting as a team, and in spite of the Sisyphean tasks that confronted us daily, we've somehow managed to survive! But we can't let up now. Please remember it is your responsibility to patrol the hallway adjacent to your classroom without fail during the student passing times. Your visible presence often means the difference between a smooth passing and a rowdy brawl.

Over and out.
Mrs. Fran Manning

Well, at least she didn't single me out, Mr. Frazier thought, admitting to himself that he hadn't "patrolled his hallway" for quite some time now. And what the *bleep* is a Sisyphean task, anyway?

Mr. Frazier almost missed seeing the attachment that was stapled to the back of Mrs. Manning's memo instead of to the front—a deliberately rebellious action perpetrated by a sullen and disenchanted student assistant named Oscar Riley, who was simply asked to staple them to the front, but who felt he was being disrespected by being told what to do all the time.

INTEROFFICE MEMO
To: All Teachers and Clerical Staff
From: Principal Manning
Re: Speaking with the Media

As you have no doubt heard, Doris Sunzeri, a sophomore student enrolled here at San Pablo High School, attempted to take her own life over the weekend. Luckily, she was discovered in time and this tragedy was averted. Whether or not you have had personal contact with this student, there is a possibility that you may be approached by representatives from the Media. If this happens, please be cautious in your response to their questions, especially those pertaining to the books young people prefer to read and cafeteria seating. Remember, ours is not a regimented environment, and students have the freedom to sit wherever and with whomever they choose at lunchtime. As to the books issue, City Schools Superintendent Mooney plans to address that concern in the near future.

Mrs. Manning, Principal

$ $ $ $ $ $

"Hey, Blue!" Mr. Frazier called out across the busy hallway right after Blue's French class. "Come over here a minute."

Blue acknowledged Mr. Frazier with a quick wave of his hand and made his way through the moving river of bodies to where his counselor was standing, dutifully patrolling his little section of the corridor.

"So where are you headed this period, my man?"

"P.E."

"Perfect. Come on into my office for a minute. There's someone here who wants to meet you."

"But—"

"No problem! Come on! I'll write you an excuse."

Tractor was idly gazing at the notices pinned on the bulletin board in Mr. Frazier's office when Blue and his counselor entered the small cubicle.

"Well, I snagged him for you, Trac. This is Blue. Our one and only Blue Avenger." Then Mr. Frazier pointed over toward Tractor and said, "Blue, meet Tractor Nishimura, one of my early, uh— counselees," he said with raised eyebrows and a puzzled smile, indicating that he didn't feel completely at ease with the word. "Let's see, Trac, how long ago was that?"

"It'll be fifteen years this June."

"No! Really? I can't believe it!" Mr. Frazier sat down behind his desk. "Have a seat, guys. Pull that stool over here, Blue. That's the ticket."

"So, are we going to see you at the reunion, Mr. Frazier?" Trac asked. "It's going to be at Spenger's, you know. I'm really looking forward to this one, since I was out of the country on our fifth and our tenth. It's going to be fun seeing all those kids again."

"Ah, yes! I did receive an invitation to that. I should RSVP pretty soon, I suppose."

"Man-oh-man! I can't wait to see old Holly Hollingshead—I mean Langsford—she's married now, I hear. She was always trying to diet, but I'll bet you a million bucks that by now she's gained at least twenty-five pounds! Boy, will I rub it in!"

"Well, if anyone can afford to bet a million bucks, I guess it's you," said Mr. Frazier, winking at Blue, who really didn't get it, since he had not yet made the connection between this unassuming young man in Mr. Frazier's office and the multimillionaire moviemaker from Marin.

"Think so?" Trac responded coolly. (Like most millionaires—and billionaires as well, for that matter—he really doesn't appreciate references to his wealth idly thrown into every conversation. It puts him in a most uncomfortable position—almost like he's expected to throw hundred-dollar bills around to everyone in the room.) "Anyway," Trac continued, "you do know where she's working now, don't you?"

Mr. Frazier shook his head. "You mean Holly? No, I have no idea where she's working."

"Well, she's over at DMV headquarters in Sacramento. Would you believe she's the personalized-license-plate censor!"

Mr. Frazier smiled. "That figures, doesn't it?"

"God, how I wanted to make that speech at graduation! I was one sick puppy on grad night when Mrs. Manning came up to me while we were putting on our caps and gowns and asked if what Holly had just told her was true. It was my own fault, though. I should've known better than to tell Holly what I was planning to do." Tractor paused and looked up at Mr. Frazier. "It was a great speech, you know. Well, you were on the committee. You read it—"

"Yes, I did read it, and it was a great speech." Mr. Frazier leaned back in his chair and rubbed the back of his neck. "But to be honest with you, Trac, the way I remember it, after Mrs. Manning was told that night—"

"When Holly squealed on me, you mean!"

"Whatever. But when Mrs. Manning got wind of the fact that you were planning to say—oh, what was that you wanted to say—you were going to start off with something—"

"Tigers suck! I was just going to shout out, 'Tigers suck,' that's all. Big deal!"

Blue was fascinated. What were they talking about, anyway?

"Yes. That was it. I remember now. Tigers suck. Well, Fran—I mean, Mrs. Manning—told me later that she asked for your word that you wouldn't say it, and that you took an *awfully* long time answering."

Tractor smiled, just enough to reveal his dimple. "Yeah, that's true. Actually, I was considering whether or not I should lie to her, because I was sure I was going to say it, regardless."

"And, obviously, she *knew* that."

"But still, when you come right down to it," Tractor said, "the whole fiasco was Holly's fault. She didn't have to run tattling to Mrs. Manning like she did. Holly was the one who threw the dead fish in the honeypot."

"Well, yes," Mr. Frazier admitted, "but then I do believe she was quite sincere about it. She just didn't think it was proper. Not proper for a graduation speech."

"Proper? Ha! But here's what I'd like to know: would it have bothered her so much if *she* hadn't happened to be the committee's second choice?" Tractor raised his eyebrows and sang out, "I don't *think* so!"

As for Blue, he didn't know what to think. He'd caught on to the gist of the conversation by then, but he couldn't believe that giving the graduation speech could mean so much to Tractor. And how could he hold a grudge *that* long?

Tractor was looking out the window then, kind of rubbing his chin with his hand, when suddenly he swirled around with a big grin spreading across his face. "Hey, you know what would be really cool?" he asked, pounding a fist into the palm of his hand. "What if I could slip one by her now—like getting some kind of hidden version of *suck* on my license plate, for instance? Yeah!" he said, quickly warming up to his own idea. "How do you say *suck* in Spanish? That might work."

Blue and Mr. Frazier exchanged glances.

"Or, then again, maybe it wouldn't," Tractor went on, speaking more rapidly now. "How about something like in a code, then?

Not pig Latin or anything so obvious, though. She's probably on to that. Just the word *suck,* but *hidden,* you know?"

"Something like S-U-K, or maybe S-U-X?" Mr. Frazier suggested, spelling out the words.

"Oh, no," Trac responded quickly. "That's too obvious. It has to be much more subtle than that."

"Well, *bleep!* Blue might be able to help you out there."

"Really? How so?"

"I've heard from Dr. Wood that he's quite a cryptographer—"

Trac looked over at Blue with raised eyebrows. "A cryptographer? No kidding!"

Blue felt himself blushing—something he always hated—even though Omaha told him once that she thought it was cute, how the red of his skin and red of his hair sort of complimented each other, and really didn't clash at all.

"Oh, no," Blue protested. "That's hardly true. I mean, just because I happen to know the Baconian Bi-literal Cipher, and—"

"Well, listen," Trac interrupted, reaching for his wallet. "If you *should* come up with something you think might work, I'll give you my business card here—" Trac hesitated a moment before handing the card over to Blue. He pulled a pen out of his shirt pocket and quickly scratched out the existing e-mail address and wrote in a different one. "I'm giving you my personal e-mail address here. This one doesn't go through my secretary, but comes directly to me. Okay?"

Blue nodded. "Sure."

"I'm really serious about this, now, so I'm counting on you to give it your best shot. This is the coolest idea I've had in months, and I expect to have some fun with it. Ah, sweet, sweet revenge!"

Blue took the business card, glanced at it briefly without really reading it, and stuck it in his shirt pocket, at the same time nursing a vague feeling that perhaps what he was being asked to do might possibly be construed as an infringement of the law.

Right there in Mr. Frazier's office, Blue's most treasured possession, his brain—if one's brain can be thought of as a possession—went into overdrive. Okay, he thought, let's look at this logically. *If* the rationale behind the existence of a license plate censor is to protect the public from offending plates, and *if* the censor's job is screening for such, and *if* the censor can find no fault with some particular arrangement of letters and/or numbers, then—hidden meaning or not—by definition that plate would be acceptable. Blue paused in his thinking to wait for a possible rebuttal. But instead, the message he got was *sounds good to me.*

Now, what was it that Tractor was saying?

"One problem is that there is a bit of a rush on this. I imagine it takes a couple of weeks to get a personalized plate, and our class reunion is—" Tractor stopped suddenly. "But wait. When you come right down to it, I guess it really doesn't matter if she actually *sees* the thing or not. Just my knowing that I've outsmarted her will be enough for me." He paused. "Although, on second thought, it *would* be fun to—"

The phone on Mr. Frazier's desk rang. "Excuse me," he said. "I have to get this."

In deference to the small size of the cubicle, Trac and Blue remained silent.

"Yes, Irene?" Mr. Frazier paused. "Okay, put her on." Mr. Frazier leaned back in his chair. "Yes, Mrs. Sunzeri. How are you? Oh, I should say! It certainly must be—what's that?" Mr. Frazier slowly reached for a pencil while nodding his head, listening to what was obviously quite a long recitation from Mrs. Sunzeri on the other end of the line. Finally he asked, "So what was the name of it again? Yes, I know it was mentioned in the paper this morning, but—yes. Okay. *Watch Me Die!* Yes. I remember it now. Well, I'm sure it'll be brought up at the next teachers' meeting—" Mr. Frazier rolled his eyes. "Yes. Well, I'm not quite sure which reading

107

committee you're referring to. There *are* several, you know. Yes. What was that? The Up with Reading! committee? No, I don't happen to have their number, but I can transfer you—what's that? Oh, right! *Definitely.* Yes. Yes, indeed. Thank you. Hold on, now." Mr. Frazier clicked the phone several times. "Irene? Can you help Mrs. Sunzeri here? Thank you."

Mr. Frazier no sooner hung up the phone before it rang again. "Yes?" He checked his watch. "Oh, *bleep!* Okay. Tell them I'll be right over. And call Officer Tracy, too, would you? Oh, you already did? Good."

He hung up the phone again and got up quickly from his chair. "Sorry. I've got to go. There's some trouble over in the gym. Apparently the toilets are plugged up again and the kids are going on another flushing frenzy. They'll flood the whole building unless somebody puts a stop to it." He rushed off without even closing the door behind him.

Tractor looked at Blue in amazement. "*A flushing frenzy? Flooding the whole building? The kids would actually do that? Jeez, I don't think the kids in my class would have acted up like that! What's happened, anyway, in just fifteen years?*" asked the producer of *Mayhem and Murder at Scream City High,* a high-grossing smash hit that did almost as well at the box office as Trac's bloody thriller of the year before called *What Are YOU Lookin' At, Deadman?*

Blue shrugged. "Times have changed, I guess."

"I *guess!*" Tractor Nishimura looked at his watch and announced that he really had to run. "Tell old Frazier I'll see him at the reunion, would you, Blue? And please give that license plate challenge some thought. I'll be asking some other folks, too, so here, why don't you jot down your e-mail address for me and I'll send you a note if someone else comes up with something before you do." He handed Blue another business card, back side up, and while Blue was writing, he added, "Oh, and say—I'd like to get a chance to talk with you more sometime soon, if we can arrange it."

Blue looked up and handed the card back. "Really? What about?"

"Oh, you know, how you metamorphosed into your Blue Avenger persona, your subsequent exploits, stuff like that—"

"Oh?"

"Yeah. Sounds like a fascinating story! Kind of different, you know? Has the makings of a musical, in a way. But I've really got to run now." He took back his business card, gave Blue a kind of salute, and walked out of the office.

Blue scratched his head. The makings of a musical? What the heck was that all about?

$ $ $ $ $ $ $

Blue met up with Mr. Frazier as he was returning from the gym. "Everything's under control. Come on back to the office. I'll give you that late pass."

As the two of them were walking back to the main building, Mr. Frazier glanced over at Blue for a moment and asked in a light, offhanded manner, "Say, Blue—you don't happen to know what Sisyphean means, do you? As in a Sisyphean task?"

"Well, yeah, I think I do. I had this book about Greek myths when I was little, and I remember Sisyphus was some bad king or other who was doomed in Hades to keep rolling this heavy stone uphill, only to have it keep rolling back down again all the time. So a Sisyphean task would mean something like endless or useless. Something like that."

"Well, sure. That makes sense," Mr. Frazier said, assuring himself that he probably had known the answer all along, but it was nice of Blue to refresh his memory.

Blue reached the door to the main building first, and as he held it open, Mr. Frazier turned his head and remarked, "By the way. I'll bet you didn't know you just shook the hand of a multimillionaire right there in my office a few minutes ago."

"Tractor?" Blue's eyes widened.

"T&T Productions. That was Tractor Nishimura."

"No kidding! Man! Pretty amazing! Jeez! Why didn't you tell me?"

109

"Well, I intended to, a little later. He'd asked me if I could arrange for him to meet you. He's always scouting around for new ideas, you know, and he seemed intrigued by the way you changed your name and saved Mrs. Manning from the bees, et cetera. But then I got called away and didn't get a chance to go into all that."

They had reached Mr. Frazier's office now, and Blue paused a moment and stared at his hand. "This is the hand he shook, but it didn't seem to turn it green."

"Nope. Just looks like the usual color to me."

"Yes, but did you notice he actually had his wallet out for a moment there? He could at least have tossed a couple of hundred-dollar bills in our direction while he had them so handy, don't you think?" Blue laughed—a short, little self-conscious laugh, as it occurred to him how unrealistic and far-fetched that statement sounded. Actually, he felt a bit embarrassed that he would even think such a thing.

But, strangely enough—or not so strangely enough—the idea had also occurred to Mr. Frazier, because he gave Blue a friendly cuff on the arm and said, "You know, I was thinking the same *bleep* thing myself!"

$ $ $ $ $ $

Editor, *The Oakland Star*

Dear Sir:

I have a complaint. In your article about the young girl attempting suicide ("Local Girl Attempts Suicide in Family Garage") you used an acronym without explaining anywhere in the article what it stood for. The acronym in question is CPFC. If this was the first time you had done this I would let it go. But it seems to happen several times a week, and is extremely annoying. Please try to do better in the future or I may have to consider canceling my subscription.

Dr. Ronald Trestle

Editor, *The Oakland Star*

Dear Sir:

Trudy Deene, your children's book reviewer, got it wrong again! As any fan of Arlene Spaniel's books can tell you, Ms. Deene's plot synopsis as quoted in the *Star* ("Local Girl Attempts Suicide in Family Garage ") was NOT that of "Watch Me Die!" at all! Obviously, Ms. Deene confused "Watch Me Die!" with the 24th book in the "Never So Miserable" series entitled "Dying to be Popular!" Also, in a previous article in the *Star*, Ms. Deene remarked that there won't be another book in this series. How can she be so sure? Just because Cristella Bassett died and went to heaven in "Watch Me Die!" doesn't mean that Arlene Spaniel can't bring her back to life again anytime she wants! Perhaps you should start looking around for a new children's book reviewer.

"A Book Lover" (Name withheld by request)

SSCHWAK

He was born with the gift of laughter and a sense that the world was mad.

—Rafael Sabatini, *Scaramouche*

It was Tuesday evening, and since Rakesh was due to pick up Sally for the book signing at Cody's at seven o'clock, dinner at the Schumacher-Avenger residence was a bit earlier than usual.

Sally removed the tuna casserole from the oven while Josh, with more noise and clatter than necessary, was getting out the plates and silverware, even though this was his week to set the table so he shouldn't have been so grumpy about it.

Blue, watching Josh's antics out of the corner of his eye, carefully positioned his knife and fork at the side of his plate and somewhat nervously cleared his throat. "So, Mom," he began, "you mentioned that you and Rakesh were old school friends. Was that at college, or—"

Sally shook her head and tossed the potholder on the counter. "No. Actually, we met in high school, down the peninsula, when I lived in Belmont. Rakesh showed up at Belmont High when I was a junior, and then we graduated together the following year. But after that, after graduation, he just seemed to vanish into thin air. Naturally, I wondered what had happened to him, because he was really very nice. And none of the other kids seemed to know, either."

"So, what did *you* think happened to him?" Blue asked, while Josh started kicking the legs of his chair and angrily flicking breadcrumbs off the table as if each one of them were alive and out to get him.

"Well, I had no idea, of course, until we met up again, you know"—Sally broke off, stealing a quick glance at Josh—"over at the Lawsons' last Saturday. Gee, he's had such an exciting life! It's hard to believe that while I've just been here, right here in Oakland all this time, Rakesh has been to so many places and has done so many interesting things."

"Like what?" Blue asked, trying to sort out his feelings. Was he happy? Protective? Jealous? He just wasn't sure. He looked over at Josh. "Quit kicking," he said.

"Try and make me."

Sally gave them both a warning glance, and then continued on with her lively recitation. "Oh, let's see. He's traveled a lot. Or did I already mention that? Anyway, he went to veterinarian school in England, and then he spent quite a lot of time in India. His parents are from there, you know. And after he came back here—well, actually, maybe it was before—he got to be quite active in the animal rights movement—"

"So when are you going to *marry* him?" Josh blurted out suddenly.

"Josh! That was rude!" Blue exclaimed, surprised to hear the very same question that was lurking in the back of *his* mind asked so bluntly and unceremoniously by his more outspoken little brother.

Sally suddenly stood up and snapped the plastic lid back on the gallon jug of milk. "Anyone want more?" she asked. "Before I put it away?"

Josh, ignoring her question, tilted his head back and looked up at the ceiling. Blue stared at his brother for a moment and then said, "No, thanks, Mom." Then, while Sally's back was turned, Blue reached over and punched Josh lightly on the arm, frowning and shaking his head disapprovingly.

Sally shut the refrigerator door, and then she walked around the table and stood behind Josh's chair, putting her hand on his shoulder. "No, honey. Nothing's going to change. Rakesh is just an old friend I haven't seen for years. Of course," she added, "I may see him now, from time to time—now that we've found each other—well, I don't mean *found* each other like we've been lost or anything, I don't mean that, but—" Sally's voice trailed off.

"Hey, that's okay, Mom," Blue heard himself say. "That's great, actually. He seems really nice, and—"

"No, he *doesn't!*" Josh said suddenly. "I hate him! And how come you just said you would see him *from time to time* but this is the third night in a row that you're going out with him!"

"Well, yes," Sally admitted. "That's true. Last night we went to a little reception for his author friend, and tonight the same man will be signing his books at Cody's, and—"

"And so *you* have to be there! Sure!"

"Josh!" Blue exclaimed again, quickly checking to see his mother's reaction.

"Josh, I—" Sally started to say, but Josh defiantly covered his ears with his hands, pushed back his chair, and rushed from the room, stumbling on a stray sneaker he had left on the floor and muttering, "I don't care—he *is* stupid! *Stupid Dr. Death!*"

Sally looked at Blue with a mixture of mild surprise and puzzlement, and then she sighed and leaned up against the refrigerator. "What are we supposed to make of that, do you think?"

"Oh, you know Josh. He'll get over it. He's just upset about Rex."

"Well, it's probably more than that. I'm no child psychologist, but I think I'm beginning to see something a little more complicated than that."

Neither one of them spoke for a few minutes, until Blue's curiosity got the better of him "So, uh—was he ever married before, or anything? Rakesh, I mean."

Sally shook her head. "No. No, he wasn't. Apparently there were one or two serious relationships. But, no. He never married.

114

Ah!" she said, as the doorbell sounded. "That must be him now." She checked her watch. "We may go out somewhere with his friend after the signing, but I shouldn't be too late."

"That's okay. We'll still be here."

Mother and son both smiled as they realized the unusual reversal of roles that had just transpired, while, at the same time, Josh was peeking out from behind his partially opened door and making very rude gestures in the direction of the unsuspecting gentleman on the porch.

A few minutes later, as Rakesh was opening the door on the passenger's side of the black van and giving Sally a little boost up, he glanced quickly back toward the porch and asked, "Hey, Sal. I meant to ask you last night—what's under that big blue tarp, anyway?"

"Oh, that. That's just cornstarch. Boxes of cornstarch."

Rakesh shrugged and made a little sideways movement with his head. "Oh, of course!" he said. "How silly of me to ask."

Sally smiled to herself with a little shiver of happiness. *Same old Rakesh.*

$ $ $ $ $ $ $

Blue had done most of his algebra homework during his honors math class, so he quickly finished the last problem and then decided to call Omaha before starting on the special assignment from Mr. Ridenaur involving those diacritical marks he had written on the board.

Since her line was busy, he set the phone on redial, and while he was waiting, he started sketching out a Blue Avenger episode in his usual four-panel format. Lately, he had begun to feature a new character in the strip, a resourceful and refreshingly independent teenage girl he dubbed Savannah Georgia Green.

On this occasion, his first panel showed spunky Savannah gagged and bound to a chair that was placed in front of a TV set permanently tuned to reruns of *The Vicki Pond Show*, a popular afternoon audience participation program whose only requirement for

115

admittance into the studio, as Blue liked to think, was certification by a licensed physician that any organ bearing the slightest resemblance to human brains had been surgically removed.

The second panel showed Savannah desperately but unsuccessfully trying to get a better look at an explosive device that was partially hidden under her chair.

Blue Avenger shows up in the third panel, poised for action, but temporarily halted by something very puzzling about Savannah's facial demeanor. Closer examination discloses Savannah's problem. Since she's bound and gagged, she can't warn Blue about the bomb under her chair. So in a wonderful demonstration of her resourcefulness, she begins to blink her eyes—five rapid blinks for *Scotu,* one short blink followed by a pause and three more blinks for *M-Sot,* and finishing up with five more blinks for *Fiotu.* (Blue's artistic talents were challenged by the need to indicate Savannah's eye blinks, but after several attempts and erasures, he was able to convey the action with the clever placement of three groups of squiggly lines around her eyes, with their corresponding words floating above like apparitions.)

The fourth panel, of course, shows Blue Avenger disarming the bomb.

With this latest adventure, Blue had now acquired a new visual gimmick in his cartooning repertoire—rapidly blinking eyes as a code for *Attention! Beware! Think! On guard! Help!*

$ $ $ $ $ $ $

At last Omaha's phone line was free. She answered after the first ring. "Hello?" she said.

"So, how's it going, sweetie?" he asked. "Anything new?"

"Oh, Blue! I'm glad you called. I was about to call you. I've been feeling really down all day, ever since this morning when I got to school and heard about Doris Sunzeri. Do you know her?"

"No. But I've been thinking about her, too, and—" Blue was all set to tell Omaha how strange it was that just thinking about Doris had actually solidified his future career plans. He thought she would find that interesting—how one person's attempted suicide could more or less set the course of another person's lifework. But this time Omaha didn't give him a chance to finish his sentence.

"Well, I do know her," she said. "See, it's kind of a long story, but I've been starting to go around a lot lately with this girl named Andrea Shirer?"

"Is that a question or a statement?"

"A statement. I met her—Andrea, I mean—in my Spanish class last term. She lives in that big apartment building you pass on the way over here to my house."

Blue remembered that Omaha had mentioned a girl named Andrea in one of the e-mails she had sent to him while he was in Venice. "Oh, yeah," he said. "Andrea. Isn't she the one you went to Fenton's with that day you got interviewed by the Question Man from the *Star?* You e-mailed me all about it."

"Yes. That's her. She's really nice." Omaha paused. "Something like me," she added.

"Right." Blue smiled and massaged the back of his neck.

"But anyway, Doris Sunzeri used to want to hang around with Andrea a lot, when Andrea was still going around with those girls who always sit at that table by the soda machine—you know, Kelly Peters and Trish What's-her-name and those kids? Personally, I always thought they were pretty snotty. Most of them, anyway. Showing off all the time, and the way they just start laughing their heads off at nothing. And Andrea—well, she said it got to be pretty bad. I mean, Doris was following her around real clingy-like just so she could sit with those other girls, and always bugging Andrea about how she really wanted to be in that group, you know."

"Wait. I'm confused. Andrea, or—"

"No. Andrea was already *in*, see? Doris *wanted* to be in. So, pretty soon Andrea got sick of it, not only of Doris—because, actually, she's kind of weird, sort of overly dramatic, you know?—but also Andrea got fed up with the whole bunch of them, since they were—oh, you know, drinking a lot, and stuff, and this was about the time she and I started calling each other on the phone—just in the last couple of weeks, really. It seems like you were going over to the DeSotos' a lot, and anyway, Andrea just started avoiding Doris whenever she could."

Blue began to detect a slight wavering in Omaha's voice. "Omaha? Are you okay?"

Omaha swallowed. Was he psychic, or what? "Yeah, I'm okay. It's just that I feel sort of guilty, in a way. See, I feel like if Andrea and I hadn't started to become so friendly, like we did, then maybe Doris wouldn't have tried to—well, you know—"

"Oh, Jeez! That's the stupidest thing I ever heard! You can't think like that. And anyway, Doris is still alive, remember? Some of the guys at school are even saying she never meant to go through with it in the first place."

"Oh, really? Well, that kind of sounds like her. But, anyway, it's really sad, isn't it? Even the idea of just *pretending* to kill yourself—upsetting your parents and all that—just because Kelly Peters and those kids aren't that thrilled about letting you sit at their table. In the first place, who'd *want* to sit at their precious table! Who'd *want* to go to their stupid parties! Like I said, all they do is get drunk, smoke stuff, and probably have sex, in one way or another."

Blue considered asking, "Hey, where's the next one?" but thought better of it. Omaha wouldn't appreciate that kind of humor at a time like this. Instead, he said, "Listen, Omaha, trust me, okay? You had nothing to do with it. It was just one of those things. If she was of that mind-set, she was going to do what she was going to do. Besides, this could have been building for years and years. What do we know?"

"You think so?"

"I'm positive."

There was a long pause. "I hope you're right."

"I know I am. But now I've got a question for you."

"Okay. What is it?"

118

"You know how you're always saying there's no such thing as free will—that people just do what they have to do?"

"Yes—" she answered cautiously, wondering what this was leading up to.

"So if that's true, like you say it is, why are we even discussing any of this in the first place? People are just doing what they have to do, right? So why should you feel guilty?" Blue moved the receiver to his other ear. Oh, how he loved these conversations with her!

Her answer came sooner that he expected. "Listen, Blue. I've told you how I feel about this before, but maybe I didn't make myself clear. So I'll try again, but pay attention this time, okay?"

Blue took a deep breath and leaned back in his chair, while a slight smile of anticipation crossed his lips.

"To start off with, you'll agree that what we call *choices* have to be made up of *something*, right? Something material. Something we can see and touch. Thoughts and memories and stuff are not made out of thin air, some kind of ethereal nothing. And what we call *decisions* are the same. They just don't appear out of nowhere, from *nothing.*" She paused a moment to let that sink in. Then she said, "Agreed?"

"Sure, if you say so—"

"Hey, are we just fooling around here, or trying to have a serious discussion? Because if we're just fooling around, I have lots of other stuff I—"

"Agreed! Agreed!"

"That's better. As I was saying, brains need chemicals and enzymes and proteins with strange names and electricity and God knows what else in order to function. They just don't *sit* there. Right?"

"Right."

"Doesn't it make sense then, that the choices we make are the choices we *have* to make? Who knows why the chemicals in one person's brain are coded to say to that person, *go hang yourself with your*

119

SaSa scarf instead of—oh, I don't know—instead of maybe saying *go polish your fingernails,* or *go to the neighborhood bar and shoot somebody*—"

Omaha suddenly stopped speaking, and her breath caught in her throat. After a moment she said quietly, "I didn't mean to say that, you know. It just came out."

Blue felt a sudden numbness in his chest. "Oh, Omaha—"

"I do think about him quite a lot. Ever since the wedding."

"Yeah. I do, too."

Omaha's thoughts went flying back to Travis and the years they had spent together—she and Travis, the wild and unpredictable half brother she had grown up with and loved, and who was still locked up in the federal penitentiary at Walla Walla, Washington, for shooting a man in a bar over something he couldn't even remember. And all these thoughts rushed through her memory while the second hand of her watch made just seven little jerky ticks. More than eleven years condensed into seven little seconds.

Blue finally broke the silence. "Have you talked with him—since the wedding, I mean?"

"Yes. A few times. I don't know why I haven't mentioned it to you. It's just—I don't know. It's just so hopeless, there's nothing to say about it. He's up for parole again in December, but I don't want to start hoping—"

"I know."

Omaha took a deep breath and let it all out in one big sigh. "So, where were we?"

"Choices. We were talking about choices."

"Well, I don't feel like talking about choices anymore. But like I told you before—remember, on our trip to Walla Walla, I told you that the way I look at it is that we have to *act* as if we had choices? I know it sounds crazy, and even kind of hypocritical, in a way, but unless we do that—unless we act like we have choices, we might as well—" Omaha just couldn't say it. She just couldn't say, *we might as well be dead.*

Blue came to her rescue. "You mean," he said, "we'd be like

poor players, strutting and fretting our hour upon the stage, and then heard no more."

"Exactly. That's good, Blue."

"It's Shakespeare. *Macbeth*."

"I know." She paused, and then said, "Hey, you want to hear something funny?"

"Sure."

Her voice dropped to almost a whisper. "Well, a couple of nights ago I was lying in bed, just sort of drifting off to sleep—you know how you do—and I was thinking about us, like what was going to become of us—after high school—and stuff like that. I was wondering mostly about you, actually. Like what you were going to study in college, and what sort of profession you'd settle in, and I could just see you in a white lab coat, doing some sort of scientific stuff, like gene research or maybe studying the brain, the biochemical makeup of the brain and all that—"

Blue had the strangest feeling, as if he were the one dreaming. He bent his head forward, straining to hear every word.

"—and I was thinking that eventually you'd start to specialize, that you'd start examining that little blob of stuff in our brains that actually *makes* the choices—that mysterious something inside people's brains that ultimately *makes* the decisions. Funny, huh?"

Something in Blue's brain, that little blob of stuff that actually *makes* the decisions—that same little blob she had mentioned—decided on the spot that he would love this girl forever. "That's pretty much what I had in mind, actually," he said.

"Really? Hey, I must be psychic. Maybe you could study about peer pressure as well. Kids wanting to fit in, and all that. You could figure out how something like peer pressure can get so far out of hand. For instance, that crowd Doris was dying to get into—" Omaha paused, mildly shocked at her own choice of words. "God! Did you hear what I just said? Anyway, I'd much rather have two or three really *good* friends, and—"

"Like me, for instance?"

"Oh, yeah. You'll do. But really, a couple of good friends, and then, you know, lots of sort of friend-friends at school, but just forget the so-called popular cliques, or whatever. They make me really nervous, if you want to know."

"What are you? Some kind of mutant or something?"

"Obviously. That's probably why you like me—"

"Hey, I *love* my little mutant baby—"

Omaha decided to play it cool, in spite of the little burst of pleasure in her chest. "Oh, shut up," she said pleasantly. "But what's wrong with people, anyway?" she continued. "Some things just don't make sense. It drives me crazy sometimes, just thinking about it."

"Me too. I feel the same way sometimes. I just read something really interesting. It's only one sentence, but it's good."

"What is it?"

"Remember when I told you I'm reading all of my father's old books? Well, I just finished *The Treasure of the Sierra Madre* and started on the next one. It's called *Scaramouche*, and it was written by this guy named Rafael Sabatini back around the 1920s sometime. Anyway, here's his first sentence: *He was born with the gift of laughter and a sense that the world was mad.*"

"What a nice beginning! Is the book good?"

"I don't know yet. I'm still enjoying the first sentence. I don't want to rush it. But there's your answer in a nutshell. The world is mad. Simple as that."

It was getting late, but neither Blue nor Omaha wanted to hang up. So they just stayed on the line, listening to the quiet together.

After a few minutes, Omaha broke the silence. "What's Blue Avenger been up to lately, anyway?" she asked. "Any more great four-panel strips to show me?"

"Interesting you should mention that. While I was waiting for you to get off the phone—"

"I wasn't on the phone. I was on the Net."

"Whatever. Anyway, I thought of a new angle, sort of, regarding Scotu! M-sot! Fiotu!"

"Really? Like what?"

"Well, actually, it's pretty stupid—"

"Yeah. Probably. But tell me anyway."

"You remember Savannah Georgia Green, don't you?"

"How could I forget *her!* My own alter ego!"

"Yeah, well, she was in big trouble. She was tied up and gagged, so she couldn't signal to Blue that there was a bomb under her chair in the usual, vocal Scotu! M-sot! Fiotu! way. So instead, she blinked her eyes—sort of matching the rhythm of the acronyms, like five blinks, four blinks, five blinks. Now, in the future, whenever they can't speak, you know, on those rare occasions when vocalizing might alert others to some possible secret plan, they'll blink instead."

"Oh, I see, *I see,*" Omaha said, much too enthusiastically.

"The important thing is, with superheroes and their girl-friends," Blue went on, ignoring her implied sarcasm, "they should always be prepared for any eventuality."

Omaha didn't respond, but as soon as the words were out of Blue's mouth, they didn't sound light and joking anymore, even to him. *Prepared for any eventuality?* Who was he kidding? He couldn't even come up with a plan to help her and her mother out of their current financial bind, and it appeared that moving day was inevitable.

"Well, it's getting late," she said, finally. "I really should start on my homework."

"Yeah, me, too. But wait. Don't hang up yet, okay? I want to tell you something. Guess who just went out on a date?"

"Uh, not Josh—"

"Guess again."

"Your mom!"

"You guessed it."

"Psychic again! Who with?"

"Some guy she went to high school with. She hasn't seen him since they graduated. He's a veterinarian, and they met up again at the Lawsons' across the street when he went over there to put their old dog to sleep."

"And she hasn't seen him since high school?"

"Yeah. Kind of a strange coincidence, huh?"

"Oh, well, I don't know. Those things happen. But has she ever dated before—since your father died, I mean?"

"Nope."

Omaha lowered her voice. "My mom hasn't, either. I don't know if she ever will." Omaha paused. "As she always says, *once burned.*"

"Once burned, what?"

"Once burned, twice shy. My mother says it all the time."

"Really? What a stupid saying. It doesn't even rhyme."

Omaha smiled. "That's what I always thought, too. But hey, thanks for calling. I feel a lot better now. Really."

"Yeah. Okay," Blue said, feeling quite proud of himself. "I'll catch you later. And, uh, sleep well, okay?"

$ $ $ $ $ $ $

After she hung up the phone, Omaha wandered out the back door and sat down on the little bench beside the dryer in the covered alcove between the house and the garage. It suddenly had grown quite dark, and just as suddenly, her mood changed, and she stared morosely across the small, moonlit patch of overgrown Bermuda grass that she and her mother mockingly referred to as *our lawn.* If she had to move, to go to another school—maybe even in another town—far away from Blue, she didn't know what she would do. She'd grown so fond of him in the few short months since that day in January when he had come into the counselors' office and told her he was about to change his name. And now she was certain that there was not another person on this earth quite like him.

"Here kitty-kitty," she called softly, cupping her hands around her mouth, and in a moment her gray-striped cat appeared, inching his way toward her while hugging the side of the garage with his back arched high and his tail held aloft like an antenna. Omaha waited patiently until he came up to her, and then she reached down and lifted the compliant cat up against her chest. *I guess I'll just have to mail it. There's no other way.*

$ $ $ $ $ $ $

Once again Blue woke up at four in the morning and couldn't go back to sleep. He turned over on his back and started to think about the possible causes of this distressing state of affairs. The dying embers of jet lag? An idea in my brain struggling to escape? Something I ate? Various combinations of those three suspected causes? For instance, how about the dying embers of jet lag combined with an idea in my brain struggling to escape? Or the dying embers of jet lag and something I ate? Or an idea in my brain struggling to escape combined with something I ate? That could happen, too. Let's see—what was that mathematical formula for that kind of problem? How many possible combinations can be made out of a group of three givens? Hmm. I think the general formula is to multiply 2 by itself n times, minus 1. So that'd be 2 x 2 x 2, which equals 8, minus 1. Seven different combinations of possibilities of why I can't go back to sleep! Jeez! No wonder I'm still awake.

Blue sat up in bed and reached for his notebook and a pencil, and soon he was attempting to come up with a coded way to write the word *suck*, in seven (or fewer) letters and/or digits. How about the old standby—backward spelling: KCUS. Well, not too original, that's for sure. Maybe something like: SXUXCXK. No, old Holly would see through that one right away. And then it happened. A marvelous solution practically wrote itself down in his notebook, due to the fact, in all likelihood, that his brain was still busy processing his evening's homework.

Blue couldn't help smiling to himself as he picked the shirt he'd worn that day out of his dirty clothes hamper and removed Tractor Nishimura's business card from the pocket. He left his bedroom door ajar so he could see his way to the computer in the den, whereupon he keyboarded a simple message to the multimillionaire from Marin:

From: BlueAvengerGuy@aol.com

To: Trac.Nish@T&TPro.com

Subject: License plate

Hi Trac:

"SSCHWAK"

Your friend, Blue

A few minutes after Blue got back in bed, he was hit with the sudden realization that *suck* wasn't the only word that would lend itself to the formula he had come up with. *But who in the world would want to have a license plate that translated into the word* duck? Blue smiled in the dark. *Am I a comedian, or what?*

$ $ $ $ $ $ $

Blue checked his e-mail first thing in the morning, and there was a reply from Trac:

From: Trac.Nish@T&TPro.com

To: BlueAvengerGuy@aol.com

Subject: Re: License plate

Hi Blue:

SSCHWAK? I don't get it. Please explain.

Trac

Blue slapped his thigh in a gesture of self-congratulation. *He doesn't get it! Great!* Then, without bothering to sit down, he tapped out a quick reply:

From: BlueAvengerGuy@aol.com

To: Trac.Nish@T&TPro.com

Subject: Re: Re: License plate

Hi Trac:

I think it's good that you don't get it! Maybe Holly won't get it,
either! Do you want to try it on some of your friends and see
if ANYONE can figure it out?

Blue

Tractor Nishimura was still sitting at his computer checking his
other mail as Blue's message came in. Trac read it and sent an
immediate reply:

From: Trac.Nish@T&TPro.com

To: BlueAvengerGuy@aol.com

Subject: Re: Re: Re: License plate

Good idea, Blue. I'll ask around and see if anyone can come
up with the solution. That way, we can find out just how
obscure it really is. I'll get back to you when I locate someone
who can explain the hidden meaning behind SSCHWAK.

Trac

$ $ $ $ $ $ $

Be prepared for unexpected riches arriving soon.
    —Message in Chinese fortune cookie

For the third time since the new term began, there was a substitute teacher in Blue's fifth-period modern history class. Since she had been called at the last minute and had no time to prepare, she hurriedly checked out a video depicting the immigrant experience on Ellis Island, and brought it along to class. Naturally, she was somewhat disconcerted by the reaction of the students.

"Oh, God! Not Ellis Island again! Sheesh!"

"We've already seen it a half-dozen times!"

"Don't exaggerate, Lenny! We only saw it twice—"

"*Three* times, you mean!"

"Hey, Ms. Krabappel, instead of watching the movie, can you give us the questions that'll be on Friday's test?"

The guffaws and giggles from fans of *The Simpsons* were interrupted by the arrival of a student messenger from the counselors' office. He handed a note to the somewhat flustered substitute, waved to a couple of his friends, and left the room.

The teacher held the folded piece of paper in her hand while she took time to explain that her name was *not* Ms. Krabappel (whoever *she* was!). It was Brazier. Ms. Brazier.

"Who's the note for, Ms. *Brassiere?*" Lenny Briggsmore called out, followed by his usual smug smile.

128

No one laughed—although some kids might have, if the jokester had been anyone but Lenny.

"Oh, Lenny, shut up," someone offered.

The girl in front of him turned and looked back at him. "It's for *you*, Lenny. The people at the kennel just noticed you were missing."

"Yeah! Report to Mrs. Manning's office right away."

"So *now* we know who was flushing all those toilets in the gym yesterday!"

Lenny sank down in his seat. Just wait. He'd show them. Just wait until he told his lunch pals about his new job—about how none of the deejays at his dad's station wanted to bother with the Unique Construction contest, and how his dad had arranged for *him* to get the assignment. All he had to do was read through the entries and pick the one he liked the best—at twenty bucks an hour. What kid wouldn't envy that?

The substitute, growing more perplexed by the minute, glanced around the classroom. "Uh, is there a Blue Avenger present?" she asked hesitantly, double-checking the note to see if perhaps she had misread the name.

Blue, starting to raise his hand, got up from his seat, and approached the teacher. "I guess that means me," he said, with his trademark blush and a nonchalant shrug.

"Rum-de-dum!" A theatrical drumroll came from the back of the room. "It's Blue Avenger to the rescue!"

"Go get 'em True Blue!"

Blue acknowledged the encouragement of his classmates with the same unique blend of modesty, sincerity, and self-depreciating humor that had won their hearts from the beginning. (Maria Hall, a student in Mrs. Wallace's sophomore honors writing class, put it best in her recent essay entitled "The Blue Avenger Factor: Analysing Student Heroes in the Twenty-first Century": *The whole idea behind Blue Avenger's popularity is one of those curious mixtures of fantasy and reality that seem to capture some elusive yearning of the human spirit.* What

English teacher could resist an essay with the phrase *elusive yearning of the human spirit?* So Maria got an A, of course, in spite of the misspelled word in the title.)

Blue unfolded the note. It was from Mr. Frazier:

To: Blue Avenger

From: Mr. Frazier

Message: Come over to my office as soon as you can—if you're not in the middle of something important.

$ $ $ $ $ $ $

"Ah, Blue! Come in. Look who's here to see you! You remember Tractor, of course, and this is his partner, Timothy Sims. Tim, meet Blue. Blue, this is Tim."

Tim reached over to shake Blue's hand. "Hi, Blue." He hesitated a moment before releasing his grip. "Say, don't I know you from someplace? You look kind of familiar."

"Uh, I don't think so."

"You never worked at Vic's Car Care over in San Rafael, by any chance, did you?"

"No. I've never even *been* to San Rafael—"

"Hmm." Tim sat back down on the stool. "Interesting."

Trac had already risen to his feet, and now he stepped over and clapped Blue on the shoulder. "Well, you did it, kid! I checked with over a dozen of my people, and not a one of them could make sense out of *sschwak*," he said, pronouncing the word as if it were spelled "shwack."

"Really? That's great!"

"Yes, but that included me as well! So I finally gave up and went to see my old linguistics professor at Berkeley this morning."

"So did she figure it out?"

"Well, she's a he. But yes, he figured it out just like that!" Tractor snapped his fingers. "And then he explained it to me. It's *perfect*, Blue! Exactly the sort of thing I was looking for."

130

"Great!" Blue repeated.

"And, incidentally," Trac continued, "when I reminded the good professor that I used to be in his class, and explained what I do now—man-oh-man, did his eyes pop out! He said he had no idea I was one of the Ts in T&T Productions. Anyway, when I mentioned that we were going to start filming a new thriller starring Taco Bell® next week, you should've seen the guy! He practically got down on his knees and begged me for a part in that movie. Happens all the time. As soon as people find out who I am, they want to be a movie star." Tractor looked directly at Blue. "How about you? You want to be in the movies?"

"Nah. I'm more the comic-book type. Thanks anyway, though."

Timothy looked over at Blue and raised his eyebrows in surprise. Then he pursed his lips in a kind of a smile and shoved his hands in his pockets. Well, that was refreshing.

Tractor shrugged. The kid probably can't sing, anyway, he thought. "Well, my old prof said he was willing to do *anything* as long as he could be in a scene with Taco. Then he started complaining—more like whining, really—that even writing an award-winning textbook on linguistics was not enough to impress his family. But maybe if they could see him right up there on the silver screen alongside Mr. Taco Bell®, well, that might just do the trick. Maybe *then* they'd consider him a real success. Can you believe that?"

"So, will he get his wish?" asked Mr. Frazier.

"Oh, sure. I'll see that he gets a small nonspeaking part in a scene with Taco." Trac laughed again. "Maybe he can play a bystander in the john. Actually, quite a few scenes in this movie take place in the john, starting with the gang rape and progressing to the multiple bludgeonings."

Blue and Mr. Frazier exchanged exaggerated grimaces. "Sounds charming," Blue remarked dryly. "My girlfriend loves those kinds of movies."

Trac missed Blue's comment completely. He was still in his own little world, envisioning his next movie as if it were already on the big screen. "No, that'd be mean, wouldn't it? Putting him in the john. But I'll find something for him. Maybe he can be the guy in the florist shop who's accidentally beheaded by the flower clippers when the cops rush the place."

"How do you behead someone with flower clippers?" Blue asked, ever the curious one. "Aren't they kind of small for a job like that?"

"Oh, my stunt people will figure out a way. They're very good. But to get back to my license plate—how'd you come up with that, anyway? It's fantastic!"

"The same way your writers came up with multiple bludgeonings and beheadings with small shears, I guess. Who can know the mysterious workings of the human mind?"

"Okay. Fair enough. But listen, before coming over here, I checked Motor V's Web site, and was overjoyed to see that *that* particular combination of letters is not taken." Tractor laughed like a gleeful ten-year-old.

They were all sitting now, but Mr. Frazier couldn't seem to contain himself. "Tell him, Trac," he said impatiently. "I've got a meeting in a few minutes, but I want to see his face when you tell him."

Trac looked doubtful. "Well, I really think it'd be better if I waited until I was sure the request would clear. Just because it's not taken is no guarantee they'll accept it—that it'll pass muster—"

"Oh, *bleep!* You know it'll clear! Even Holly won't be able to read anything objectionable into S-S-C-H-W-A-K," he said, spelling out the word.

"Oh, okay," Trac agreed. He looked at Blue. "But what I'm going to say now will only hold water if the plate clears. Right?"

Blue was confused. "Uh, pardon? I don't get it. Hold water if the plate—what?"

"What I'm saying is that you shouldn't expect to get the money if for some reason the application is turned down. If I don't *get* the license plate, see?" Trac glanced at Mr. Frazier. "That's why I didn't want to say anything about the money until we know for sure."

132

"The money?"

"Okay, Blue. Here's the thing. You must know by now how much this means to me, so what I want to do is show my appreciation in a monetary—"

Blue's heart started pounding hard, as if it were trying to pump him into another dimension, or maybe even into another world.

"—in a monetary way for your efforts."

Now Blue began to feel faint, and his mouth was as dry as the eraser on the end of a bank teller's pencil. Suddenly, all he could think of was that four-panel strip he drew on Sunday afternoon after coming back from Omaha's house. The fourth and last panel, drawn in black and white, suddenly became bright with color in Blue's mind. His towel headdress looked as blue as the bluest sky, and the steel-gray burglar-proof safe and the green American bills spilling out of it looked as real as the multimillionaire now sitting beside him in Mr. Frazier's office.

"So how does seven thousand dollars sound? A thousand dollars for every letter."

Blue's knees began to tingle and his legs went numb. *What is happening here? Could it be possible I actually managed to discover a secret route, a passage to a miracle that could only happen in the comics? What other explanation can there be? Offers of seven thousand dollars cash don't just fall out of the blue! There's got to be some other explanation!*

Tractor was mildly amused at Blue Avenger's reaction. Ah, yes! he thought. How well I remember the days when seven thousand dollars was a lot of money! How well, indeed. But just look at the kid! He's as pale as the proverbial ghost.

Oh, Omaha, my sweet! I have not failed you! You won't have to move away for your last year of high school! You won't have to get a job! You won't have to resign from the swimming team—oops. Hold it. Not resign from the swimming team? Maybe that's going a bit too far. But wait! Wheels! At last I'll be able to buy a real, running car!

Perhaps, if Blue Avenger had not been so deeply moved by this unbelievable turn of events, if he had not sat there practically

133

immobile for the better part of a minute with thoughts of Omaha and her mother and San Pablo High's formerly all-boy swimming team and a car of his own, all swirling about in his brain—perhaps, if there had not been this unnecessary delay, then maybe—just maybe—Tractor Nishimura would not have had time to conceive of an inspired and guileful complicating component to his original offer—something he would call your Other Option.

"I don't think you're listening, Blue—" Trac was saying.

"Pardon? What?"

"I said, I don't think you're listening. I was just explaining your Other Option."

"My Other Option?"

Timothy Sims suddenly stood up and turned away, muttering under his breath. *Oh, jeez! Not another one of his weird little experiments!*

"That's right. As I was saying, if you prefer, you can take a pass on the seven thousand dollars in cash, and, instead, donate *one million dollars*—of my money, of course—to worthy causes of your own choosing! It's money I would not otherwise donate, so this contribution would ultimately be made possible by your generosity in foregoing your own cash reward."

"One million—" Blue began.

"Yes. One million smackeroos! But the rule is, you *must* give it to charity—all of it. Neither you, nor your friends, nor your family will be able to share in this windfall. And I check on things like that, believe me!"

Tim rolled his eyes and uttered a long, drawn-out *Sheeesh!*—which Trac ignored completely.

"You will receive no material gain whatever, should you choose to take the million, but think of the good you can do! It's up to you. And actually, either way you're the winner! Keep the money, or multiply it and give it away. Whatever makes you the happiest."

Blue's heart was like a bouncing ball. First it shot upward at the words *seven thousand dollars*, as he pictured himself helping Omaha and her mom out of their present financial bind, and then, of course, buying that car!

The thought vaguely crossed his mind that he could sock away any surplus into his college fund—for now he had a real, genuine career goal. But then he remembered the insurance settlement from his dad's accident that his mother was saving for his and Josh's education, and also that promised scholarship from the Peace Officers Association. He could count on that as well. So now he was back to a car.

And then, suddenly, the bouncing ball almost went out of sight at the words *one million dollars*. Forget Omaha, forget a car, and just *do good?* Blue was utterly and thoroughly confused.

Mr. Frazier was confused as well. Tractor hadn't mentioned this so-called Other Option when he had first suggested the reward he had in mind for Blue. But after a minute Mr. Frazier declared himself a player. "So how do you like them apples, Bluie!" he said. "So what'll it be? Take the seven thousand and run, or give a cool million to causes dear to your heart? A million bucks! That's *ten thousand* little ol' one-hundred-dollar bills, you know. Or *twenty thousand* fifty-dollar bills! Any way you look at it, that's a *bleep* of a lot of moola!"

Blue was stunned. He closed his eyes and saw himself clearly, staring wild-eyed and frightened out of a four-inch square panel. Above his head, enclosed in the cartoon bubble, were the words HELP! PLEASE! I'M TRAPPED IN HERE AND CAN'T FIND THE EXIT!

"Now, kid, for a little free advice," Trac was saying. "No sense broadcasting this around, or you'll be bombarded by everybody and his brother—not to mention his sister, aunt, uncle, mother, father, niece, nephew, cousin, friend, neighbor, and ad infinitum—and that's just for starters. You can't *imagine* how many people come oozing out of the woodwork when they smell the odor of fresh, green money."

"Uh, Mr. Frazier?" Student Office Assistant Oscar Riley was standing in the open doorway that connects Mr. Frazier's office to the main executive offices' reception center. "Mrs. Manning wanted me to give this to you. She says it's urgent."

"Okay. Well, give it here."

Mr. Frazier swirled his chair around and reached for the envelope. "What's this?" he muttered. "Let's see. Oh, yeah. It's from downtown. Ah! From Superintendent Mooney."

Trac cleared his throat and touched Blue's arm. "So, anyway, as I was saying, once you have a little money, people really start to—"

Mr. Frazier held up his hand, motioning to Trac. "Hold it a minute, will you, Trac? I'm trying to figure this out. It's supposed to be urgent." Then he scanned the double-sided paper in his hand for a moment and proceeded to read it aloud, muttering at first, but gradually speaking more clearly. "Let's see—blah, blah, blah— oh, yeah, here we go. *It is time for us to act on the potentially perilous atmosphere possibly being perpetrated on pupils in all our schools (K through grade 12) as exhibited not only by the recent attempted suicide and the dismal showing of our varsity football teams, but also by the numerous comments that have reached my desk from parents concerned about the increased symptoms of depression they are seeing in their children, caused, in part, they think, by the plethora of grim and depressing novels which their children—our students—seem to enjoy so much."* Mr. Frazier glanced around the room with a pained expression on his face. "Does that make any sense to you guys?" He shrugged and went on reading. *"And while we are pleased to see the extraordinarily high page counts reported during this year's Up with Reading! campaign, there is growing concern among parents and teachers that depressing reading is not our only problem. In addition, other highly inappropriate materials (i.e., explicit sex manuals, certain so-called men's magazines, and the like) are being submitted as 'pages read' for this competition."*

Mr. Frazier stopped reading again, this time smiling suggestively and raising his eyebrows before continuing. *"Therefore, to facilitate the formation of a vision plan on these serious problems, we have obtained the services of Edumation Consultants, Incorporated, a nationally recognized firm with an outstanding reputation in the fields of teenage depression, inappropriate reading materials, and other pertinent subjects. They are happy to have this opportunity to help us."*

Mr. Frazier looked up again and shrugged. "Well, that's good, I guess. But there's more. Uh—*Edumation Consultants, Inc., will provide us with leadership in team building and the development of the interpersonal skills needed to delineate our mission statement that will be incorporated into our district curriculum. Teachers then will have a basis for formulating the goals and objectives that will be used in their individual classroom lesson plans. Therefore, we are calling a Special Emergency Two-Day Workshop—*" Mr. Frazier stopped again. "Okay, here we go. Here's the meat of the thing—*calling a Special Emergency Two-Day Workshop this Thursday and Friday. Consequently, we will be canceling all classes for students in all the secondary schools in the district on Thursday, and in the elementary and middle schools on Friday. Please inform your students and their parents immediately. This office will also notify the* Oakland Star *and all local radio stations. Teachers and administrators, please don't miss this compulsory two-day meeting. Attendance will be taken. Sincerely, Ralph Mooney, Superintendent."*

Mr. Frazier sighed and tossed the paper on his desk. "So did you get that, Blue? No school on Thursday."

Blue nodded, but it seemed to him as though Mr. Frazier's voice were coming from a dark cave or tunnel, miles away from where they were standing.

As for Tractor Nishimura, well, his mind was really on his newest experiment. This was going to be *very* interesting. Of course, the kid can't lose: Blue Avenger comes out ahead either way. Seven thousand dollars is not to be sneezed at—especially for a guy his age—yet the feeling of goodness and power that comes from choosing who will be the beneficiaries of your largesse to the tune of one million bucks, well, certain people would derive a great deal of pleasure from that as well. Now we'll just see which path this Blue Avenger guy decides to take. Oh, being rich truly does have its unexpected and peculiar rewards!

STRESS BALL CRAFT

Stress Ball Craft: **Materials Needed:**
- *Small Balloon*
- *Cornstarch*
- *Funnel*

Instructions: *It is easiest to make this stress ball with two people so you have more hands . . .*

—The Internet: http://familycrafts
.about.com/c/ht/00/07/
How_Stress_Ball0962934821.htm

Hey, the Internet's full of surprises, Josh. And kids like you are sitting ducks.

—Omaha Nebraska Brown

Blue was still in a giddy sort of daze when he got home from school. All he knew for sure was that he was going to do his best to keep the events of the afternoon strictly to himself until the final word came down from Sacramento. Then he would decide about the money. Besides, he was beginning to fear that Trac's old schoolmate Holly might be smarter than Trac thought, plus surely by now she must be aware of all the sly and devious tricks employed by those attempting to sneak one past her, the belea- guered license-plate censor.

Blue spied Josh through the front-room window—where he was sprawled on the floor, watching television—and knuckled his usual "shave-and-a-haircut" on the door. While he was waiting for Josh to let him in, he heard a familiar voice calling to him from the other side of the blue-tarped mound. "Hey! David! Wait a minute!"

It was Marvin Lasher, cutting across the lawn in his customary loping stride, wearing his WELCOME, ALIENS! baseball cap and holding his cell phone in one hand and a cup of coffee in the other.

"Oh, hi, Marv. What's new?" Blue said, deciding not to make an issue of the "David" thing this time.

"Well," Marvin said, "I was wondering just when you were planning to get that cornstarch moved out of there. Your mom told me the story behind it, but, you know, it's a real eyesore, with that blue tarp draped over it like that. God, it looks like you've got an elephant crouching under there."

"I know, Marv. I've been meaning to get to that, but I just haven't had the time."

"Yeah. Well, the thing is, I'm hosting a meeting of the Psychedelics Club tomorrow night, and it kind of reflects on the neighborhood, you know?"

Blue scratched his head. "I guess what I *could* do is move it all to the backyard—at least until I figure out how I'm going to dispose of it."

"Sure. That'll work for me. I'd help you with it, but I've got to get busy cleaning up my house. Some of the members may want to use the john, and I'm afraid they'd be grossed out unless I do a few chores in there."

"So what's going on with the Psychos, anyway? You guys unearthed any aliens yet? How are the ESP experiments going?"

Marvin laughed. He was used to David kidding him about his belief in things out of this world, but it really didn't bother him, because he was absolutely and positively sure of everything he believed in, and he could take any kidding anyone could dish up. They would learn the truth soon enough. "Hey, you want to come

139

to the meeting? Our guest speaker is this guy who actually had a one-on-one in-person conver with Whitley Strieber!"

Blue was puzzled for a moment. And then he remembered Marvin's peculiar short-speak. "Conver" was conversation. "A one-on-one conver with Whitley? *No kidding!*"

Marvin leaned over very close to Blue. "You can pooh-pooh all you want, David, but it's starting to happen." His voice fell to a whisper. "*Some really strange stuff is starting to happen!* Just listen in to KFIB tonight at eleven if you don't believe me. You'll see. People are calling in saying that suddenly all their dreams are beginning to come true! And these are *real people*, mind you! Like for example, this one lady said she's been sending articles to *Baby Life*, or some such magazine like that, for over twenty years—jeez, her 'baby' is in the U.S. Navy now, sailing somewhere off the coast of Greenland! But she's been sending stuff to them all this time, and just yesterday she got a letter saying they wanted to publish her latest submission!"

"Well, knock me over with a feather," Blue said. "Imagine that."

"And then this other guy called in to report that he's been trying to get his dog to obey the fetch command since he was a pup, and now, after five years, the dog finally caught on! He's fetching everything in sight. He can't get him to *stop* fetching!"

Blue nodded, trying not to smile. "Amazing."

"Okay, okay. I'll admit that one's kind of off the wall. But there's more. Like, this woman called in just last night. She said she and her boyfriend work at this donut store here in Oakland, see, but they hate it. Especially her boyfriend. She said they've been dreaming of starting up a health food franchise but they didn't have the money and were having trouble getting a bank loan. Well! What happens! Out of the blue, her boss in the donut store hands her this envelope—addressed only to her first name. She opens it, and what do you think it is?"

"Uh, she won the Publishers Clearing House Giveaway?"

"No," Marvin said mockingly. "She didn't win the Publishers

Clearing House Giveaway. But listen to this: in the envelope was a cashier's check for twenty-five thousand dollars!"

A little chill ran across Blue's back. "Really?"

"I tell you, David—something strange is happening! I can actually feel it in my gut! When people's dreams start to come true, you can bet your life it's not an accident! Something *very unusual* is about to happen on this little planet Earth. Some unknown force is at work all around us. So my advice is just this: keep your wits about you, keep an open mind, and stay receptive to whatever comes your way."

Blue put his hands in his pockets, lifted his shoulders in a slight shrug, and looked at the ground.

Marvin was about to start back toward his house, but then he suddenly stopped and said, "Oh, David! I almost forgot. I've been meaning to ask you. What do you know about that black van I've seen parked in front of your house a couple of times? Is that someone you know, or what?"

"Oh, yeah. It belongs to an old friend of my mom's. He's a vet."

Marvin Lasher was not convinced. "A vet, huh? That's curious. I seem to remember you guys don't have any pets!"

"No, Marvin. *He's a friend.* He and my mom went to high school together."

Marvin nodded, still suspicious. "But, hey, don't forget what I said, okay? Keep an open mind, David. That's all you need to do."

Blue gave the blue tarp a little kick as he passed it on the way back up to his porch. It sounded crazy, but could Marvin really be onto something this time?

$ $ $ $ $ $ $

"Mom says for you to call her," Josh said, as Blue stepped over his supine body on the way to the kitchen.

"Why? What's wrong."

"Nothing, I don't think. She just told me to tell you to call her, that's all."

"Well, it must be *something*, or she wouldn't have called, would she?"

Blue picked up the phone in the kitchen and dialed his mother's work number, wondering what could be the matter. As she once told the boys, "My patients really hate it when I leave them there in the chair with a mouthful of dental paste, even if it is mint flavored. So don't call unless the house is burning down, okay? On second thought, don't even call me then. Call the fire department, and then run outside."

"Hey," Josh called out. "Do we have a funnel around here? I need a funnel and I looked all over and I couldn't find one."

"I'm on the *phone*, Josh—yeah, hi, Mom."

"Oh, Blue. You're home. Listen, Rakesh and I were talking and we think it might be a good idea if we all went out to dinner tonight. Well, not exactly dinner—but not fast food, either. Something in between, so he could try to get to know Josh a little better. And you, also, Blue," she added quickly.

"Tonight?"

"Well, yes. Early, though. Probably about five-thirty. As soon as I get home."

"Sure. I guess—"

"Wait! I just thought of where we could go! Fenton's! Josh always likes to go there. We could just have sandwiches. And soup. And then ice cream. Josh would like that. So if you guys could just be ready when I get home, I could tell Rakesh to come over around five-thirty. And listen, if he gets there before I do, you and Josh be proper hosts, you hear?"

"Oh, Mom! Jeez! What do you think we're going to do? Leave him standing on the porch?"

"No. Of course not. Oh! Wait! Here's an idea. Do you suppose Omaha would be able to come along?"

"Omaha?"

"Yes, if she's not busy, of course. She'd be kind of like a buffer, you know? She gets along so well with Josh. I'm sure he wouldn't complain so much about going if Omaha were coming along with us. Could you ask her? I know it's a school night and all, but we wouldn't be out late."

"Sure. I'll ask her."

"Okay, then. I'll be home around five-thirty."

When Blue hung up the phone, there was Josh, hovering in the doorway.

"What's wrong? What did she want?"

"Nothing. We're going out to dinner, that's all." Blue had just dialed Omaha's number and was waiting for her to answer.

"So do we have a funnel or not?" asked Josh, rummaging around in the utensil drawer for the third time.

"Wait a minute, Josh. Can't you see I'm on the phone?"

Omaha picked up the receiver after the first ring.

"Fenton's? That'd be great," she said. "But is it okay if I come over now? Mom's just leaving for work, so she could drop me off at your place." She paused for a moment. "Josh is there, isn't he?"

"Yes. Our little chaperone is in. And any time is okay."

"Ask her if she has a funnel," Josh said quickly, pulling on Blue's shirtsleeve. "Don't let her hang up! Ask her if she has a funnel!"

"Just a minute, Omaha. Josh is rattling on about something. Just a sec, okay?" Blue put his hand over the mouthpiece. "Now what *is* it, Josh?"

"I need a funnel for my stress ball craft! Remember I was telling you—"

"Yes! I remember. But I don't think we have one."

"I *know* we don't have one! That's what I'm trying to tell you! So ask Omaha if she has one!"

"Hey, Omaha, do you have a funnel we could borrow?"

"A funnel?"

"Yeah. Josh needs a funnel."

"I think we have one here someplace. I'll bring it over. And listen, is Rakesh going to be at this little shindig?"

"You got that right."

"And my purpose is to exert a calming influence on a certain rambunctious somebody?"

"Right again. You are *so* smart, and so socially savvy. It's amazing."

"Thank you. But Mom's getting ready to leave. See you in a few minutes."

"Tell her not to forget the funnel," Josh said urgently.

"Too late. She already hung up. And listen, I'll be outside. I'm going to start moving those cartons of cornstarch to the backyard. I sure hope it's not going to rain for a while."

$ $ $ $ $ $ $

"Stress ball craft? You want me to help you make stress ball craft?" Omaha asked, after Josh had answered the door and let her in. "What's that?"

"Well, it's these little things that you squeeze when you're stressed out. You make them out of balloons and cornstarch."

"Really? Well, maybe I could, later." She glanced around the front room, down the hallway, and then toward the kitchen. "Where's Blue?"

Josh motioned to the backyard with several short jabs of his thumb. "Didn't you see him? He's carrying the cornstarch to the backyard."

"Oh." Omaha hesitated for a moment, wondering if perhaps she should go out and help him.

"I got all the instructions off the Internet," Josh said.

"What?"

"For the stress ball craft. See?" He handed the printout to Omaha. "This was on a craft site I found. Every class at my school is supposed to look for things they can make and sell during the final week of Up with Reading! Month, and whoever comes up with the best project in each class is going to get an award! At a special assembly and everything! And since my stupid brother has

144

all that cornstarch he has to get rid of, I thought I could find something that I could make out of it, and—"

"Yeah! I see! That's a great idea, Josh! Bordering on brilliant, even. But the thing is, it's getting kind of late, and, uh, your mom will be here in a few minutes. Maybe we should wait until we get back from Fenton's."

"No! I want to do it now! We have time! Come on, Omaha! *Please?*"

"Oh, all right. I guess we could try." Omaha tousled his hair (which he loved) and started skimming through the instructions:

HOW TO MAKE A STRESS BALL FROM YOUR FAMILY CRAFTS GUIDE

This squishable stress ball craft makes a fun gift!

Difficulty Level: Average

Time Required: 20 minutes

Here's How:

1. Get a small round balloon. Do not use water balloons; they are too thin.

2. Blow up the balloon until it is about 4–5 inches around, but do not tie it.

3. Pinch the top of the balloon shut an inch or 2 from the hole.

4. Place a funnel inside the opening of the balloon while pinching it shut.

5. Fill the top of the funnel with cornstarch.

6. Slowly let go of the top of the balloon so the cornstarch can slide into the balloon.

7. Continue adding cornstarch to the funnel until your balloon is filled to about 3 inches.

8. Pull up tightly on the opening of the balloon and pinch out any extra air.

9. Tie the balloon closed as near to the cornstarch as you can.

10. You can decorate your stress ball with stickers or permanent markers if you like.

Tips:
1. This project is easier to make with 2 people!
2. You might need to tap the funnel or stir the cornstarch occasionally to keep it moving into the balloon.
3. If you decorate your stress ball watch what kind of markers you use. Some markers will leave stains on your hands when you are squeezing the stress ball.

Omaha glanced up with a puzzled look on her face. She went over the instructions again, a bit more carefully this time. "Josh, honey," she said, finally. "I don't know about this. I'm not sure this is going to work."

"Why not? Sure it will! I got it off the Internet!" Josh reached into a package of balloons and drew out a small yellow one. After puffing into it a few times, he pinched it off and held it up for Omaha's inspection. "That's about four inches, isn't it?"

"Yes, but listen Josh, I—"

"Okay. I'll keep pinching it here, like the instructions say. Now, can you stick the end of the funnel up on the end of the balloon here?"

"Like this?"

"A little further."

"How's this?"

"That's good. Now I'll keep pinching while you pour a little cornstarch into the funnel."

"All right, but—Yipes! Holy Moses, Josh—" Omaha reared backward, shielding herself with one arm as a huge puff of white powder shot up from the funnel and hit her smack in the face and completely obliterated every trace of purple on the front of her purple-and-white-striped T-shirt.

Josh stared at her in amazement. "What *happened?*" he exclaimed. "You must have done something wrong!"

"*Me?* You little idiot," she said, gingerly wiping under each eye with the side of her index fingers as she headed off to the bathroom.

Just then the doorbell rang. Josh could see Blue out the kitchen window, busily stacking the cartons in the backyard, so it was up to him to answer the door. Still stinging from Omaha's uncharacteristically harsh rebuke, and holding the now deflated balloon and the funnel together in one hand, he stood on his toes and peered through the little peek hole in the door. Oh, no! Dr. Death! What's *he* doing here? He opened the door anyway.

"Well, hello there, Josh! Ready for a big treat at Fenton's?"

"Huh?"

"No one told you? I'm taking you kids and your mom for sandwiches and ice cream at Fenton's—"

"No one told me *you* were coming," Josh muttered. "And my mom's not home yet."

"Uh, is your brother home?"

"He's out in back, stacking cornstarch."

"I see. Well, may I come in?"

"I guess so."

"So, what's with the funnel and balloon?"

"Nothing. I'm just making stress ball craft."

"Oh, great!" Rakesh's dark eyes seemed to sparkle. "It's great fun making stress ball craft, isn't it," he said, wondering what on earth stress ball craft was. Rakesh really loved kids, and animals as well, of course. Animals probably more than kids, actually, but only because he had studied them, and treated them, and tried to ease their pain for as long as he could remember.

Josh eyed his mother's friend suspiciously. "Well, it takes two people—" he suggested.

"Well, you're one, I'm two! So we're all set! Right?"

"I guess so." Josh headed toward the kitchen. Rakesh followed. Hey, could they be bonding *this* soon?

Josh handed the funnel to Rakesh and again blew up the balloon, at the same time leaning over the counter and rereading the instruc-

147

tions. "Okay," he said. "That's about four inches. So while I pinch it here, two inches from the end, you're supposed to stick the end of the balloon onto the end of the funnel."

Rakesh set the funnel down on the counter, small side up, and using both hands, deftly slipped the end of the balloon over it, just as he was instructed. "Like so?" he asked.

"Good," Josh said, still pinching the balloon closed. "Now we hold it up like this, and you're supposed to fill the funnel with cornstarch. Now fill it all the way up to the top. I think that's what Omaha did wrong. She didn't fill it full enough. That's it. That's good—"

Just then Omaha appeared in the doorway, towel still in hand. "No! Stop!" she yelled.

But, alas, the warning came too late.

Pffft! "Ahkkkk!" Rakesh, the dark-skinned Indian gentleman, was suddenly transformed into a rare form of albino Indian, covered from the waist up with a cup and a half of finely powdered Wanner cornstarch, unquestionably the finest quality cornstarch in all the land.

Miraculously—no, not miraculously—rather, following the immutable laws of physics, most of it missed Josh, since he was not in the line of fire, so to speak, but the kitchen counter and half of the stove were not so fortunate—if inanimate objects can properly be classified as such.

"Joshua Schumacher! What on *earth* is going on in there! Rakesh! Are you all right?" It was Sally, home from work, standing in the doorway, with Blue positioned a few feet in back of her.

Josh suddenly turned almost as white as Rakesh. "Oh. Hi, Mom," he said, with an innocent little wave.

"It—it's okay, Sally," Rakesh said, with a slight sputter, accompanied by a surprisingly genial smile—under the circumstances. "It's just a little experiment Josh and I were working on. I believe it's called stress ball craft. It's really quite all white." He laughed at his own unintentional pun. "I mean," he corrected, "it's quite all *right!*"

148

But Sally wasn't buying it. She knew her son. "Joshua! I can't believe you would actually *do* such a thing! Now, apologize to Dr. Chandra this *instant!* And you'd better make it good!"

"I don't think he really meant any harm, Sally—" Rakesh put in quickly.

"No, really, Mrs. Schumacher—" Omaha chimed in.

Josh was looking puzzled. Was he supposed to apologize or not?

"Well! What are you waiting for! Let's hear it!" Sally said, cutting short any doubt in Josh's mind.

Rakesh had his handkerchief out by then and was cautiously starting to wipe around his mouth and eyes with a light dusting action, causing the white powder to suddenly take on a glorious new life.

"I—I'm sorry—" Josh started to say, looking down at Rakesh's shoes and then slowly bringing his eyes up to view the entire person. Oh, God! Did he look funny! Try as he might, Josh just could not stop himself from snickering, and then laughing outright. His usual progression in a case like this would be to fall down on the floor, but something told him that would definitely not be appropriate on this particular occasion. In the meantime, Blue had caught Omaha's eye, and they, too, began to smile.

"All right! That's it!" Sally said. "There will be no Fenton's tonight!"

Rakesh stepped forward and gently took Sally's arm. "No, no," he said. "It's really quite all right. I'm sure it was not intentional. Let's just go on with the party, as we planned."

"Well," she said, hesitating. "It's up to you, of course."

Rakesh began to remove his jacket, and Blue reached out to take it. "I'll shake it off outside," he said.

"Thank you, Blue. And I'll go wash my face in the bathroom, if I may—"

"Certainly!" Sally gave Josh her sternest look. "I'm going to change my clothes now," she said. "But just remember, you're not off the hook yet, young man! We'll talk about this again when we get home!"

"Whew! That was close," Omaha whispered, when she and Josh were alone again in the kitchen.

Josh, suddenly sober, sniffed and ran his hand under his nose. "Yeah."

But Omaha was curious. She couldn't help it. She had to know. "Hey, Josh," she whispered. "Let's try it one more time, okay? This time *I'll* pinch the balloon and *you* can pour in the cornstarch."

"Well," Josh said, haltingly. "Okay, if you think it might work. Because I really *do* want to get that award for the best idea in the class. I never got an award for *anything* in my whole life." Josh wiped his eyes, first one, then the other, with the back of his wrist. Then he reached for the instructions again and began to read them.

Omaha was immediately repentant. She gently took the printout from his hand and set it aside, out of his reach. "I'm just teasing," she said. "It won't work. But it's not our fault, really. It's the instructions. But that's a good lesson for you, huh? Just 'cause it's on the Web doesn't mean it's true. That site was probably posted by a quirky science teacher trying to have some fun."

"Actually," Josh whispered hoarsely, "Rakesh *did* look pretty funny. And surprised, too."

"Hey, the Internet's full of surprises, Josh. And kids like you are sitting ducks." She tousled his hair again. "But this time *I* got fooled, too! Don't worry, though. I'll help you think of something better. You'll win that award yet, if I have anything to say about it!"

"Honest?"

"Just you wait and see!"

$ $ $ $ $ $ $

Omaha usually didn't pay much attention to people's shoes, but she couldn't help noticing those adorning the feet of the woman sitting at the next table over at Fenton's. Even Omaha recognized a genuine pair of Rainbowlies, the very latest in inexpensive but highly advertised casual shoes to take the entire country by storm, even generating this short news item on the usually staid financial pages of the *Wall Street Journal:*

Wow-Whee!
Rainbowlies Rule!

Sales of the new bargain-priced Rainbowlies flip-flop shoe, with its famous slogan, "It's Special, It's Unique, It's YOU!" have just hit the $5,000,000 mark, according to company officials. Much of the credit for the company's phenomenal success has been given to the Bowles and Benny Advertising Agency for waging a brilliant, award-winning campaign that made thousands of ordinary women feel special and unique just for choosing Rainbowlies.

A few minutes after Rakesh and the others had finished their soup and sandwiches and were ready to order their ice cream, Omaha noticed that several of the servers were gathering around the Rainbowlies lady's table. The first server in line was bearing a chocolate sundae topped by a glowing birthday candle, which he was carefully shielding with his cupped hand. As the woman smiled benignly, the sundae was placed in front of her male companion, who appeared to be slightly embarrassed, but not unduly surprised. Several tables of diners gamely heeded an invitation to join in the song: *Happy birthday to you, Happy birthday to you, Happy birthday dear Hmm-Hmm, Happy birthday to you!* After the birthday man blew out his candle, the lady with the new shoes ($79.95 at Bon Marché) presented him with a small package, which he immediately opened. Omaha was close enough to hear his comment. "Oh, honey! I didn't really *need* a new wallet, but this is great! And look at that inlaid caribou! Cool! Thanks a lot!"

If even a tiny trace of guilt appeared on the face of the woman, it was not at all apparent to Omaha, who, after all, would have no reason to suspect it.

$ $ $ $ $ $ $

Even though Josh was behaving well within acceptable limits, Sally still kept darting frequent warning glances in his direction. In his nervousness, he had already torn two paper napkins into tiny shreds, and then he accidentally tipped over his water glass, which, luckily, happened to be empty. Omaha could tell he was still quite upset about the surprising and disappointing outcome of the stress ball craft construction project, and, probably, her own rebuke as well. And his mother's mistaken and highly unfair assessment of his intentions in regard to Rakesh's misfortune certainly didn't help. While the others were talking, Josh was busying himself by constructing small pyramids and towers out of the half-dozen little individual coffee creamers allotted to their table, one of which had just fallen to the floor. Josh leaned over and picked it up, and then began to fiddle around with it, nervously twirling it between his fingers.

Not surprisingly, Rakesh was doing most of the talking, contributing what he could to keep the general tone of the evening from deteriorating even further. And Omaha was doing her part by asking questions whenever the conversation began to lag, even while Blue, sitting beside her, seemed oddly preoccupied.

"But how come it seems like there are so many *extremists* in the animal rights movement?" Omaha asked, after Rakesh had talked briefly about the contributions of well-known people such as Jane Goodall and Steven M. Wise. "Like, I read that some of them were throwing blood, maybe—I don't remember if it was blood, exactly, but I think it was—on those fur-coat models in New York or somewhere. I think it was at Macy's or somewhere." Omaha blushed slightly and tucked a loose strand of hair behind her ear. Oh, boy. I hope I don't sound like a complete airhead. I should pay more attention to details when I read—

Rakesh shrugged and smiled weakly. "Yes, that's true. Some do more harm than good. But all in all, things are improving, slowly but surely. People are becoming more conscious of the fact that animals do indeed feel pain, just as we humans do, and that it is our duty to prevent it, whenever possible, and alleviate it when we can. And there *are* organizations that work toward this that are not so extreme—" Rakesh glanced at Josh, sitting across from him, and then at Blue, whose right elbow was on the table, crossed with Omaha's, their hands clasped together. "But as far as pet euthanasia goes, I'm all for that, and always have been." Now he looked directly at Josh. "There comes a time when the kindest thing you can do for an aged and suffering dog is to put it painlessly to sleep."

Now Omaha squeezed Blue's fingers and gave his hand a little jiggle, trying to get his attention. "So, Blue, what do you think?"

"Huh? What? I'm sorry, my mind was on something else. Sorry."

Omaha shrugged and gave Rakesh a lame little smile—a wordless apology for Blue's momentary preoccupation, which, of course, was not his fault. Because even if he had tried, he wouldn't have been able to halt the activity in those specific sections of his brain that were suddenly aglow—now that they'd had sufficient time to fully understand and process certain recently acquired facts. *I may soon be rich! It's true! Seven thousand dollars for me—or one million to give away! This can't be true! This can't be true!*

Josh, however, was certainly paying attention. At Rakesh's words *pet euthanasia,* he was reminded once again of the good times he'd had with Rex—poor Rex, now laid to rest under the grape arbor in the Lawsons' backyard. Was his old pal *really* that sick? Josh could feel the tears welling up, and in an attempt to keep from crying, he purposely stiffened his entire body, including his grip on the little coffee creamer—when suddenly—pop! Omaha screamed and Sally gasped as a cascade of Crystal Dairy Cream shot straight across the table and landed with the force of a water gun blast directly on Rakesh's shocked and surprised face, which he had tried to protect by raising his arms, a reflex action that came a split second too late, and which only succeeded in knocking over his milk shake glass and spilling its contents onto Sally's lap.

"Oh, *no!*" Josh breathed, dropping the empty container onto the table and quickly covering his eyes with his hands.

"*Joshua!*" Sally exclaimed, standing up and lunging over to grab him by the collar, her lap awash in chocolate milk shake, while Blue and Omaha sat speechless in their old-fashioned ice cream parlor chairs.

"Well, how about that!" Rakesh said, calmly pulling out several paper napkins from the holder and carefully wiping around his nose and eyes. "You got me again. Persistent little guy, aren't you?"

"I'm—I'm *really* sorry!" Josh stammered, without any prompting from Sally this time. "It was—like, I didn't even *know* it was going to do that!"

Sally, taken aback at Josh's unsolicited apology, seemed strangely stymied, like a rocket ready to blast off with nowhere to go.

Omaha quickly waylaid a passing server and snatched his table-wiping towel right out of his hand. "Here, Mrs. Schumacher, let me help wipe—"

"*Please,* Omaha!" Sally exclaimed, in an agitated voice she had never before used in Omaha's presence. "Please *don't* call me Mrs. Schumacher! You make me feel like my own mother-in-law, and she's been dead for years!"

"Oh," Omaha replied, almost timidly. "Sorry."

Sally was immediately remorseful. "Oh, Omaha, honey, I didn't mean to snap at you like that." She took the towel from Omaha and gave her hand a little reassuring pat. "But I've been meaning to ask you that for some time now. So, please, just call me Sally. Okay?"

"Okay." Omaha paused a moment, quickly glancing at Blue, as if for approval.

Rakesh, mostly dried off now, again caught Josh's eye. "I accept your apology, Josh. But I hope you'll understand if I seem to be a little wary of you in the future. I think at this point, the onus is on you to at least foster civil relations between us." Rakesh squeezed Sally's hand under the table, and added, "But I know you mean well, and I do hope we can be friends in the future."

154

Josh didn't know the precise definition of *onus*, but the meaning was clear. As far as Dr. Death was concerned, he'd just better knock it off—even though today's little episodes truly had been accidents.

"Do you understand what I'm saying?" asked Rakesh.

Josh immediately glanced at his mother.

"Don't look at me," she said lightly, extremely pleased that Rakesh seemed to be handling the matter in his own unique way.

Josh, blinking his eyes like mad, nodded his head, and then idly picked up another little coffee creamer that was lying next to his empty plate.

"Please put the little creamer down, Josh, dear," said Sally, with an obviously exaggerated smile. And they all laughed, even Josh. Just like on TV.

SWEET REVENGE

. . . and I'll be merry in my revenge.
—William Shakespeare, *Cymbeline*

"You know what?" Tractor asked, poking his head into Tim's office.

Tim didn't look up from the complicated flow chart on his computer screen. It was almost four in the afternoon already, and he was way behind schedule. "No, what?"

"I'm thinking of calling Holly, you know, over in Sacramento, and asking her if she'd like to do lunch tomorrow."

"Oh, yeah? I thought you said before that you hated her guts."

"I never did say I hated her guts! Where'd you get that idea! I just want to even the score a little, that's all. I mean, hearing me say, 'Tigers suck!' from the stage at my graduation wouldn't have killed anybody! Do you think that would've *killed* anybody! So what I'm going to do is just call her up and tell her that I want to bury the hatchet—you know, before we meet up again at the reunion—and then I'll just slip that coded suck-word right under her nose and *smack*, right onto my new license plate!" Tractor looked up at the ceiling and brought his hands together as if in prayer. "Revenge! Sweet revenge!"

"Oh, spare me," Tim muttered, turning back to his computer screen. He loved this guy like a brother, but when was he going to grow up!

"Anyway, I'm thinking, I could take her out to lunch, see, and explain how I wanted this special license plate and everything, and then I would ask her if she could *personally* expedite it for me, as a special favor for an old high-school buddy, see? And then, when she looks it over and doesn't see anything wrong with it—"

"Oh, *I* see!" Tim said, without looking up from his work. "Then you'll feel very superior, and smarter than her, and it'll make your little hurt feelings from fifteen years ago go away." He stopped keyboarding and gazed at the screen a minute. Actually, if Tractor *did* suddenly grow up, T&T would certainly lose touch with their biggest target market, that's for sure. He rubbed his stubby fingers together. He'd been sitting there too long without a break. "So, what will you tell her it means?"

"Tell her what *what* means?"

"*Sschwak*, of course," Tim said. "Since you can't tell her the truth, you'll have to make up something."

"Really? Will she even ask what it means?"

"Sure she'll ask. They always want to know what it means. I thought you downloaded an application form from DMV's Web site. It's printed right on there." Tim paused. "At least it was when I applied for mine."

"No. I just checked to see if my word was already taken, that's all. And it wasn't."

Tim turned back to the computer and quickly closed the spreadsheet he was working on. Then he found DMV's Web site and printed out the special-interest license plate application form in just under two minutes. "Here," he said. "Read."

"Hmm. I see. The application will not be accepted unless the meaning is explained," he read. "So, what'll I tell her? What could *sschwak* mean?"

"Well, you could have each of those letters stand for something, you know, like your license plate could be an acronym. Maybe make up a sentence like, uh—" Tim grabbed a pencil and quickly scribbled something on a scratch pad. "Okay, let's see. S-S-

C-H-W-A-K," he spelled. "How about this: Saturday someone came home with a kangaroo."

"*Saturday someone came home with a kangaroo?* What's *that* supposed to mean? Why would anyone want to put that on their license plate?"

Tim shrugged. "How should I know? But you have to tell her *something.*" He scribbled some more words on his pad. "If you don't like that, here's another one, then: So someone clever has wed a knot-head." Tim thought a second, then added, "You could tell her your sister just got married, see? And the guy was not very smart. Something like that."

"Tim, I don't even have a sister! Jeez! Where's a pencil? I can do better than that." Tractor scratched his head and started to write. "Ah! I've got it! Listen to this: Swiss sweethearts can't hug without asbestos knickers."

"Asbestos knickers! Sheesh!" Tim burst out laughing.

"What's so funny?" Tractor asked, a slight grin beginning to spread across his face in spite of himself. And the next minute they were both overcome by a fit of silly giggling that would put even Josh Schumacher to shame.

When they finally settled down again, Tractor picked up the phone and punched in the number of his personal secretary, who happened to be at her desk just across the hall.

"Hey, Denise, can you try and get a woman named Holly Langsford on the line for me, please? She works at the DMV in Sacramento. Yeah. Department of Motor Vehicles. I'll wait right here in Tim's office. Thanks."

$ $ $ $ $ $ $

While Tractor Nishimura was at Rancho Sueño waiting for his call to go through, back in the real world of Oakland, California, Omaha Nebraska Brown was walking home from school with her new friend, Andrea. Suddenly, an idea popped into Omaha's head. In her mind's eye she could see quite clearly how she might improve on the flawed formula for stress ball craft that Josh had discovered on the

Internet. It was really a deceptively simple scheme, but it just might work. At the very least, it was worth a try.

"Hey, Andrea, do you mind if we stop in here a minute?" Omaha asked, as they were coming up to Rudy's Market. "I need to see if they have some really large balloons."

Andrea didn't notice Omaha's smile, or perhaps she would have asked about it. It would be difficult to explain, however, and probably Andrea wouldn't see anything funny about it. But Omaha was just picturing how Blue would illustrate the very moment when she got her idea, if he were to draw it in his comic strip. She knew he'd use that cute little light bulb he drew so well, hanging in a raggedy little cloud right above her head. She loved the way he drew that little light bulb.

Sure enough, in the toy section they found just what Omaha was looking for—a package of extra-large, heavy-duty, twelve-inch balloons in assorted colors.

$ $ $ $ $ $ $

"Holly Langsford speaking. Thank you for waiting. How may I help you?"

"Hello, Holly? It's Tractor Nishimura, from high school."

"Tractor?" she asked, after a short pause. "Is it really *you?*"

"Wait. I'll check. Yep. It's me all right."

He was rewarded with a short little nervous laugh, and then a string of nonstop questions. "So how did you know where I worked? What have you been up to, anyway? What's going on? How come you didn't show up at our tenth reunion?" Holly was getting right in stride now. "Or our fifth, either—"

"Ah, just too busy, I guess. Actually, I think I was out of town both times. But listen, I was just thinking—"

"Trac," she broke in, "about that incident at graduation, I'm really sorry, you know. I hate to bring it up, but we'd better clear the air. It was something I *had* to do. I mean, we *were* pretty good friends up until then, but—"

Tractor held his hand over the receiver and signaled over at Tim. "She says she's *really* sorry about that incident at graduation," he mouthed.

"—but it was *my* graduation, too, you know," Holly was saying, "and I just, well—gosh darn, Tractor, I think you're really a nice guy, I've always thought that—but let's face it, we don't see eye-to-eye on your penchant—I guess that's the right word—your penchant for vulgar and really inappropriate language, and all my relatives were going to be there, and I—"

After a few halfhearted attempts to interrupt her, Tractor finally spoke out. "Well, Holly, that's all water under the bridge now, isn't it? Bygones are bygones, and all that. But the real reason I'm calling is that I plan to be passing through Sacramento tomorrow about lunchtime, and I was wondering if maybe we could get together—rehash old times. Kind of like get a head start on the reunion."

Tim rolled his eyes. *Passing through Sacramento.*

"Oh, *golly*, Trac, that'd be great!" Holly exclaimed. "So does that mean all is forgiven? But hey, listen," she went on, not waiting for an answer, "did you ever get married, or are you still a carefree bachelor?"

"Nope. Not married. Too busy, I guess." *All is forgiven? Ha!* "But what about you? Any kids yet?"

"Yeah! I've got two little girls! One's six, and the other will be four in August—"

"Really? That's great! Well, you probably have to get back to work there, so I'll let you go now. Anyway, I'll pick you up in front of Motor Vehicles tomorrow about noon, then? Okay?"

"Wonderful! You know where the office is, don't you?"

"Yeah. I've got a map right here. Well, not right here, but I've got a map."

"Okay, then. I can't wait to see you, Tractor. It's been a long time."

"Hey, same here! See you tomorrow." Trac hung up the phone and smiled at Tim. "Done," he said, snapping his fingers.

Tim glanced at his watch and suddenly decided it was quitting time. "Can you imagine how Blue must be feeling right about now?" he asked, grunting a bit as he leaned heavily over his desk to straighten out some papers. "Yep, I can just picture him now, sitting around waiting to hear if his idea will come to fruition, and if it does, whether he'll take the cash or exercise his—" Tim just couldn't bring himself to use the phrase *Other Option*.

Tractor suddenly grew thoughtful. He stood up and shoved his hands into his pockets, jiggling his loose change and keys. "He does seem like a nice kid, doesn't he?"

Tim looked up quickly. "Yes. Yes, he does." He surveyed his desktop one more time and scratched under his ample chin. "Say, isn't he off school tomorrow because of that special teachers' meeting? Maybe he'd like to ride along with you to Sacramento, see firsthand what Holly decides to do with your—"

"—with my application," Tractor said, finishing Tim's sentence, as he often did. "Good idea. It would give me an opportunity to talk with him a little, see if there really is a musical buried there in his persona somewhere, or possibly some kind of sweet, young teenager-type movie—"

"Sweet, young teenager-type movie!" Tim exclaimed with one of his hearty laughs. "Did you really say that?"

Tractor sighed deeply and furrowed his brow, looking as stern as he could. "Maybe you're forgetting who's the creative half of this business."

"Oh, right. Sorry," Tim said in that half-mocking, half-serious tone they often used with each other.

Tractor reached into his pocket for his wallet. "Listen, can I use your computer a sec? I've got Blue's e-mail address right here, and it'll only take me a minute to send him a message."

$ $ $ $ $ $

As fate would have it, Blue was sitting at his computer at that very same instant, writing a note to his friend Louie. Blue had been so

161

busy all week that the only contact he'd had with Louie since they returned from Venice had been exchanging a few words in math class.

But now, hearing the familiar computer voice telling him, *You have mail,* he stopped writing to Louie in midsentence and picked up Tractor's message. It immediately set his heart racing. Have lunch with the famous Holly herself! Wow! That means I'll find out about the money tomorrow!

Blue hastily typed his response, explaining he'd have to check with his mother, but he was sure he'd be able to go. He typed in his phone number and asked Tractor if he would mind calling him sometime after six that evening, when he could give him a definite answer. Then, just for fun, Blue Avenger gave himself a pinch. Yep. He passed the test. He was really there.

$ $ $ $ $ $

Omaha got right to work as soon as she arrived home from Rudy's. First, she selected a blue balloon from the package and blew it up as large as it would go. Then she pinched it closed and held it like that for several minutes. When she finally let the air out, it displayed the usual aftereffects of a deflated balloon. It was stretched out a bit larger than it was before it was blown up, and it was quite limp and pliable. Since the funnel was still at Josh's house, Omaha fashioned a makeshift one out of a manila folder, taping the ends and trimming the uneven edges. At first it was slow going, trying to fill a deflated balloon with cornstarch through a manila folder funnel. But, presently, she got a wooden chopstick from the drawer and began to agitate the cornstarch within her makeshift funnel. Soon, after repeatedly settling the contents by tapping the partially filled balloon on the tabletop, it was full to the top. She stretched out the end of the balloon as far as she could and tied a knot. Then she trimmed off the excess "stem," leaving just a slight remnant of blue balloon showing beyond the knot.

And there it was! She squeezed it. She tossed it. She squeezed it again. It was perfect! A perfect stress ball! She immediately got on the phone and dialed Blue's number. Josh answered.

"Hi, Omaha. Want to talk to David? He's out in back staking down the tarp. I could go call him——"

"No, that's okay. You're the one I wanted to speak to, anyway. And you know what? I did it, Josh! I figured out a way to fill up a balloon with cornstarch without having it all blow up in your face. If you don't win that award now, I'll eat my hat!"

Omaha was surprised to see her mother's car pull into the driveway a few minutes after she had explained her simple procedure to Josh. Since Margie was working the night shift, she wasn't due home until after midnight, and it was only a little before five.

Omaha unlocked the front door and swung it open.

"Well, it's happened," Margie announced, walking in and tossing her sweater on the couch. "We're officially on strike."

"Oh, God. That means you don't get paid?"

"That's the way it works, honey."

"For how long?"

Margie shrugged and walked into the kitchen. "Don't know," she said, filling the coffee carafe with water. "Depends on how long it takes for management to give in to our demands." She put the coffee into the filter and turned on the machine.

Omaha began to get just a hint of a stomachache. "So, when does the rent *really* go up, anyway? Did the old bat say next month, or not until May?"

"Next month, I'm afraid, although I didn't get an official notification yet. I think she's supposed to send a registered letter or something. But, listen, I don't want you to start worrying about this. We'll be okay. You know we're not going to starve. Plenty of people are much worse off than we are." Margie reached into her pants pocket and pulled out several lottery tickets, which she tossed on the table. "Besides, one of these is a sure winner. The kid at the Quick-Stop told me so," she said with a wink.

"God, Mom! That's just wasting your money!"

Margie turned and looked at Omaha for a second with the same expression she had used when Omaha was little and would stand there defiantly with her hands on her hips, stamping her foot and saying, "No *way!*"

But Omaha was not about to be deterred by a mere facial expression. "Blue told me that if he could afford it, he'd buy a huge ad in the paper with the faces of a million people—or whatever the odds were for that week's lottery—and draw little circles around all of them except for one, which would be so hard to see no one would even notice it. Then he'd put a big headline over it that said *losers*. He said that might give people a clearer picture of what their chances really were."

"Oh, he did, did he?"

Margie opened the cupboard and took down a coffee cup. "You want some?"

"No, thanks."

"Well," Margie said, "I've started to call around, you know, I mean—I'm starting to look for a less expensive place to live. We have to stay within our budget, and except for food, our rent is our biggest expense."

Omaha motioned to the lottery tickets on the table. "Maybe we could start by cutting out—"

"What's that?" Margie said sharply.

"Oh, nothing."

"We have some savings, of course," Margie continued. "But I don't want to go dipping into those. Like I said before, if we could just find a less expensive place to live, we could make it okay. I mean, what do we need a yard for? And I never bother putting the car in the garage. An apartment would do just as well—"

"Yeah, but *where?* That's the thing. You know I don't want to change schools."

Margie looked away and sighed.

"Hey! What about that apartment building where Andrea lives? I don't know how much they pay, but it's probably a lot less than here."

"I've already talked with the manager over there. They've got half a dozen people on the waiting list, and she told me they rarely have vacancies. But I did find something over toward Hayward that might—"

"Hayward! God, Mom! I just said I don't want to change schools!"

"Well, you know as well as I do what the problem is. We have to consider our safety. You know that as well as I do, Omaha. We certainly could find something cheaper here in Oakland, but, personally, I don't wish to be serenaded by gunfire each evening."

"It's not that bad."

"Okay, then. Every *other* evening."

"Yeah, Mom. Very funny." Omaha started tapping her foot on the floor. "I could get a job. I could look for a job. I mean, we only have to hold out until next year—next June, actually. My senior year—and after that we could move to Hayward, or wherever you wanted."

Omaha didn't mention college. Although Mr. Frazier had assured her she'd get some help with college, she could just end up at a junior college somewhere. Who knows? Anyway, she could worry about that later.

"Okay. I'll tell you what," said Margie. "This is the end of March, right?" She began ticking off the months on her fingers. "So we've got April, May, and June. Then school's out. And that's what you're worried about, right? Well, a lot depends on how long we'll be on strike. Without my salary, it's going to be rough staying here for three more months. I mean, really, kid, we don't need a whole *house* all to ourselves."

"I don't want to change schools, Mom. I mean it. I *can't* change schools—" Omaha thought she might begin to cry. "God, haven't I changed schools enough times already? I haven't even been at San Pablo a *year* yet!"

Omaha's voice was getting shaky. She didn't want to risk talking anymore. But she couldn't stop thinking about her senior year, coming up right after the summer. Senior year! The very *worst* time to change schools. And just when Blue and I seem to be getting closer every day. And what about Andrea? Just when I've found a really great friend, someone who thinks like I do, yet— "Hey, Mom!" Omaha said suddenly. "I wasn't kidding about getting a job. What if I *could* get one? I'm sure I could earn enough to at least make up the difference in the rent. On the way over to Blue's house yesterday, I noticed that Donut Pros had a sign in their window— they're taking applications for counter girl and a donut maker. Maybe they need somebody to work on weekends, like on Saturdays and Sundays. I could do that. It's kind of far to walk, but it's right on the bus line, so you wouldn't have to take me. So that's good, isn't it?"

Margie didn't answer. She was sitting at the kitchen table now, staring at her coffee cup and thoughtfully running the tips of her fingers along her hairline.

"I'd have to quit the swimming team, though. And I really hate to do that, especially since Mr. Frazier says that's the kind of stuff college admissions officers always look for. But, gosh, maybe they look for kids who had jobs, too. Do you think they do?"

Margie still didn't answer. She was thinking about Omaha's father—Johnny Brown. What did I ever see in that guy, anyway? And how did it ever last as long as it did? But then, in a way, maybe it was my own fault, too. Maybe, instead of trying to ditch him the way I did after he walked out on us, maybe I should have gone the other route. Maybe I should have sued the bum for child support—even if we weren't married—instead of letting him off the hook the way I did. Oh, Lord! My whole life has been nothing but a travesty. Look at me—forty-five years old, never married, a mother of two kids—one of them in jail and the other volunteering to get a job to help pay the rent. What a mess I am. What a washout. What a genuine four-star, grade A, all-American first-class failure.

"Do you, Mom? Do you think that admissions officers tend to favor kids who had jobs in high school? I mean, if they also kept their grades up, too, of course."

Margie rested her chin in her hand and gazed at her daughter until Omaha finally smiled a little puzzled smile and said, "What's wrong? Why are you looking at me like that?"

"Like what?"

"Oh, I don't know. Sort of like you never saw me before. Like you didn't even know who I am."

"Well, that's silly, isn't it?" Margie said, suddenly reaching over and playfully poking Omaha in the ribs, just as she used to do when she was a baby.

"Hey! Quit it!" Omaha said, quickly doubling up with her arms folded in front of her, and grinning like a three-year-old.

Margie grinned back. Maybe she didn't do so bad after all.

$ $ $ $ $ $ $

Blue answered the phone when it rang a little after six that evening.

"Hey, Mom?" He called out a minute later. "Where are you?"

"I'm in here," Sally answered from her bedroom. "Who is it? Is it for me?"

"No. It's for me. You know there's no school tomorrow, because of that special superintendent's meeting?"

"Yes—"

"Well, would it be okay if I drove over to Sacramento with this multimillionaire guy I met in Mr. Frazier's office the other day, and had lunch with the woman from the Motor Vehicles Department whose job it is to censor personalized license plates?"

Sally Schumacher stood still a moment, her head cocked. What a kid! "Sure, honey," she said, playing along. "That would be fine."

SUCCESS!

That man is a success who strives quietly to make his corner of the world a little bit better.

—Coffee mug: Hallmark Card®, Inc.

That man is a success who brings out the best in others and gives the best of himself.

—Ibid.

"There she is!" Tractor said, turning the key in the ignition without taking his eyes off the attractive blonde woman who had just walked through the main door of the Motor Vehicles office in Sacramento and was now standing in the sunlight, shading her eyes with her hand and peering out over the parking lot.

Trac and Blue had arrived early and had been waiting for her in the short-term parking zone nearby. "I'm really surprised," Trac said, unable to hide his disappointment. "She hasn't gained any weight at all! In fact, it looks like she's even lost some!"

Blue instinctively turned to look for cars behind them as Tractor backed out of the cramped parking space. "All clear in back," he said.

Tractor swerved the car to the right, pulling into the lane reserved for waiting passengers. He stole a quick glance at Blue. "Nervous?" he asked. "A little nervous, are you?"

Blue smiled and straightened his shoulders. He knew Tractor was kidding him, but all the same he imagined he was wearing what Josh referred to as his *stupid outfit*—his father's old blue fishing vest, together with a blue towel wrapped around his head à la Lawrence of Arabia—the getup inspired by the original Blue Avenger, the cartoon hero he himself had created. "Nervous? Of course not," Blue replied coolly. "Blue Avenger is never nervous."

Something in the tone of his voice caused Tractor to take another look at the teenager sitting beside him. Although he sounded serious enough, there was a kind of appealing playfulness about him, as if he were not quite real, yet not purely playacting either. Tractor was instantly intrigued. Although the two of them had been together for several hours—first during the ride over from Oakland, and then later waiting in the parking lot—this was the first time Tractor sensed what seemed to him to be almost another dimension in this slim, red-headed kid who called himself Blue Avenger. Tractor now regretted that most of the conversation on the way over had been about Trac himself—about making movies, and making money, the real lowdown about the actors he knew, and how his life had changed after becoming rich. It seemed that Blue would never run out of questions.

"So you'll jump out here and let her sit in front, right?" Tractor suggested.

"Right."

Blue swung open the car door, hopped out, and gave Holly his best Blue Avenger smile. She was not quite sure what to make of it. "Tractor's right in there," Blue said, with a dramatic sweep of his arm.

Holly bent her head down to get a better view. "Oh, Tractor!" she exclaimed, glancing back at Blue a moment before climbing into the front seat. "It really is you! Oh, God, look at you! You haven't changed a bit!"

"And neither have you, Holly! You're looking great!"

After carefully checking to make sure Holly was safely seated—with no part of her anatomy or clothing in jeopardy—Blue closed the car door after her with all the grace and aplomb of a doorman from the Ritz. Then he himself hopped nimbly into the back seat and firmly slammed the door.

"I shouldn't be gone from the office for more than an hour or so," Holly said, double-checking her seat belt. "Shala's going to cover for me, but still—"

"An hour or so? Sure, we can do that. Do you know of a place close by? I noticed there's a Denny's® just down the street, if we're desperate. But I'd really like to take you someplace with a bit more class."

"No. Denny's® is fine," Holly said, silently complimenting herself on her *own* class, exemplified by the fact that she'd been in Tractor's presence for all of ninety seconds and hadn't so much as *hinted* at his millions. Now she swiveled her head around and looked questioningly at Blue, calmly sitting in the back seat.

"Hi. I'm Blue," he said with a smile.

Blue? Holly quickly glanced at Tractor, looking for guidance. He reassured her with a slight nod—yes, that was indeed the young fellow's name. Holly, still slightly flustered at seeing Tractor after so many years, but wishing to appear calm and in control, attempted a casual quip. "Blue, huh? Would that be your name, or your state of mind?"

Tractor rewarded her with a pained expression disguised as a smile, while Blue was smart enough to realize she was only trying to be funny, and her question didn't really require an answer.

"Actually, his name is Blue Avenger, and he's quite a famous guy," Trac explained. "At least he's pretty well known in Oakland, especially among those folks who follow the doings of the Oakland City Council."

Holly suddenly leaned forward in her seat so she could turn her entire torso and get a really good look at Blue. "Blue Avenger's Weepless Wonder Lemon Meringue Pie!" she exclaimed. "I don't believe it! You're the kid in Ask Auntie Annie's column! I'll be darned! I actually *made* your pie. And you're right! It didn't weep!"

Holly, her face slightly flushed after this bit of excitement, turned around again and settled back into her seat. "I'll be darned," she said again. She reached her hand out and touched Tractor's shoulder. "Hey, Trac, where in the world did you ever meet *this* celebrity?"

"Oh, just call it serendipity," Trac said, feeling somewhat deflated. "Well! Here we are!" he added, pulling into Denny's® parking lot. *"Le Restaurant Denné."*

$ $ $ $ $ $ $

Superintendent Mooney was at his wits' end. Nothing was going as planned. He and his various department heads had hammered out an agenda for the Special Emergency Two-Day Workshop, and they were barely into the first hours of the first day and already chaos and confusion reigned. Dr. Mooney had just tried to quell one of the minor altercations in Focus Group One—which was meeting in the San Pablo High School library—involving the book publisher's representative on the Up with Reading! committee and a disgruntled writer who said she had sent a manuscript to his company over eight months ago and hadn't heard even the slightest peep from them yet. Even though the superintendent had not been able to placate the unhappy author, at least he had managed to solve the problem temporarily by assigning her to a different group. That accomplished, he was now on his way to see how Focus Group Five, convened in the drama classroom, was coming along.

Mrs. Phoebe McPherson and her vociferous little group called Watchword! were there in force, chanting their catchy little phrases whenever possible and stretching out their allotted time at the microphone from two minutes to five or six or more, and even then, the Edumation Consultants facilitator practically had to drag them off the small stage.

171

"We're here, as is our mission, to ensure that unsuitable reading material is kept *out* of the hands of our children," said Mrs. Mc-Pherson, when it was her turn to speak. Staring directly at Mrs. Bernice Ryan, the chairperson of the Up with Reading! committee, she added, "We feel strongly that the Up with Reading! committee dropped the ball *big time* this year! Not anywhere have they stipulated what *kind* of reading material is acceptable for earning points in their ill-conceived contest."

She stooped down and withdrew from her briefcase a sheaf of papers secured with a thick rubber band and shook them in the air like a bird airing out its feathers in preparation for takeoff. "These represent but a small portion of the letters, e-mails, and phone calls Watchword! has received from concerned parents—and, yes, from teachers as well—since the beginning of this contest. Let me share a few of them with you."

She pulled a sheet of paper off the top of the stack and announced, "This is from a father of three: *I counted fourteen swear words* in the first chapter alone *of the book my son is reading in an effort to help his school win the Up with Reading! contest. What the hell is going on here? Is this what you call Ed-u-ca-tion? I call it in-ex-cus-ible!*"

Mrs. McPherson looked over the top of her reading glasses at the standing-room-only crowd in front of her, since Focus Group Five was one of the most popular of the several dozen in progress at the workshop. "Fourteen words in the first chapter alone, people!" she said. "What do you think of that?"

Marianne Jergens, the student representative from the Up with Reading! committee, politely raised her hand. "I've never exactly counted, but I usually hear at *least* fourteen swear words in the hall-way before I even get to my first-period class, so I don't think—"

"There! You see! That's exactly what I'm talking about!" Mrs. McPherson pulled out another letter. "This one is from the mother of a twelve-year-old girl." She cleared her throat and began to read: "*Since when are the pages from magazine articles with titles such as* How Good a Kisser Are You? *and* Ten Hot Hints to Improve Your Sex Life *considered eligible for the Up with Reading! competition now in progress in our schools? Who is in charge here?"* Mrs. McPherson again focused on Mrs. Ryan, raising her eyebrows accusingly. She withdrew another letter. "Now, this one is from——"

The facilitator from Edumation Consultants lightly tapped his microphone, which immediately emitted a short burst of high-pitched screeches. "I'm sorry, Mrs. McPherson, but your time is up."

"Just let me finish this one more letter. It's my last one."

"No, I'm sorry. Your time is up."

"But——"

"He says your time is up!" Mrs. Ryan called out.

"Let her read one more!" intoned a deep male voice from the audience. "You people just don't want to hear this!"

"When your time's up, your time's up!" shouted out a man in the last row.

"Book burners!" A shrill voice called out. "This is how it all started in Germany!"

A very pregnant middle-aged woman in the front row slowly turned around to face the others, gripping the back of her chair for support. "You want to let these children just read whatever they want?" she asked. "Is *that* what you want for our babies? They're reading all these depressing, sexy books and then they commit suicide, like that youngster last Sunday."

"Well, at least they're reading *something*——" a pale woman wearing a huge black turtleneck sweater said quietly—too quietly to be heard by anyone except the man sitting next to her, who immediately jumped up and declared, "She never committed suicide! She's just as alive as you and I! Please, get your facts straight before you speak!"

"As you and *me!*" someone corrected rudely. "Just as alive as you and *me!*"

A strained and tremulous female voice quickly joined the fray. "No! That is not correct!" As those in attendance quickly glanced around to see who was speaking, an elderly woman slowly rose to a half-standing position and, clutching her workshop agenda tightly in her hand, turned stiffly and surveyed the room. Indicating her name badge with a gentle pat of her fingers, she announced, "My name is Miss Steward, and I've been a teacher of English for forty-six years. You and I is correct. In this case, the *I* is not the object of a preposition, so—"

"Will someone please call Dr. Mooney? This is getting ridiculous!"

"Here he comes now," remarked a woman sitting near the open door. "He's coming down the corridor."

An eager-looking young man, appearing slightly incongruous dressed in a gray business suit and wearing a WarpSpeedPlus™ baseball cap, popped up from his seat as if he were jet-propelled. "May I just take this brief opportunity, while we're waiting for Dr. Mooney, to say a few words on behalf of the remarkable Warp-SpeedPlus™ reading program, a scientifically designed system which has proven itself to be—"

"—a poor second to the far superior KidsFirst™ reading improvement program!" a shrill voice called out.

"Oh, both of you pipe down!" instructed Mrs. McPherson.

The facilitator from Edumation Consultants flopped down in his chair, muttering to himself, "I'll have my head examined before I come again to this crazy town."

Dr. Mooney entered the room and strode up to the microphone. "First of all," he said, standing up tall and looking over the anxious faces in front of him, "I want to say that we at the Downtown Office are very pleased and surprised at the early returns from our schools in the Up with Reading! competition. Why, those pages are getting read faster than you can tip over a cow!" he exclaimed, choosing to use a bit of his trademark jaunty humor.

Immediately the assembled crowd broke out in near frenzy, a noisy mixture of wild applause, catcalls, and stomping feet. It took several minutes before Dr. Mooney and the Edumation Consultants facilitator could bring things back under control.

Dr. Mooney held up both hands, fingers spread, and waggled them back and forth until the room settled down enough for him to be heard. "Thank you," he said, immediately deciding to take the easy way out. "But now I must announce that the morning sessions are hereby closed. Lunch will be served in the school cafeteria, with beverages supplied at no extra charge by the Pepsi® Corporation. Thank you all for coming, and for those of you who are here in an official capacity, I'll see you here this afternoon. Have a nice lunch."

Principal Manning, who had served as chairperson for Focus Group Ten, ran into Mr. Frazier on the way to the cafeteria. "Let's hurry," she said, "before the line gets too long. I hope there's something besides the usual fare today," she added, unaware that the luncheon was being catered by McDonald's®, with beverages supplied at no charge by the Pepsi® Corporation, who hoped very soon to win a contract giving them exclusive rights to every soft drink dispenser in every school in town for the next twenty years.

The line was already extending past the coffee machines by the time they reached the cafeteria. Mrs. Bernice Ryan was the last person in the queue.

"Well! Hello, Bernice!" said Mrs. Manning. "How have you been? Has your committee gotten any enabling feedback so far this morning?"

Mrs. Bernice Ryan pursed her lips and shook her head. "Absolutely not!" she declared. "In fact, I'm just going to have a bite to eat and skedaddle right out of here!"

"Why, for heaven's sakes?"

"Well, first thing this morning, before we even had time to defend ourselves, those Edumator Consultants had the nerve to tell us outright—tell us, the Up with Reading! committee—that our efforts were entirely misdirected!"

"*Edumation* Consultants," corrected Mr. Frazier.

"What?"

"The name of the consulting company is Edumation Consultants, not Edumator."

"I don't care *what* their name is! They're a bunch of idiots, as far as I'm concerned. They said it's now common knowledge in education circles that when we have these contests between the schools, challenging them to see who can read the most pages, what happens is that the kids who are already readers just lie around like slugs, reading reading reading, racking up the pages, while the kids who *should* be reading just give up and let the others do it all. They said we should concentrate not on trying to get *some* readers to read a *lot*, but to get a *lot* of readers to read *some!* And they even suggested that recent research backs them up on this, although I noticed they didn't cite any hard references! I tell you! I'm leaving, right after lunch. I have better things to do with my time, thank you!"

The line had now moved up sufficiently to enable the three of them to get a glimpse of the food being dished up to the hungry participants.

"What *is* this?" exclaimed Mrs. Ryan, reading aloud from the sign propped up on a nearby easel. "*Food catered courtesy McDonald's®!* Now that is the last straw," she said, turning on her heel. "Excuse me, but I'm out of here, pronto!"

$ $ $ $ $ $ $

The conversation at Denny's® got around to money even before the sandwiches arrived. "You know, Tractor, I'm wondering, do you consider yourself a success, now that you've become a millionaire? In other words, does hitting it big and making a lot of money like you did automatically entitle you to be called a 'success'?" she added, writing exaggerated quotation marks in the air.

Tractor was totally surprised by her question. What was she *talking* about! Of *course* I'm a success! "Well, sure," he said quickly. "I'm doing what I dreamed of doing ever since high school, and while I don't mean to brag, I believe I've done very well." He thought about her question a moment longer and then repeated what he had already said. "Yes. Definitely. I would say I'm a success. Why? Wouldn't you?"

"Well, that depends," Holly replied. "That's what I'm trying to get at. I mean, does being a success involve more than money? I suppose, like you said, if you're doing what you've always dreamed about—well, I—" Holly looked away for a moment, and then she looked down at her hands and trifled with her rings a bit. "I was just thinking about this coffee mug I have at the office, and it's got this little saying printed on it that says *That man is a success who brings out the best in others and gives the best of himself,* and I just wondered whether you thought that definition would fit you, that's all."

Tractor folded his arms on the table and leaned forward, looking directly into Holly's eyes. "Oh, Holly—you're a hard one, you are," he said. But by the curve of his lips and the firm resolve of his little smile, she knew that she really hadn't touched him at all.

"But listen," he said, breaking out in a genuine smile now and gesturing toward the street, "it's a big world out there—plenty of room for both of us, right? So we'll just keep doing our own thing—hey!" he exclaimed. "Remember, back in high school, when *doing our own thing* was our—oh, what would you call it? Our mantra?"

"Yes. I do," Holly agreed, more or less relieved for the moment that Tractor took her veiled attempt at censuring him so lightly. "And I imagine it's the same for kids today as well."

Tractor turned to look at Blue, sitting beside him in the booth, and nudged him with his elbow. "How about it, Blue? Are you and your friends still into *doing your own thing?*"

But Blue really hadn't been paying much attention to this conversation. What he was doing—without letting on to the others—was taking his own pulse rate. His heart had been racing like mad ever since they'd arrived at the restaurant, and the pounding in his chest and throat reminded him of the sound the raindrops made when they fell on the garbage can lid just outside his bedroom window. *Dut dut dut-dut dunk, dut dut dunk dut-dut.* So there he was, slightly turned toward the wall, holding his arm close to his body while the fingers of his right hand pressed against his inner left wrist. He had counted up to seventy-eight already, and the second hand on his watch still had a ways to go before reaching its starting point.

"What?" Blue asked, when Tractor nudged him. "What did you say?"

"Hey, what are you doing there?" Tractor laughed, grabbing Blue's hand. "What are you doing? Why, look at that!" he said, smiling across at Holly. "What a nutty guy. He's sitting here taking his pulse!"

"Who's taking whose pulse?" Blue asked, blushing. "I'm just checking the time, that's all. Let's see here, it's exactly seventeen minutes after twelve noon. Pacific Standard Time."

Blue didn't believe in ESP, of course. That was Marvin Lasher's department. But he sure wished he could somehow signal to Tractor to please get on with the business at hand! Please, *please* produce that application and show it to the lady! I can't take this suspense much longer! My whole future with Omaha may be riding on this deal!

"Oops, heads up," Holly said. "Here's lunch." She waited until the food was all set out in front of them—a simple salad with no dressing for her, hamburgers and fries for the guys—before asking Blue if he'd ever seen Tractor's *first* movie, the documentary called *Life at Mansanar.*

"No. I've never even heard of it."

"You really don't know about it?"

"Nope."

"Well, it's been shown on PBS several times now," Holly said. "They always seem to bring it back around pledge time. You really should watch for it. It's excellent!"

Blue turned to look at Tractor, who was busily engaged trying to keep the onion slices from sliding out from between the two halves of his hamburger bun.

"Did Tractor ever tell you how he happened to get such an unusual first name?"

Blue shook his head. He had wondered about that from the beginning.

"Well, he explained it in his intro to the documentary. He said

178

that when his grandparents were sent over there, to Mansanar, they had to dispose of all their possessions, and it seems that his grandfather had just made the final payment on this brand-new tractor, and he didn't know what to do with it. He couldn't take it with him, of course. So just before he had to go off to the camp, he asked a neighboring farmer—a Caucasian, of course—if he'd keep it for him until the war was over. Well, unfortunately, when—"

"I'll finish the story, Holly," Tractor said, wiping his mouth with his paper napkin, which he then crumpled up with his fist. "When the war was over, and my grandfather went back to claim his tractor, he found that the neighbor had moved away in the interim, and no one knew what had become of it."

"The tractor? Jeez, that's awful," said Blue. "So what did he do?"

Tractor shrugged. "What could he do? Nothing. Anyway, he missed that tractor as if it were a living, breathing creature. In fact, he never went back to farming, even though he loved it. He and my great uncle pooled what little money they had and started up a neighborhood fish market in Oakland."

"Oh, gee. That's really sad, isn't it?"

"Yeah, but his kids—my father, especially—got really sick and tired of hearing about that lost tractor all their lives. So when I was born, my dad and mom just decided to put an end to it, once and for all. The way my parents tell it, the first time my grandfather saw me, they placed me in his arms and said, 'Here's your new Tractor. Now we don't want to hear about that *other* one ever again.'"

Holly quickly wiped a little tear from her eye. "Great story, isn't it? You really should see that documentary sometime, Blue. It's marvelous."

Tractor was just sitting there with a faraway look in his eyes. Finally he said, "Listen, Holly. Give it up, will you?"

"Yes, well, I've seen a couple of your recent movies, Trac, and I know you're capable of—well, never mind," she said, realizing she really didn't have time now to tangle with him over this, providing she could even get him to listen to her.

There she goes again, Tractor thought. *Little Miss Goodie-goodie. I can't stand it when she starts on her moralizing kick. It's like that* Tigers suck *thing all over again!*

Tractor took a deep breath and forced a smile, consoling himself with the thought of that marvelous, double-dealing prank just waiting to happen.

"So," he said brightly, "tell us about your job, Holly. Barry Goode—you know he sells used cars now in Oakland, don't you? Well, old Barry told me that you're the chief license-plate censor here at Motor V. Is that true?"

"Yes, that's true."

Blue couldn't swallow fast enough. He wondered why he had so much trouble with his saliva glands. Whenever he felt stressed, his mouth became either as dry as toast or wet as water.

"So, uh—how do you like it? Do you have certain guidelines, or—"

Holly sighed and shook her head. "The way things are going, I estimate I'll be out of a job within five years."

Trac tipped his head to one side and smiled a kind of cockeyed smile. "Why? Why do you say that?"

Holly hesitated a moment. "Well, let me put it this way: I don't suppose you've looked at a modern dictionary or thesaurus recently, have you? Either of you?"

Tractor shook his head. "No. Not recently," he said, while Blue admitted that he occasionally dipped into his whenever he had a report to write.

"Well, I use mine quite often, but the other day I finally got around to reading the introduction in the front of the book. I wonder if it would surprise you guys to know that in the introduction to *Bartlett's Roget's Thesaurus,* the editors come right out and admit that censorship is long gone. In fact, that may even be an exact quote—*censorship is long gone.* Words that were once labeled as taboo or obscene in older versions are no more, since today, those words are encountered everywhere—in books, on the Internet and

TV, and in movies—right, Tractor?—and, of course, in everyday speech. Even that good old four-letter Anglo-Saxon standby—you know the one I mean—is simply labeled as 'informal' in the thesaurus. So, like I said, if guys like you, Tractor—guys in the TV and motion picture business—just keep on plying your trade as you have been—having no qualms whatsoever regarding the nature and number of foul words that come spewing out of your characters' mouths—if you keep on doing that, there'll soon be no restrictions whatsoever, even on license plates, and I'll be out of a job."

"Oh, God! *No!*" Tractor gasped, even before she had finished her sentence, burying his head in his arms and repeating, "No, no, no, *no!*"

Blue and Holly looked at each other across the table. Neither one of them spoke as they watched Tractor, his head still on his arms, both fists pounding on the table, and him muttering, *"No! No! No!"*

"Oh, come on, Trac," Holly said finally, not certain what to make of this unusual display. "You're not the least bit funny," she added, winking at Blue. "So cut out the theatrics, will you? I'm sure you couldn't care less if I lost my job."

Tractor put his hands over his ears and made a little moan.

Blue didn't know what to think. He just looked over at Holly with a helpless shrug.

"Oh, let him be," Holly said, trying her best to stifle a smile, for Tractor's antics *were* pretty funny. "Let's not encourage him with the attention he obviously craves. He's just reverting to his true nature. Just a silly but strangely gifted overgrown little boy, who has absolutely no concept whatsoever of appropriate speech or behavior."

That did it. Tractor slowly raised his head, took a deep breath, and leaned against the back of the booth. Then, surprisingly, he started to laugh—that intense, quiet, shaking kind of weird, joyless laugh that soon spreads around to everyone at the table for no apparent reason at all.

"Well, I'd better be getting back to work," Holly said after a bit. "This has been just like old times, hasn't it? We can talk some more at the reunion, okay?" she said, looking at her watch and sliding out of the booth.

"Right." Tractor picked up the check, ignoring Blue's look of alarm.

Wait, wait! Blue wanted to shout. *We can't leave yet! You didn't do what we came here for!*

Alone in the back seat of the car on the short ride back to the Motor Vehicles office, Blue was still trying to understand what went wrong. What was going on here, anyway? Why hadn't Tractor even *mentioned* the license plate?

When they were just a block away from their destination, Blue decided to give the back of Tractor's seat a little kick—as a sort of reminder. When there was no obvious response, he kicked it again. By the time they had come to a stop, he had kicked it a total of nine times, to no avail, when suddenly he heard the sound of his own voice, speaking quietly but firmly. "Say, Trac—weren't you going to ask Holly to do you a favor? You know, that special license plate application you were telling me about?"

Tractor smiled a little victory smile. He had won his impromptu game of License Plate Chicken, no matter that his opponent didn't even realize he was playing. Tractor snapped his fingers. "Oh, that's right," he said. "Thanks for reminding me, Blue."

He had pulled up to the passenger loading zone now and had stopped the car. Holly was preparing to get out, when Trac said, "Oh, excuse me, just a second here, Holly," and he reached across her and removed a sheet of paper from the glove box and then carefully adjusted the check he had attached with a paper clip. "I wonder if you'd mind sending this through the proper channels for me."

In the back seat, Blue was holding his breath.

"What is it?" she asked, taking the paper from him. Of course, she recognized it immediately. "Oh, I see. You want personalized plates, do you?" Her eyes scanned the paper. "So what's this— *sschwak?* What's that supposed to mean?" She quickly glanced down to the bottom of the form to read the typed explanation there, while Tractor turned around and signaled for Blue to get out of the

car and go around and open her door for her. Hey, no reason for the kid to know about the little white lie on the application, he thought. No use risking the kid getting on his high horse about that.

"Ah, I see," Holly said, scanning the wonderfully inventive explanation that Tractor had dreamed up the night before: *"Sschwak" is the title of an upcoming kiddie movie to be produced by T&T Production Company early next year.* "Yes," Holly said, unbuckling her seat belt. "That looks fine."

And then, acting on a sudden inspiration, Trac added softly, "It's still pretty hush-hush, but we've almost got Reynolds Wrap® in the bag to play the part of the wacky Major Sschwak, and he's always a big hit with the kids." Feeling an urge to gild the lily, he added, "And you'll be pleased to know, Holly-girl, we're holding the line on this one, as far as language is concerned, in deference to the tender age of our targeted audience."

"Well, I'm glad to hear that," Holly said. "Maybe there's hope for you yet." She smiled through the window at Blue, just as he was opening the door for her. She slipped her arm through the shoulder strap of her purse and stepped out of the car, still holding onto Tractor's application, which was now flapping in the breeze against her hand. Then, holding onto the edge of the door, she bent over and poked her head back in for a few final words with Tractor. "About your application, I'll send it right through. Your plates should arrive in a couple of weeks. And thanks again, Trac. I'll see you at the reunion."

"Great!" Tractor called out, giving her a little good-bye salute.

Holly smiled at Blue and offered her hand. "It was wonderful meeting you, Mr. Blue Avenger. And thanks again for coming up with that wonderful recipe!"

Blue nodded, mumbled something he hoped was polite, and collapsed in the front seat with barely enough strength left to close the door behind him.

JOHNNY BROWN

We all have moments when all seems right with the world, when everything that's important to us—family, friends, career—is in perfect harmony. And we take joy in whatever form it comes. Guardian understands.

—Advertisement for the
Guardian^{SM} Life Insurance
Company of America

In a few minutes Trac and Blue were back on the freeway again, heading west toward Oakland. Trac glanced quickly at Blue, who seemed to be thoroughly immersed in his own thoughts. Trac smiled, just barely enough for the dimple to show. "Well, what do you think?" he asked.

Blue took a deep breath and exhaled slowly, the way people sometimes do after completing a difficult task or finishing a hard day's work. He sensed that Trac was about to toy with him, not maliciously, of course, but more in a playful way, just exercising the prerogative of a rich guy prepared to give away a great deal of money.

But Blue could play that game, too. "What do I think about what?" he replied, wearing an expression as devoid of emotion as he could muster, even though he felt as if he were floating on a bed of feathers six inches above the seat. *Seven thousand dollars to keep, or one million to give away! Unbelievable!*

184

Trac checked his side-view mirror and merged into the passing lane, whisking away an imaginary fly from his forehead. *What do I think about what?* Say, this kid was all right.

Neither of them spoke for several minutes, but long silences made Tractor jittery. "So what did you think of Holly?" he asked, trying a different tack.

"Holly? She seems real nice."

"Yeah, but she'll seem a lot nicer to me once I've got my new plate."

Blue shrugged. "Whatever it takes, I guess."

Tractor adjusted the visor to block out the afternoon sun. "I suppose all this seems pretty silly to you, right?"

Blue didn't know how to answer that. He just wished he could calm down a little. This whole episode was just too way-out weird and unpredictable, even for a comic-book hero.

"Actually, I can't explain it, either," Tractor admitted. "Except that I've always liked to give myself little challenges, and then see if I can—you know, accomplish them. But this time it kind of backfired on me." Without waiting for Blue to ask what he meant by that, Tractor immediately changed the subject. "You decided about the money yet? Do I shell out a mere seven thousand, or is this little diversion going to set me back a mil?"

Blue sighed again and massaged his neck, slowly shaking his head. "It's not so easy. There's a lot to consider—"

"Okay, let's see," Tractor said. "Today's Thursday, right? Maybe you want to think about it for a couple of days. Talk it over with your parents, and maybe your girlfriend, if you have one. Do you?"

"Have a girlfriend?" Blue hesitated. "Actually, yes. I do, now." He glanced out the window. It seemed so strange to be able to say yes to that question for the first time in his life.

But Trac didn't pursue the matter. Instead, he asked, "How about this Saturday, then? You can give me your answer on Saturday. That'll give you tonight and all day tomorrow to think about it. That sound okay?"

Blue nodded again. But Tractor had used the word *parents,* and Blue couldn't allow the misimpression about his father to stand. "I guess I should tell you, there's only my mom and me—and my little brother, of course. My dad died three years ago."

"Oh, I'm sorry. I didn't realize that. I'm sorry."

"That's okay," Blue said, swallowing hard, but giving no other sign of discomfort.

"Saturday it is, then," Trac said. "Let's see. Where shall we meet?"

Blue looked up in surprise. It wasn't up to *him* to make that decision. But, hey! How about the five-star Claremont Hotel and Resort up in the Berkeley hills? Or the fabulous Mark Hopkins, over on Nob Hill in San Francisco. Never been to either of those!

"Think of someplace?" Trac asked, noticing Blue's little smile.

"Oh, no. Not really."

"Okay, then, we'll make it simple. Let's meet at that donut shop around the corner from your house. Donut Pros—say about ten o'clock?"

"The *donut* shop?"

"Yeah. Donut Pros, ten o'clock Saturday morning."

"Well," Blue said, hesitating slightly. "The only thing is, I'll probably have to bring my little brother along. See, my mom works on Saturdays, and—"

"Sure. That's fine. No problem. Bring him along."

"I can't believe this is happening, you know," Blue remarked, after a long pause.

Tractor kept his eyes on the road ahead. This would be good for the kid, having to make such a decision at his age. He might actually surprise himself by what he decides to do. He might find out something about himself. "Hey, you want to hear something funny?" Trac asked. And once again he just kept talking without waiting for a response. "I made up this little word game a couple of years ago. After I got rich," he added with a grin. "I call it World-Wide-Word-Watch, and the way it works is that I think of

186

a word, and then I wait for someone to say it. And when they do, I present them right there and then with a cashier's check for five thousand five hundred fifty-five dollars and fifty-five cents, along with my congratulations for saying the lucky word."

Blue was dumbfounded at such an idea. Was this guy for real? "How come all the fives? That your lucky number or something?"

"Oh, no. I just like the way it trips lightly over the tongue. You want to know who the latest winner was?"

They both turned to look at each other, and for a second their eyes met. As soon as Blue saw the mixture of anguish and amused irony in Tractor's face, he didn't even have to ask. He knew exactly who the winner was. "But I didn't see you give her a check—" Blue began.

"Of course not. Are you kidding? I just couldn't bring myself to do that."

Blue felt a sudden cold chill of disillusionment come over him, and he slumped down in his seat. "But don't you—"

"No," Trac broke in. "This one I'm going to have to mail. It's bad enough that she won, but presenting it to her face to face—well, *that* I just couldn't handle."

Blue nodded and sat up a little straighter. "Yeah. I guess I can understand that," he said with a big smile.

$ $ $ $ $ $ $

Timothy thought it was the funniest thing he'd ever heard. "So tell me again. How did she happen to say it?"

"Oh, shut up."

"No, really. How did she say it? Did she say that you were plying your trade, or that somebody else was plying *their* trade? I know you said it had something to do with trade plying."

"I don't know why you're so happy about this."

"Who said I'm happy?" Tim couldn't resist smiling. "I'm content," he said, repeating a line from *Lovers and Other Strangers*, one of their favorite old movies.

"Well, maybe *you're* content, but I would've preferred to get a good whipping rather than have her—of all people—be the one. It seems almost impossible, after all these months with no winner, and then *she* hauls off and says it."

"What did she do when you told her that she was the lucky winner? I'll bet she was sure surprised."

"Are you kidding?" Trac shook his head. "I didn't say a word. But Denise is putting the cashier's check in the mail tomorrow. Maybe it'll drive her nuts, wondering where it came from, and why."

Tim glanced up a moment before scribbling a short memo on an itemized bill three pages long and then tossing it into a wire basket with the others. "So have you picked your new word yet? Or maybe now you've learned your lesson and are ready to give up your Wide-World-Watch-Word game and move on to new and greater challenges."

"No. It's too late," Tractor said, deciding to ignore Tim's sorry attempt at humor based on simple word-order reversal. "I've already got my new word. It's *whip!* As in *whip, whipping, whipped.*"

"Does that include *whup* as well? When I misbehaved, I used to get whupped, not whipped. Does that mean people who use the colloquial won't be eligible for your prize? Trac, is that *fair?*"

Tractor shrugged and looked at his watch. "I'm outa here," he said. "It's much too late in the day to have to listen to the sordid details of your whuppings." Trac turned to go and then remembered something. "Listen, are you doing anything this Saturday at ten? I'm meeting Blue at Donut Pros, and he's going to give me his answer about the money. You want to be there?"

Tim leaned back in his chair and raised his arms in a slow stretch, accompanied by a few moans and groans. "You know, I can't believe you don't feel even the slightest bit of guilt—presenting a kid his age with a choice like that. I'll bet he or his parents could really use that kind of money. What about college? Don't you think he's worried about that? Don't you think he's trying to save for college? You know, Trac, you've got this little streak in you that—" Tim stopped himself. Did he really wish to go any further with this? They'd discussed it before—Trac's little manipulative games, placing people in psychologically challenging positions and noting their reactions. Tim shuffled some papers around on his desk until he came up with his datebook. "Saturday at ten?" he asked, flipping the pages. "Sure, I'll be there. Are we filming it?" he asked, with just a hint of sarcasm.

"Now, there's an idea! If we decide to go with a Blue Avenger movie, we could splice it in! Cinéma vérité!"

"Right. Do you want to do anything that afternoon? I'm free all day on Saturday."

"Well, actually—you won't believe this—but afterward I'm going to a meeting of the Donut Shop Collectors Club of America. It's going to be over at the Dream Fluff in Berkeley—"

"There really is a donut shop collectors club? That's hard to believe."

"I found it on the Internet, and then I got in touch with this guy in Berkeley named Jared—really nice guy, sells toothbrushes, I think he said—and he invited me to their regular monthly meeting, which they have on the last Saturday of every month. Jared wants to see my photos, although he wasn't too impressed with my ninety-two shops. He said one guy in the club spent a couple of days in Dallas last year and got over ninety-five just in that city alone! Can you believe that? But Jared liked the idea of photographs, and said maybe they'll start doing that, too."

"Sounds just like you. Bringing new and exciting innovations wherever you go."

"You got that right. New and exciting innovations is my middle name."

$ $ $ $ $ $ $

Omaha was getting tired of sitting by the phone all day, but early that same morning she had walked over to Donut Pros and filled out an application, and when Mrs. Phom took it, she said she would read it over and give her a call later in the day if she wanted to schedule an interview.

Also, since she was sitting by the phone anyway, Omaha was hoping she might get a call from Blue as well, even though she didn't know what plans, if any, he had made for their unexpected day off from school.

So when the phone finally rang at a little before five in the afternoon, Omaha picked it right up after the first ring. But it wasn't anyone from Donut Pros. And it wasn't Blue. It was from a woman at the hospital asking to speak to Margie.

"I'm sorry, she's not here," Omaha said. "May I give her a message?"

"Yes. Is this her daughter?"

"Yes."

"Well, this is a friend of hers—Mary Ellen, from the business office?"

"Oh, yes. Hi."

"When she comes home, would you please tell her that we have a registered letter up here addressed to her? I signed for it, but we'd like to know if she wants us just to forward it to her or if she'd rather pick it up herself."

"Okay, I'll tell her," Omaha said, wondering why the old witch sent the raise-in-rent notification to her mother's work address rather than to the house. "Actually, though, I think she's over there at the hospital right now, with the pickets—or the picketers, whatever you call them."

"Oh! Okay. Well, in that case, maybe I'll just go downstairs on my break and look for her myself. Thanks."

"You're welcome."

Phooey! Omaha flopped down on the couch and stared at the phone, *willing* it to ring—just for the fun of it. She knew that couldn't possibly affect whether it would ring or not. It was just something to do. Mrs. Phom probably wasn't going to call at all.

Omaha picked at a little pimple on her chin. *They always want somebody with experience, and the only thing I could put in that*

190

blank space where it said "Experience" was my job feeding old Mrs. Caruso's goldfish last December while she went to stay with her daughter for two weeks. Maybe I shouldn't have written that bit about Splashy—where I said I trained him to poke his nose up against the glass whenever he saw me, and that even Mrs. Caruso said he looked much healthier when she got back than he did when she first brought him home from the fish store. But I had to fill the space up with *something*.

Again the phone rang, this time surprising Omaha and making her jump.

"Hello?"

"Hello. This is Mrs. Phom, at Donut Pros. Is this Omaha?"

"Yes—"

"Well, Omaha, I can't promise you anything, because I've already decided to hire someone else—someone a little older than you, who's had some experience—"

Oh, right! Same old story—

"—but if you'd like to drop by on Saturday, anyway, we could talk, and I could keep your application on file in case we—"

"Oh! Sure!" Omaha broke in, and then was instantly chagrined to think she had interrupted Mrs. Phom in midsentence.

"Good. Come in on Saturday then, anytime between, oh—say nine and noon. I'll be here all morning."

"All right! And thank you very much for calling!"

Holy Moses! They're going to keep my application on file! I just may get a job yet!

$ $ $ $ $ $ $

Even though Margie hadn't seen a sample of Johnny Brown's handwriting for over five years, she immediately recognized it on the registered letter Mary Ellen handed to her outside the hospital. Of course, she didn't let on to her friend that it was anything out of the ordinary. "Oh," she said. "Thank you. It's from an old friend of mine in Italy."

After Mary Ellen finished her cigarette and went back inside, however, Margie left the little group of picketers and walked directly over to her car, unlocked it, and climbed inside.

She tore the envelope open very slowly, carefully preserving the Italian stamps and the postmark: Roma, Italia. A check floated into her lap as she unfolded the single sheet of paper:

Dear Margie:

After thinking about how I could begin this letter to you for almost an hour, I decided to just start it off by telling you how I've been thinking about how to begin it for almost an hour, and in that way let the problem itself become the solution to the problem! (You must remember how much I enjoyed—and still enjoy—that sort of roundabout thinking!)

How have you been? Both you and Omaha have been on my mind off and on ever since she made her surprise visit to me here in Rome on 17 February, the anniversary of the death of my hero, Giordano Bruno. Now, are you sitting down? If not, please do so, because I have some super-exciting news!

MY LIFE'S DREAM HAS FINALLY COME TRUE!! I AM ABOUT TO BECOME A GENUINE, PUBLISHED AUTHOR!!! (Because, as Omaha may have told you, I finally finished the book I've been working on all these years, and now I have found a publisher right here in Italy!!)

I can't tell you how happy it makes me to be able to send you the enclosed check for $4500, which represents a fair percentage of my advance against royalties, all things considered.

It is the best vindication I know for the fact that I left you and Omaha on that fateful day five years ago in order to pursue my dream. And I hope that in some small way it will permit you and Omaha to share in my great personal triumph. (And just to help put that in its proper perspective, my editor at BiblioItalia Publishing Company informed me that they had rejected over 2,500 manuscripts last year alone!)

I always knew that success was within my reach! I only needed to be free, and have the chance to try.

Sincerely,

Johnny

P.S. Please note that the check is postdated for April 2. The chief teller at my bank here in Italy has assured me that the funds will be transferred to my checking account in the U.S. by that date. Don't worry, Margie, the check won't bounce.

J. B.

It's true that a generous check such as the one Margie now held in her hand couldn't have come at a better time. Omaha would be so relieved! Even so, Margie had to force herself to stuff it into her purse as fast as she could before succumbing to an almost irresistible urge to tear it into a million pieces and scatter them to the wind.

Margie resolved not to say anything about this sudden windfall until the check actually cleared the bank on Monday. As it happened, however, she could only manage to keep the news from Omaha for just a day and a half—all the way to Saturday morning—which was really quite remarkable, considering how much she longed to set her daughter's mind at ease.

$ $ $ $ $ $

KFIB's chief deejay—the one, the only—Bobby Briggsmore, couldn't believe his eyes as he read the I'm Unique, Too! contest entry sent in by a young lady with the melodious name of Omaha Nebraska Brown, a student at San Pablo High, the same as his son, Lenny. He read her entry over for a second time, and then carefully refolded it and slipped it back into its envelope, tapping it on his desk a few times while deciding what to do.

Finally, he made up his mind. Although it was very cleverly done, it was just not worth the risk. The quips and taunts and double entendres that were sure to come after Lenny spilled the beans would go on forever and simply drive the poor girl crazy.

So instead of placing her entry in the container with the others that he was saving to take home for Lenny to read and judge, Mr. Bobby Briggsmore, known only to a chosen few as "the deejay with a heart," opened his briefcase and tossed Omaha's envelope inside. (And while he was there, he removed the jumbo can of salted cashews, the little plastic bag filled with candy kisses, and the jar of sliced dill pickles, because he was on in just five minutes, and it was going to be another long night at the station.)

After his shift was over, while waiting in the to-go line at the Benny Burger® Drive-in, Bobby Briggsmore removed the envelope from his briefcase and stuffed it into the grinning mouth of the Benny Burger trash can, where it would never again see the light of day.

$ $ $ $ $ $ $

Blue was startled when he heard Josh turning his key in the lock and opening the front door. Knowing his little brother would be bounding into his room any second, he quickly shoved the sheet of paper he was writing on into his desk drawer and called out, "Hey, Joshpot, I thought Mom told you to let yourself in around the *back*, and not the *front!*"

"Oh, yeah. I forgot," Josh said, tearing around the corner into Blue's room, carelessly bumping into the partially open door with his book bag, which then dropped to the floor as the door swung wide open and banged against the plastic garbage can beside Blue's desk.

194

"Hey! Watch it! You don't have to knock the house down, you know."

"Oh. Sorry. But listen! You know what? I think I might get that award for thinking up the best idea for our class to make money during Up with Reading! Month!"

"No kidding."

"Yeah! You know how Omaha told me a way to make stress ball craft out of those bigger balloons so you don't have to try and fill a balloon with cornstarch when it's already full of air—"

"Why do you always call it stress ball *craft*, anyway? You're not making stress ball *craft*, you're just making stress balls."

"Well, don't blame me! That's what they called it on the Internet, on those instructions on the Internet. They called it stress ball craft."

"Well, it's still just *stress balls*. Leave off the *craft*. It sounds dumb."

"Yeah, well, anyway, when I showed Ms. Knight how to do it today, she really loved it! And then when I told her we have all this free cornstarch in our backyard, well, boy! You should've seen her! She said that was the best idea for a class moneymaker that's come in so far, and unless a miracle happens before tomorrow, I'm going to get the award!"

"Well, that's good. But who's Ms. Knight?"

"My teacher, stupid! Who do you think! Anyway, when—"

"Aha! I thought you told me a couple of weeks ago that your teacher's name was Ms. Hamster! Remember? You said her name was Ms. Ima Hamster! And then when I questioned you about it, you just said really, *really*, that was her name, and didn't I believe you. So, Mr. Smartguy, how do you explain *that?*"

Josh scratched his head and said, "Hmm," and looked puzzled, but only for a moment before brightening suddenly and adding, "Oh! Well! I guess I forgot to tell you she decided to change her name—just like *you* did, David! People can change their names whenever they want to—"

"Get out of here, please, and take your book bag with you. I've got stuff to do. And close the door behind you."

Once Josh was out of the room, Blue retrieved the sheet of paper he had been writing on. It was divided into two columns, one with a $7,000 heading, and the other with $1,000,000. The first column was very short, with just two items, while the second one was getting longer by the minute.

$7,000

1. Help Omaha with rent increase until after senior year. (Knowing her, probably in the form of a loan.)
2. Buy good, cheap used car. (Get Uncle Ralphy to check it out before purchase.)

$1,000,000

1. Donate to Councilwoman Peters' voter initiative campaign in favor of the bullet ban.
2. Arrange for a grant to set up a local suicide hot line for troubled teens (and maybe adults as well).
3. Purchase big ads in selected California newspapers depicting photos of millions of lottery losers, and identify them as such—LOSERS!
4. Arrange for a generous grant to the Jonathan Barger Proteomics Research Center. (Find the write-up about them in that recent copy of *News!* magazine for their address.)
5. See about feasibility of supplying polypropylene underwear to freezing children throughout the

world. (That stuff is really
good!)

6. Talk to Rakesh regarding
   worthy animal welfare
   organizations. (Mom should
   like that—)
7. Donate to the Shakespeare-
   Oxford Society to help
   finance their studies of
   who really wrote Shakespeare.
8. Give grant to PBS to rerun
   Fawlty Towers for a new gen-
   eration of viewers.

Just as Blue was beginning to have second thoughts about
Fawlty Towers—like maybe that was too frivolous, giving money so
people could watch a silly British comedy on public television
while financial support was desperately needed for medical research
into AIDS, and cancer, and the development of new or improved
vaccines for anthrax and other biological warfare diseases—just as
he was beginning to feel a real sense of responsibility about the
possibility of giving away one million dollars, the phone rang.

"Get the phone, will you, Josh?" he called out.

"I can't! I'm in the bathroom!" came Josh's muffled reply.

Blue dashed down the short hallway, vaulted over the low coffee
table in the front room (an exhibition of physical prowess he never
demonstrated when his mother was at home), and made it to the
phone in the kitchen by the third ring. "Hello," he said.

"Blue? Hi. Are you busy?"

"Oh, hi, sweetie. No. Not really."

"You sound busy. What are you doing?"

"I'm—uh, I'm just making a list. Nothing important. What's
happening?"

Omaha quickly decided to tell him her news first, and then find out what was bothering him. (By the way he sounded, she knew it was something.)

"Well, I just wanted to tell you that this morning I filled out an application at Donut Pros, and the lady there just called me back and wants me to go in for an interview—"

"An application to *work*, you mean?" Blue interrupted.

"Yeah. To work! There's just one little problem, though—she already *hired* somebody. But she wants to interview me anyway, and put me on the waiting list. Isn't that great?"

"Well, I don't know. Like, it depends. When would you—"

"I told her I could work all day on Saturdays and Sundays, and maybe some mornings before school. They open at 4 A.M., you know. It would have to be in the mornings, because she told me they're usually sold out by the time I get out of school. She wants me to come in on Saturday morning for my interview. I'm kind of nervous, though, because I've never—"

"Saturday morning?" Blue hunched his shoulder and pressed the receiver tight against his ear.

"That's what she said. She said anytime between nine and noon, so I'll probably go in about ten."

Blue leaned up against the wall. "About ten?"

"That's right."

"About ten," Blue repeated.

"Yeah! What's wrong with ten?"

"Nothing's wrong with ten. But listen. I need to think about something. I'll call you back in a little while, okay?"

"Sure."

Blue hung up the phone and went back to his room, sitting on the edge of his bed and asking himself, well, where do I start? Maybe by thinking about why I'm so *suspicious* of every little coincidence all of a sudden. But isn't it *amazing* that of all the places Omaha could be at ten o'clock on Saturday morning, she's going to be at Donut Pros—at the very same time and very same place where I'm going to have to make a pretty darned important decision? Does she have a part to play in all of this? If so, what is it? Why does my life seem to be progressing along just like a story, unfolding in a planned and orderly manner? *Almost like the plot of a well-constructed comic strip.*

The sound of the flushing toilet and Josh's footsteps in the hall suddenly brought Blue back down to earth. He stood up and studied his reflection in the mirror hanging on the back of his door. Okay, time to think logically. What are the chances of that happening just by chance? Is it really that unusual? Is it really that much of a coincidence? The job opening at Donut Pros, for instance? Omaha noticing the sign in the window? Nothing too unusual about that. Omaha filling out an application? So? She needs the money. The donut shop lady calling back? Of course she would call back. Making an appointment for an interview on Saturday? Well, why not? Omaha has school tomorrow. Saturday's the logical day. And the time? Omaha said she'd probably go in around ten o'clock? That's perfectly normal. A nice, convenient time. Nine would be too early, eleven getting close to lunchtime. Ten is perfect. So what's the big deal? Everything is perfectly normal. Nothing strange about it at all.

Josh was back in the front room now, lying on the rug, watching his program on television. Blue stepped over him on his way to the kitchen and got Omaha back on the line. As soon as he heard her voice, he knew he had to tell her about the seemingly miraculous situation he found himself in, and about the big decision he was called upon to make. He felt certain that he knew her well enough to know she wouldn't presume to tell him what he should or should not do—that this was a decision for him, and him alone, to make.

Starting from the beginning, he told her everything—all about his first meeting with Tractor Nishimura in Mr. Frazier's office on Monday morning, about SSCHWAK, and Holly, and the World-Wide-Word-Watch and how she used the word *ply* and now Trac's going to send her a check for $5,555.55, and even the *Fawlty Towers* versus the AIDS and biological-warfare-vaccines dilemma, and right on down to his own ten o'clock appointment at Donut Pros on Saturday with the multimillionaire from Marin.

Omaha didn't know what to say. Maybe, if he had asked her what she would do in his place, she would tell him. But he didn't ask, and she respected that. And, anyway, she didn't *know* what she would do.

She suddenly found herself not only biting her inner lip, but also twirling a strand of hair around her fingers, babyish habits she had given up years before. "You know, Blue," she said softly, "ever since you changed your name, it seems like—well, the things that happen to you—to us, really—are so—" Omaha's voice was getting softer and softer, until she was almost whispering. "It's almost like it's not *real*, you know? And now—this! My God! A millionaire would be bad enough, but a *multimillionaire?* It's all just too much. It's"— and she was really whispering now —"*it's comic-book stuff!*"

But Blue wasn't going to allow himself to get pulled back into that abyss again. He just laughed and said, "Some imagination you have there, Omaha. But listen, I've got about two hours of homework to do yet, and since when do comic-strip characters have to do homework?"

"Well, I don't have any homework. I did it already."

"Oh-oh. That's scary."

"Listen, Blue—"

"Yeah?"

Omaha wanted to tell him that she knew what he was thinking, but if he *did* choose the seven thousand dollars, she wouldn't take a penny of it. But somehow the words wouldn't come. Could she really be that selfish? Instead she was appalled to hear herself saying, "Did you hear the nurses went on strike yesterday? I sure hope the donut girl they hired decides to quit pretty darn soon. I really need that job."

$ $ $ $ $ $

Blue might just as well have stayed home from school on Friday for all the attention he paid in class. No matter how hard he tried to concentrate, his thoughts kept returning either to the decision he had to make the following morning or the sheer unlikelihood of being in such a position at all.

Ordinarily, he would have had no qualms about discussing a matter of such import and potentially far-reaching effects with his mother, but somehow, in this case, he wanted to be entirely on his own. He wanted to find out what kind of person he really was.

He waited until the house was quiet and both Josh and his mother were in their rooms before getting out his pencil and drawing paper. Now, to see what Blue Avenger would do.

The first panel explained the problem—Blue Avenger looking at two stacks of thousand-dollar bills. One was labeled "$7,000 TO KEEP" and the other, "$1,000,000 TO GIVE AWAY."

The second panel was almost identical, the only change being Blue's growing frustration, illustrated by drops of perspiration flying off his face, and his hands desperately running through his hair.

In the third panel, Blue is leaning suggestively toward the seven thousand dollars with a little balloon above his head depicting a girl's face and an automobile.

The final panel shows him suddenly lunging for the million, with as wonderful an expression of goodness and self-satisfaction on his face as Blue could possibly draw.

When it was done, Blue stared long and hard at his handiwork. Well, he thought, I guess that's that.

THE THEORY OF EVERYTHING

Scientists have come up with theories in the shower, on barren mountains, while driving to work and even in their sleep.
—James Glanz, *New York Times*

Like most CPAs and accountant-types in general, Timothy Sims is an extremely conscientious and punctual individual. In fact, he is so punctual he sometimes crosses over the time line into the too-early zone. But his innate thoughtfulness always shines through, and he wouldn't think of arriving at the doorstep of his host until the appointed hour, always waiting patiently in his car until time catches up with him, or, to put it another way—in deference to those who believe there is no such thing as time—he doesn't ring the doorbell until the hands of his watch are in the position earlier agreed upon by himself and his host.

The scheduled Saturday meeting for 10 A.M. at Donut Pros did not call for any such consideration, and it was just after 9:30 when Tim parked his yellow Mercedes 500 SLC in front of the row of newspaper-dispensing machines just around the corner from the donut shop. He bought a copy of the *Oakland Star* to read while he was waiting for the others. Once inside the shop, he ordered a cup of coffee and only two plain glazed, resisting the urge for an apple fritter as well, in token compliance with his doctor's orders. When Mrs. Phom began to serve up his coffee in a Styrofoam® cup, he quickly said, "Oh, make that for here, please," whereupon she transferred the already-poured coffee into a genuine ceramic Donut Pros mug and set it down on the counter with a friendly nod and a smile. Hmm, Tim thought. Styrofoam® Cup. *"Styro"* Cup. Not bad. I'll try to remember to suggest it to Trac.

Tim was pleased to see that the very same table by the window that he and Trac had occupied the previous Sunday was free. He quickly took note of the supply of little packets of sugar and little containers of cream resting on top of the napkin dispenser and deemed them sufficient for his needs, and, with his newspaper still held securely in place under his arm, he carefully placed his coffee mug and the red basket with the two glazed donuts on the table and was about to sit himself down when a sudden movement just outside the window attracted his attention. A quick glance revealed two bicycles and their riders, with their helmets in place, coming to a stop and proceeding to dismount.

"My God!" Tim muttered, enacting a classic double-take—first one quick glance followed by a prolonged stare. That kid on the bike! It's the same kid I almost whacked with the door of my car!

And a few seconds later, as Blue—now dismounted—removed his helmet, Timothy received another surprise revelation. Jeez! It's Blue Avenger! I *knew* I'd seen him someplace before! And the other boy, well, he must be the younger brother Trac had mentioned.

Tim watched as the two boys locked their bikes together and leaned them against the foot-high round cement planter next to the curb. Blue was checking his watch while the younger boy, clutching what appeared to be a Game Boy® in one hand, sat down on the edge of the planter. A moment later, however, he stood up and climbed on top of it, struck a pose, and then leaped off. Again he climbed on the planter, and again he leaped off. And again, and again, and yet again.

Having a younger brother himself, Tim recognized Blue's reaction to the kid's antics, an attitude that could best be described as annoyed tolerance. By the way Blue kept looking up and down the busy street, it was obvious that he was waiting for someone.

Presently, an older-model Ford coupe pulled up and parked in the ten-minute zone in front of the shop, and Tim watched as a young, dark-haired girl paused long enough to pass a piece of paper about the size of a check back to the driver. Had he been close enough to hear what was being said, he would have understood the reason for the somewhat agitated exchange that followed:

"But Mom! Can't I at least tell Blue? I have to tell *him!*" Omaha pleaded (for it was indeed she who was in the car).

"No! You gave me your word, Omaha! Before I showed you that check, you *promised* you wouldn't mention it to anyone until I gave the all clear! You *heard* me say that, didn't you? We are *not* going to mention this to anyone until after it clears the bank. I know how people are, Omaha, and you don't. I don't care how stupid you think it is, but I refuse to be left holding the bag, explaining how your father snafued again!"

"*Snafued?* What's that!"

"Messed up, that's what! I don't want to have to explain how he didn't follow through on one of his wild promises again. And besides, if the check *is* good, it should clear by Monday afternoon. You can wait that long, can't you? Come on, honey. Please! We should be happy about this—not arguing!"

"I *am* happy about it, Mom! But I still think it's stupid, having to wait." Omaha took a breath and decided to cave in. "But, okay. I won't say anything," she said. "And anyway, thanks for the ride. I'll see you later."

Omaha stepped out of the car just as Blue came up from the curb to meet her. Josh made a final spectacular flying leap off the planter for Omaha's sake, and together the three of them walked into Donut Pros.

$ $ $ $ $ $

Tim really didn't expect that Blue would bring his girlfriend along, but he was pleased to see her there. "Over here, Blue!" he called out with a wave of his hand.

"Oh!" Blue said, surprised to see Tim there so early. He quickly nudged Omaha and said a few words to her, and then, leaving Josh pressed up against the glass of the donut display case trying to decide between a chocolate sprinkles and a gooey raspberry Bavarian, they both walked over to where Tim was sitting.

"I see you've come a little early, too," Tim said pleasantly, standing up and giving Omaha a friendly nod and smile.

"Hi, Tim," Blue said. "This is my friend Omaha—"

Tim quickly extended his hand before Blue could complete the introduction. "—and I'm Tim," he said. "I'm really glad Blue brought you along today. I've been wanting to meet you."

"Well, it was really kind of a coincidence," Blue said. "She's here to—" He stopped and glanced at Omaha. Maybe he should let Omaha explain what she was there for, if she wanted to.

Omaha was surprised to find her usual composure had suddenly deserted her upon meeting her first bona fide millionaire—make that multimillionaire.

Omaha looked up at Blue, hoping that he'd finish the sentence he'd begun, but instead, he just smiled at her and quietly rubbed her back.

"Uh, yes," she said, trying to pull herself together. "Hi. It's nice to meet you, too. I'm here to—I mean, I applied for a part-time job here, and the lady wanted to interview me this morning. That's her there," she added, her voice trembling slightly, but only enough for Blue to notice. "Behind the counter. That's Mrs. Phom."

Tim nodded. "Oh, yes," he said, waiting expectantly to hear whether Omaha had anything further to add.

Actually, she didn't, but she suddenly found herself talking again anyway. "See, my mom and I sort of needed the money, since the nurses are on strike and our landlady just raised our rent, but now—" Omaha caught herself just in time, before she mentioned Johnny Brown's surprise check. She looked up at Blue, hoping again that he would come to her rescue.

This time, taking her cue, he did. "They may even have to move," he said, drawing her closer to his side. "Probably pretty far away—"

Timothy Sims was instantly won over by Omaha's quiet and forthright manner, and he was deeply touched by the sight of these two young people, so obviously in love, faced with the unhappy prospect of a possible separation. At that moment, Tim appreciated more than ever the mental torment that Blue must be going through in trying to choose between Tractor's offer of a personal reward and his so-called Other Option, which now seemed to be not only unnecessary, but downright cruel. For most kids, Tim realized, it would be no contest; they would take the cash without any qualms at all. But he sensed that for Blue, the realization of the amount of good that could be accomplished with one million dollars would weigh heavily against his own personal desires.

Suddenly and without any warning at all, a brilliant idea flashed through Timothy Sims's brain. And in the following instant of time, his brilliant idea became doubly brilliant. Not only could he manage to come to Omaha's aid, but in so doing, he could also— just for this once—play by Tractor's rules. Just this once, he could actually *become* the imaginative and creative half of this partnership, instead of the steady, dependable, rule-abiding drone. And, at the same time, he might actually turn part of Tractor's world on its ear. All in all, it was too much to resist.

"Listen, Blue," the new Tim said, as he pulled a five-dollar bill from his wallet. "Why don't you go fetch a donut and a cup of coffee for your girlfriend here." He turned to Omaha and asked, "You do drink coffee, don't you?" And when she nodded, he repeated his request to Blue. "Yes, go on. Go get her a donut and some coffee, and for yourself as well. And here, take this," he added, pressing the bill into Blue's palm. "My treat. Go on, now."

Omaha looked at Blue, lifting one eyebrow in that half-humorous, subtle way only he could understand and appreciate. "I'll have a chocolate glazed, please," she said. "And a medium coffee."

Tim drew out the chair next to him and motioned for Omaha to sit. "Here, sit down. That's it. Now, do you have a specific time scheduled for your interview? Punctuality is extremely important to employers, you know."

"No," Omaha replied, even more flustered than before by Tim's sudden attention. "Mrs. Phom said anytime before noon."

"Good." Tim now bent his head as close to Omaha's ear as he dared without attracting undue attention. "You know all about the reason for this meeting between Blue and Tractor, I presume?"

Omaha nodded. "Oh, yes."

"Okay then, listen closely," Tim whispered urgently. "I want to help you, and Blue, too, in a way."

Omaha's eyes widened. "Help me do what?" she whispered back.

"You'll see. But for now, just listen. Here's what I want you to do. After Trac gets here, and just as soon as you can manage it—*before* Blue gives Trac his answer about the money—I want you to say the word *whip*. Say it naturally, just in conversation. Do you think you can manage to do that?"

"Say *whip?* Why?"

"I can't explain it now," Tim said, checking Blue's progress at the counter. "Just say it. *Whip, whipped,* or *whipping.* Say any one of those: *whip,* or *whipped,* or *whipping.* Come on, trust me," he said, gently grabbing her forearm and giving it a quick shake. "You can do that. You can think of something." And then, noticing that Blue was already collecting his change from Mrs. Phom, he leaned toward her ear again and whispered, "Oh, and listen. This is just between you and me, right? Our little secret."

Josh was coming toward them now, carrying a red plastic basket containing a chocolate sprinkles, a raspberry Bavarian, and a half-pint carton of milk, with his trusty Game Boy® still clutched in his other hand. Blue was following closely behind, somehow managing to balance two mugs of coffee along with a basket containing three chocolate glazed—one for Omaha, two for himself.

Tim sat up straight now, giving Omaha an exaggerated wink and making a little clicking sound with his mouth.

Omaha felt a sudden shiver. *Holy Moses! He's given me Tractor Nishimura's new Word-Watch word! He's just given me a chance to win $5,555.55!*

$ $ $ $ $ $ $

Moments after Blue returned to the table with the coffee and donuts, Omaha noticed that Mrs. Phom was smiling and motioning to her. (Actually, Mrs. Phom had no reason to question Omaha further. The simple fact that the young lady had demonstrated her dependability by showing up for her appointment was all she needed to know.)

With the words *whip, whipped, whipping* still echoing in her brain, Omaha excused herself and started to walk over to the counter. But in the few seconds it took for her to get there, the *whip*-words gave way to a whole new series of ideas. I really don't need this job anymore, Omaha was thinking. My father's check should be enough to tide Mom and me over until I finish high school next year. And I'm not even including the possibility that I could be $5,555.55 richer as soon as Tractor shows up, simply by uttering a certain word in front of him. *Unless*—and here Omaha had a sudden flash of inspiration—*unless I could somehow get Blue to say the word!* Holy Moses! If I can get *him* to say the *whip*-word, he would get the money. Then, since he'd already have the money to help me out, he'd be free to choose Tractor's Other Option—which I know he really, *really* wants to do. But the *best* thing is that on Monday I could surprise him with the news about my father's check, and that he could then use the *whip*-money not to help me, but to get himself a car! A *car!*

"Thank you for coming in today, Omaha," Mrs. Phom was saying, pulling Omaha away from her thoughts and back into reality.

"Oh, you're welcome," Omaha replied, now trying to keep her eyes focused on Mrs. Phom instead of looking back at Blue and imagining how happy he'd be winning a $5,555.55 jackpot without even *entering* the lottery!

"I have your application on file, and I'll give you a call as soon as I have an opening," said Mrs. Phom. "You can tell me then whether you're still interested in the job."

"Oh, that's great," Omaha said. "Actually, something may come up before then. I'm—well, I'm not sure."

Mrs. Phom nodded and smiled. "We'll just wait and see what happens, then. Thanks again for coming in."

"Thank *you*," said Omaha. She walked back to the table by the window and took her seat next to Tim, who was now telling Blue about his very first adding machine, an old hand-cranked model from the 1940s.

Omaha started in on her chocolate glazed, not making any attempt to join in the conversation. Instead, she was trying desperately to figure out a secret way in which she could get Blue to say the *whip*-word, not only so that he could get the money, but also, partly, because of Tim, for she had taken an instant liking to him and was just beginning to realize that no matter *who* said the *whip*-word that morning, Tractor would immediately get suspicious, and he'd probably accuse Tim of letting the cat out of the bag. And if the word came from *her* mouth—and if Tractor accused Tim of giving away the word, as she suspected he would—then poor Tim would find himself in a very awkward position indeed. He would either have to admit the truth, or lie about it.

Omaha felt a sudden rush of adrenaline as she delved further into the many facets of this whole unbelievable state of affairs. It was beginning to be as exciting as watching one of those big money-giveaway shows on television. She dipped the last bite of her chocolate glazed into her coffee and held it there for a second before popping it into her mouth. It was soggy and warm and chocolate. Surely, she couldn't be imagining that! All of this *must* be true!

Now, she thought, how can I get Blue to say the *whip*-word? That's the question! How can I get Blue to say it without anyone else catching on?

"Ah! Here's Trac now!" said Tim suddenly.

Outside the donut shop, Tractor tapped lightly on the window glass and waved at them as he walked past. Tim stood up and reached for an unoccupied chair and moved it over to their table as Tractor entered the store and approached them.

"Oh, thanks, Tim," Trac said, sitting down and placing a little box on the table. "Hello again, Blue! Big day, huh?" he added, with a mischievous wink. Then he turned and looked at the girl on the other side of the table. "And you must be Omaha. I didn't expect to see you here. You *are* Omaha, I presume," he said, more like a statement than a question. He glanced briefly at Josh. "And you're Blue's little brother, right? What was your name again, pal?"

Omaha remained sitting there with her mouth slightly ajar, sizing up this multimillionaire newcomer, while Josh merely looked up for a second, muttered that his name was Josh, and went on with his game.

Trac indicated his amusement at Josh's nonchalant air with a shrug and a fleeting grin, and then he announced that he was going to get some coffee and some more donuts. But first he pointed to the little box on the table and looked at Omaha. "Have you ever seen a donut shop collection, before?" he asked.

Omaha wasn't sure she had heard him correctly. "A what?"

Tractor opened the box and removed the ninety-two photographs of donut shops. "It's my donut shop collection," he explained, handing the stack of prints to Omaha. "I'm going to take them to a meeting of the Donut Shop Collector's Club this afternoon. Hey, I'll bet you guys didn't know that there are over ninety-five donut shops in Dallas, Texas, alone." He waited a moment for the enormity of that statement to sink in, and then he said, "Be back in a sec."

Omaha's brain suddenly lit up like a Christmas tree, or so it would seem if viewed by scientists watching the moving dots lighting up the screen during a magnetic resonance imaging procedure. She had just formulated a marvelous plan and was now beginning to implement it. Although she appeared to be flipping through the donut shop photos in a seemingly careless manner, what she was *really* doing was slyly rearranging them in such an order that the first letters in the donut shop names would spell out the phrase SAY THE WORD WHIP. She was sure that if she gave Blue the high sign, he would catch on immediately.

Luckily, there were ninety-two shops from which to choose. Everything was going along swimmingly until she came to the *h* in the word *the*. She had looked through all the photos, but couldn't find one donut shop in Trac's whole collection that started with the letter *h*. Beginning to panic, she quickly flipped through all of them again, but still no letter *h*. Okay then, she thought, I'll just skip the *the*. Blue is quick enough. He won't need it. Actually, I could simply spell out SAY WHIP. Oh, no! There's that *h* again! I'm going to have to think of something else, and quick!

$ $ $ $ $ $ $

Tractor was delayed at the counter by several indecisive donut lovers in the line ahead of him, trying to decide among the twenty-three varieties in the case. One stout woman in a pink jogging suit took what seemed like forever choosing between a chocolate cake with coconut and a crumb raised glazed for the final selection in her box of one dozen, until, finally, Mrs. Phom was obliged to call for her husband's help. But he was in the back just starting to put another batch in the fryer and couldn't come to her aid.

As involved as we are in the fortunes (literally and figuratively) of Blue and Omaha in this important juncture in their lives, we must take a short time-out here—even at the risk of losing our so-called narrative momentum, which, for some lightweight readers and critics, may prove to be an insurmountable obstacle. Nevertheless, in part because we're obliged to wait for Tractor to get to the head of the donut line and make his purchase before getting on with it, but mostly because of the huge import of a future event which needs to be aired, we must veer off our course momentarily, trusting that those aforementioned readers, unceremoniously jerked from their complacent dependency on orderly plot progression, can find both the strength and will to persevere. (After all, it's no worse than having one's reading cut short by the ringing of a phone, or the announcement of one's desired stop on the bus or subway line, or even a teacher beginning to pace the aisle between the desks, for it's a rare book that's read straight through, without interruption, from beginning to end.)

But our chief task remains, and that is to take a moment out to pity poor Mr. Phom—for, as fate would have it, fame and fortune are destined to pass him by, falling instead to the lot of yet another donut maker—a brilliant young graduate student in physics working part-time to help support himself while attending Princeton University, three thousand miles away and a mere fourteen years from now. Yes, it most certainly will be his supreme good fortune to suddenly have an epiphany while watching the peculiar action of donuts frying in grease—the way the hot bubbles emerge from the molten oil, then suddenly enlarge and float recklessly about before annihilating each other in a mysterious dance of death, only to rise again, like the phoenix, reborn, some of them flooding over the now partially browning donut and exploding violently, sometimes flinging themselves out of the boiling cauldron into the vastness of space and utter timelessness, even while the frying donuts them-selves bob around like demented denizens on a golden sea, always following predictable patterns according to precise mathematical formulas, before they coalesce into one grand vision in the fertile brain of the part-time donut maker at Princeton. Already well versed in the many aspects pertaining to his particular field of study, but now armed with the vital missing element contained in his newly acquired insight gained from the lowly donut fryer, the young scientist will arrive at the lab after his stint in the donut shop, and, working nonstop throughout that day and the following night, he will greet the morning light with the long-awaited final solution, the formula for the complete unified Theory of Everything. "Now, why didn't I think of that!" a chagrined Stephen Hawking will be heard to exclaim. "I guess you never had a chance to watch donuts frying in grease," the elated but still humble young donut maker will reply. From Homer Simpson to the long sought-after final unification of physics, at last, donuts will have gained the respect they deserve.

$ $ $ $ $ $ $

"My turn? Already?" Tractor asked. "Okay, then," he said, pointing to his selections. "I'd like two of those chocolate old-fashioneds, please, and a couple of those chocolate cake with peanuts—"

"Those are almonds, sir—"

"Almonds? That's fine. And maybe that crumb cake there, and the one next to it. What is that? Blueberry? Let's have two of those. That should do it, for now."

Tractor paid Mrs. Phom and ambled back to the table.

"Here, kids. Help yourselves," he said, setting the basket of donuts in the middle of the table before sitting down and taking a sip of coffee. Then he slid a paper napkin over to Blue, patting it gently and at the same time pulling a pen from his shirt pocket and placing it on the table beside the napkin.

"Decision time is drawing nigh," he said with a quiet, dramatic flourish. "If you'd like to indicate your choice on the napkin there"— Tractor looked at his watch —"I'll give you some extra time, say, ten or fifteen minutes? Will that be sufficient?"

Blue nodded. "Yep." He could feel his heart pounding in his throat, even though his decision had already been made the night before. Bending his head low and shielding the napkin from sight by placing his curved left hand around it, he wrote in very small numbers, $1,000,000. Then, heaving a giant sigh, he turned the napkin over to hide what he had written, and he suddenly found himself filled with a feeling of profound and unexplained fright. A moment's reflection revealed its source: the fate he had feared the most had actually come true. He was merely a helpless clone, a living counterpart of the cartoon character he himself had created.

He looked across the table at Omaha. He wondered why she had been shuffling the photos around so much, but now she had stopped doing that and was quietly holding the entire donut store collection in her hands.

Their eyes met again, and her tentative but hopeful expression just tore at his heart. She had not asked for his help. She would never do that! But how could he desert her in this, her greatest hour of need?

With a sudden, impulsive move, Blue wadded up the napkin on which he had just written and stuffed it in his pocket. There is a time for altruism, and a time for selfishness, and for Blue, helping Omaha was akin to helping himself—self-interest of the highest order. But he didn't care.

He reached over and grabbed another napkin from the pile in the center of the table. Tractor watched in amusement as Blue once again wrote down some numbers, and although Trac could see that action plainly enough, what he couldn't see was the intense feeling of relief and happiness welling up in Blue's heart and mind. The craziness was over! He was *not* a slave of his own creation! He was Blue Avenger, teenage boy in the flesh!

Trac now turned his attention to Omaha. "So, what do you think of my donut shop collection?" he asked. "I have ninety-two there, you know. They represent three years of intense collecting. But then, of course," he added, with good-humored self-depreciation, "I've never been to Dallas."

"Oh! I think they're great!" Omaha responded enthusiastically. "You should see these, Blue," she said. "They're pretty amazing!"

Omaha took a few seconds to align the pack of photos by gently striking it on the tabletop as one would do with a deck of cards.

And then, in an inspired bit of intentional distraction, she pointed out the window and said, "Oh, look! A hummingbird!"

And as quickly as the others turned to look, Omaha gave Blue's ankle a not-so-gentle kick. Holding out the photos to him, yet not releasing her grip even as his fingers reached around them, Omaha began a hurried but unmistakably rhythmic blinking of her eyes. Of course, the silent message they relayed was "Scotu! M-sot! Fiotu!"

$ $ $ $ $ $ $

Omaha was approaching her finest hour. Realizing that Blue would need some time to concentrate on the task she had given him, she skillfully engaged the multimillionaires in the one topic of conversation she knew would hold their interest—the movies.

And in the meantime, just as she expected, the talented code-breaker was keeping careful track of the first letter of each of the shops in the order she had arranged, until all five words were spelled out and the hidden message was revealed:

Tastee Donuts
Express Donuts
Lou's Living Donut Museum
Li'l Orbits
Chris's Doughnut Barn
A to Z Donuts
Ted's Ragtime Do-nuts
Ace Donut Shop
Nathan's Original Donuts
Donut Star
Pat's Buttercream Donuts
Izzie's Donuts
Amy Joy Donuts
New York Donuts
Oh My Donuts

Jeanne's All-Nite Donuts
O'Henry's Donut Shop
King Donuts
Ev's Donuts Plus

$ $ $ $ $ $ $

Tim was getting nervous. What was wrong with Omaha, any-way! She had been conversing with them for almost five minutes now and still hadn't figured out a way to say Tractor's word. Could it be she didn't have as much on the ball as he had given her credit for? And what about Blue? He had already changed his mind once. What was going on with him?

"One movie I really *hated*," Omaha was saying, "was *The Laugh Machine*—you know, that one about the female comedian. The acting was okay, I guess, but the jokes were so lame."

Under the table, Blue felt another sharp kick. It hurt, but it served its purpose.

"Maybe she should have told the one about the cat and the piano," Blue said, catching Omaha's quick nod of approval out of the corner of his eye.

"I don't believe I know that one," Tractor said. "Let's hear it."

"I hope I can remember it." Blue swallowed and moistened his lips. "Well, it seems that this musician had just moved into a small apartment way up on the fifth floor of this really old building in the Bronx or somewhere. The rent was fairly cheap, and the building was pretty dilapidated. It didn't even have an elevator. Well, finally, when the musician was all moved in, he invited one of his friends to come over and check out his new digs."

Omaha put her chin in her hand and idly fingered the handle of her Donut Pros mug, trying to appear relaxed and natural, but she was certain that if the others looked, they would surely see her heart wildly thumping under her blouse.

"Well," Blue continued, "the friend climbed up all those stairs, and once he had made it up to the apartment, the first thing he noticed was the huge grand piano sitting there taking up most of the space in the front room. 'Man!' the friend said. 'You even got your piano up here! How did you ever get that huge thing up those four flights of stairs?'"

Suddenly, to Omaha's great dismay, she noticed that Josh was beginning to squirm around in his seat. The Game Boy® was put aside, and Josh was hanging on every word. Omaha had no trouble reading the signs. As usual, Josh was preparing to jump in and holler out the punch line a moment before Blue could speak the words himself. Omaha's biggest challenge was just moments away.

Blue polished off his second chocolate glazed in one bite and went on with his story. "'How did I get that piano up those four flights of stairs?' the musician repeated. 'It was easy! The cat did it!' he said, indicating the small gray alley cat napping on the couch."

Omaha was fully armed now, poised and ready to strike.

"'Well, that's just ridiculous!' the musician's friend exclaimed. 'How could that little cat carry a grand piano up four flights of stairs?' 'Easy!' said the musician—"

Josh immediately jumped up in his seat and shouted out, "I— *blaugh!*"

"'I *whipped* him!'" Blue exclaimed, at the very moment that Josh's face and mouth were suddenly splattered with the contents of two small containers of half-and-half, shot diagonally across the table by an instantly apologetic Omaha.

"Oh, Josh!" she said, covering her mouth with her hands in alarm. "I'm *sorry!* I was just playing around with these little coffee creamers, and I guess I squeezed them too hard!" She grabbed a bunch of napkins and passed them over to him. "Here," she said. "Did any get on your shirt?"

"Nah," Josh said, standing back from the table a bit and wiping off his face, not quite sure whether to believe her or not. And even after the half-and-half was wiped away, the puzzled expression remained.

Tractor Nishimura was strangely quiet. He was leaning back in his chair now, arms crossed, surveying the scene like the movie director he was. The exploding coffee creamers shtick was a surprising twist for him, and only added to his overall bewilderment. Finally, he looked straight into his partner's eyes and asked, "Okay, Tim. What do you know about this?"

Tim glanced quickly at Omaha and then at Blue. "Nothing, Trac," he said earnestly, automatically raising his right hand. "Nothing, I swear."

His reply was so swift and so honest that Tractor had no choice but to believe him. With a little sigh, he reached for his wallet and removed the cashier's check that was nestled between his driver's license and his American Express card, and made out in the amount of $5,555.55. "Hand that pen back over here, will you please?" he asked Blue.

As Tractor was writing the name *Blue Avenger* on the check, Tim quickly sneaked another look at Omaha. She met his glance, but just bent her head to one side, pursed her lips, and shrugged.

"Here you go, kid," Trac said, handing over the check to Blue. "Congratulations. You're the winner of my final World-Wide-Word-Watch. Two winners in one week is more than I can handle."

"But—what did I say?" Blue asked, glancing up from the check with a wide, unbelieving smile, flushed with the knowledge that he was suddenly $5,555.55 richer.

"The word was *whipped*," Trac said. He smiled weakly and then added, "I must admit I have a weakness for off-the-wall humor—but this one really cost me."

"Ah, come off it," Tim said lightly, still trying to figure out what had happened. "You can afford it."

Blue grinned at Tractor and then held up the check for Omaha to see. "Look! I'm rich!" he exclaimed. After a pause, he added, "What do you know about *that*?"

Omaha smiled, knowing full well what he was *really* asking, but all she said was, "Holy Moses! Five thousand five hundred fifty-five dollars and fifty-five cents!" Then she laughed. "Hey, that's really fun to say!"

"Okay, folks," Tractor announced. "The fun's over. Now it's decision time." He handed the pen back to Blue. "So, what'll it be? Your final decision. The seven thousand, or the one million—"

"The seven thousand or the one million of *what?*" Josh broke in, suddenly extremely interested in what was happening at this most unusual donut party, complete with exploding coffee creamers, talk about World-Wide-Word-Watches, and checks for $5,555.55 being passed around like donuts. Well, almost.

"Josh! Shh!" Omaha said, putting her finger over her lips. "Blue has to concentrate."

"No. No, I don't," Blue said, grabbing the last napkin still left on the table. "It's easy now."

This time he didn't hide what he was writing. He just spelled it out in large, capital letters: ONE MILLION DOLLARS, PLEASE!

$ $ $ $ $ $ $

Tractor and Tim lingered in the donut shop after the kids had left, refilling their coffee mugs from the large thermos at the counter.

"I've been thinking, Tim," Trac said, "my little experiment involving Blue's decision—whether he would opt for himself or for others—was really skewered when he won the five thousand five hundred fifty-five dollars and fifty-five cents." Trac smiled a kind of mirthless smile that didn't even reveal his dimple. "Actually, you know, that *is* fun to say."

Tim leaned back in his chair and gazed at the ceiling, his folded hands resting on his stomach. "Yes, I agree. The five thousand no doubt took the pressure off him. I guess you heard him immediately asking Omaha about helping her with her rent—even before the check was dry?"

"Yeah—I did. And when he came to the punch line in his little story, I also heard the sound waves reaching all the way to my wallet, eventually, as it turned out, to the tune of one million bucks."

Tim stared down at his hands, lacing his fingers and forming mother's table, the way children do when reciting the old rhyme. "But have you realized yet that what you were doing to Blue—forcing him to make such a decision—was *really* not very nice?"

"Not very nice? How can you say that? Either way, he would come out a winner—"

"Oh, come on. You know what I mean."

Tractor took a very deep breath and closed his eyes. Then he put his elbows on the table and began to rub his temples with the palms of his hands. Finally, imitating Tim's posture, he, too, leaned back in his chair and folded his arms. "Okay, Timmy," he said, addressing his partner by a diminutive he rarely used. "It's time we laid our cards on the table. I believe I'm beginning to see some elaborately thought-out plan here. A plan designed to give me a little dose of my own medicine, perhaps?"

"And has it worked?"

"Maybe. Maybe a little. We'll have to wait and see." Tractor picked up one of the tiny creamers from the table and playfully aimed it at Tim's head. Then he said, "Now let's hear the truth. Did you or did you not betray my trust and tell Blue Avenger my current World-Wide-Word-Watch word?"

Tim raised his hand as if taking an oath in a court of law. "No, Tractor. I didn't. I give you my word. I did *not* tell Blue Avenger your secret word."

Tractor reached across the Formica® table and the two men shook hands, each one now just a little bit more like the other.

$ $ $ $ $ $ $

Blue, Josh, Sally, Rakesh, Omaha, and Margie all went out to Fenton's that night. Blue's treat.

"This has sure been *some* week," Blue said, after they had finished their sandwiches and were starting on their ice cream. "*Some* week, when you stop to think about it."

"That's right," Sally agreed, squeezing Rakesh's hand under the table. "It's been, well—it's been pretty unusual, all right."

"For us, too," Omaha said, feeling right at home now, surrounded by her mother, and Blue's family, and even Rakesh, whom she had liked as soon as they met. "Right, Mom? Remember, last week when we were really struggling—trying to figure out what we were going to do about our rent, and moving and everything, and now, because of Blue—" Omaha smiled. Actually, this was kind of fun, letting Blue feel like he was saving the day for them, when, really, he was going to get the surprise of his life on Monday. "—but because of Blue," she continued, "we'll be able to stay where we are! Right, Mom?"

Oh, God, Margie thought, as she weighed both paths now open to her. While the thought of announcing the arrival of a check that *could* bounce was extremely embarrassing, being put in a position of accepting money from her daughter's boyfriend—for heaven's sake!—that was even worse!

"Well," Margie started—deciding in her mind to just take the plunge and let the devil take the hindmost. "Actually, Omaha and I do have an ace in the hole, so to speak."

Omaha looked up, extremely surprised.

"What happened was that I—that is, Omaha and I—received quite a handsome check in the mail from her father yesterday, who recently had the good fortune of selling his book to a publisher in Italy. I originally planned to wait until the check actually cleared the bank before speaking of it, because, as you may know, sometimes those dealings with foreign banks can get pretty fouled up."

Blue looked as if he had been struck by lightning. Omaha suddenly threw a protective arm over his shoulder and said quietly, "I had to promise not to tell you until we were sure the check was going to clear. But I'm *sure* it will. My father's probably so proud of himself for finally getting his book published, he wouldn't dare spoil this show of generosity with a no-good check."

"But what about me?" Josh exclaimed. "What about *my* week? Ms. Knight told me yesterday that I was going to get the award for the best idea for raising money for Up with Reading! Month!"

"Hey, that's great!" Omaha said. "I told you that would happen, remember?"

Josh nodded. "Yep," he said.

"A real success story!" Rakesh added. "We're proud of you, Josh!"

"Well, actually, there's just one little problem," Josh said, licking hot fudge sauce off the handle of his spoon with more attention than necessary.

"Really? What's that?"

Josh blinked his eyes a couple of times and looked at the ceiling, a familiar gesture that Blue could read like a book.

"Like what? What's wrong now?" Blue asked quietly.

"Oh, half the class is mad at me, that's all. Trevor, especially. Trevor is mad because he thought his idea was better than mine, and so some of his friends are mad at me, too. He said making stress ball craft—I mean, stress balls—is stupid."

"So, did he have a better idea?"

"Are you kidding? Man, it was potty! He wanted all the kids to bring in all their old toys and junk and have a giant garage sale. And the only reason he wants to do that is so he could get rid of all his useless Pokémon™ cards." Josh shook his head back and forth and said, "Sheesh!"

No one spoke for a moment.

"Well, as far as we're concerned, you're still a success," Rakesh said.

Josh raised his sundae glass up to his mouth and let the melted ice cream slowly dribble in. Sally started to reprimand him, but decided to just let it slide this time.

"Here's a suggestion for you, Josh," Rakesh said suddenly. "Maybe you could ask Trevor if he would like to become your partner."

Josh looked up but didn't say anything.

"What I mean is, have you given any thought about *after* Up with Reading! Month?"

Josh shook his head. "No," he said, cautiously looking at Rakesh out of the corner of his eye.

"Well, I was just thinking that if people bought your stress balls on *that* day, you could probably still be in business *after* that day. Only, then *you* could keep all the profits. Right? So you could ask Trevor if he wanted to be partners, don't you see? It's a lot more fun doing something like that with a friend, don't you think? You could supply the cornstarch, and maybe Trevor could buy the balloons—make some arrangement like that."

"Hey!" Omaha exclaimed. "That's a great idea! You guys could probably make a lot of money. And you could call your company T&J Productions," she suggested, giving Blue a friendly nudge.

"I think I like J&T Productions a *lot* better," Josh said brightly, obviously taken with the idea. And everyone laughed. Just like on TV—again.

For the ride home, Josh asked his mother if maybe he could sit in the front seat, with Rakesh, and even though safety experts recommend that children sit in the rear seats of automobiles at all times, Sally allowed that it would be okay, just this once.

$ $ $ $ $ $

It was after eight when they got home from Fenton's that evening. Blue fooled around checking his e-mail and watching a stupid TV program with Josh, who kept laughing his head off over nothing, mostly because he had just spoken to Trevor and was in a particularly happy mood.

After a while, Blue went to his room and got out the chart he had made on Thursday—the paper listing all the possible recipients of his million-dollar windfall that he had come up with so far. He soon realized that this was going to be a lot more difficult than it looked.

The phone rang just as he was trying to figure out a workable method for deciding which of his eight causes to keep, which to eliminate, and how to add new organizations for consideration.

The call was for him. It was Timothy Sims.

"I've been thinking about you and your million most of the day," Tim said. "By any chance has Tractor called to talk to you since this morning?"

"No," Blue said. "The last I heard, he just told me he'd have his lawyer get in touch with me to work out the details."

"Okay. Well, I've just talked with him—Tractor, that is, not the lawyer. And he agrees with this plan I've come up with, which is this: how would you feel if I added a million of my own to the pot, and then instead of just giving it all away and being done with it, we could set up a kind of charitable trust for you. You know how those things work, don't you?"

Blue noticed that his fingers were starting to shake a little, and his voice was getting a bit tremulous. "Well, uh—no. Not exactly."

"It's a simple idea, really. The main thing is you never spend your principal. It's put to work making interest, and that's the money you end up giving away. I'm sure you've heard of them."

Blue tried to speak, but no words would come. He swallowed several times and tried again. "But, uh, I mean—would this *really* be okay with Tractor? Remember how he kept calling the one million dollars my Other Option? So, will he *really* go along with this?"

"Oh, certainly," Tim said, with a little businesslike laugh. "It's still your Other Option. Nothing will change. None of this money is for you, personally."

Blue was beginning to feel very peculiar—like his feet and legs were starting to get numb and he was no longer in contact with the floor.

"So, what do you think?" Tim asked. "It's up to you, really. You can decide what to do with the million and be done with it, or we can set this thing up on a more permanent basis." Tim paused. "We might want to call it the Blue Avenger Charitable Trust. How does that sound?"

"It sounds—well, actually, it sounds sort of unbelievable."

"Yes," Tim agreed. "I suppose it does. But I'll get our lawyer to set it up next week, and be back in touch then. Okay?"

"Okay."

"And, by the way, Blue—"

"Yes?"

"I do want to congratulate you on your decision. Even Tractor admits now that it was a dirty trick to play on you—"

"Oh, no! No. It's okay. It's fine."

"I'll talk with you next week, then."

"Wow. Thanks a lot, Tim. Thanks a million, actually!"

Blue hung up the phone and floated back to his room. There, still on his desk, was the four-panel strip he had drawn just the night before. Blue picked it up and sat down on the edge of his bed. In the final panel, Blue Avenger had chosen the million dollars, just like Blue Avenger. Blue Avenger studied the expression on Blue Avenger's face. If he didn't know better, he would say it looked almost human. Not bad, for just an amateur.

"What Are YOU Lookin' At, Deadman?"

JOËLLE DUJARDIN—EXXON® GASOLINE—ROCKY NEVINS

INSISTON FILOFAX®—HANK GOMEZ—DJ WRIGHT—NANCY REESE

"Want to scare your pants off? A Masterpiece of the Genre!"

—Angela Aguilla, Syndicated Columnist

"Mayhem and Murder at Scream City High"

Starring Teenie-Jo & Dottie, the Hilarious Nadeau Sisters!

And featuring an All-Star Supporting Cast, including "Fetch" the Dog

"Rollicking & rowdy nonstop hi-jinx at America's favorite high

school!"

—Bobby Briggsmore, Radio KFIB

T&T PRODUCTIONS